CAPTURE OR KILL

Tom Marcus, former MI5, grew up on the streets in the North of England. He joined the British Army at sixteen and went on to become the youngest member of the Armed Forces to pass the six-month selection process for Special Operations in Northern Ireland.

He was hand-picked from the Army into MI5 as a Surveillance Officer. He left the Security Service recently, after a decade on the frontline protecting his country due to being diagnosed with PTSD.

An extraordinary battle and recovery took place, which led Tom to write his first book, *Soldier Spy*. Having been vetted and cleared for publication by MI5, it's the first true ground-level account ever to be told. For the first time in the Security Services' history, a Surveillance Officer has told the real story of the fight on our streets and his debut book went straight to number one on the *Sunday Times* bestseller list.

Tom now consults on projects within TV and film including the TV dramatization of his book *Soldier Spy*. *Capture or Kill* is his first novel.

Due to the ongoing specific threat to Tom Marcus, MI5 insist he keep his identity hidden and he continues to work with the Security Service and other agencies to ensure he stays safe.

BY TOM MARCUS

Fiction

CAPTURE OR KILL

Non-Fiction

SOLDIER SPY
I SPY

CAPTURE OR KILL

TOM MARCUS

PAN BOOKS

First published in the UK 2018 by Macmillan

This edition published 2018 by Pan Books
an imprint of Pan Macmillan
20 New Wharf Road, London N1 9RR
Associated companies throughout the world
www.panmacmillan.com

ISBN 978-1-5098-6359-4

1 3 5 7 9 8 6 4 2

A CIP catalogue record for this book is available from the British Library.

Typeset in Janson Text by Palimpsest Book Production Ltd, Falkirk, Stirlingshire

Printed and bound by CPI Group (UK) Ltd, Croydon, CR0 4YY

Visit **www.panmacmillan.com** to read more about all our books
and to buy them. You will also find features, author interviews and
news of any author events, and you can sign up for e-newsletters
so that you're always first to hear about our new releases.

This book is dedicated to my wife.

Without you, I would have been lost a long time ago.

Semper Vigilat.

CAPTURE
OR
KILL

PROLOGUE

Standing in the doorway of my flat, I take one last look. It's clean and orderly, the home of a righteous man. And yet, beneath the surface, I know it could be defiled. There may be bugs hidden somewhere, spies listening to my every word. Well, if so, they will have heard many prayers, but not our plans. I put my phone on the shelf by the door before walking out onto the landing. With your phone, they can track you wherever you go. And of course, they can record what you say. Which is why Mohammed and I never communicate electronically. If we need to meet, we fix the place the night before, during last prayers at the mosque. Only the two of us know the plan. We never meet in the same place twice and never inside a building or an open space like a park. Following these rules keeps us alive, and lets us hope we may, in the future, live in a different world from this corrupted one.

I walk down the stairwell and leave my block of flats, walking calmly but purposefully, watching for anyone who looks out of place or who is paying too much attention to me. I see no spies, but I have to be sure. Before crossing the street,

I wait at the traffic lights, looking both ways. The light changes to green, but I don't cross yet, instead I wait for cars or people to react to me, stopping suddenly or changing direction. Still no sign of anyone.

Moving onto the other side of the road lets me look up and down the street, checking for anyone hiding in their cars. There's a phone shop on the corner and I check that the owner is alone before entering. He nods to me as I walk past the counter and out of the side door into a narrow alley, which leads to the back of the houses behind. If anyone follows me down here, I will know they are spies.

The alley is dark. I put my hood up and look back onto the street. In the darkness I am like a ghost; no one can see me. But the end of the alley is lit up like a TV. Anyone looking down here to try and see me would stand out.

Still clean. I turn and walk to the other end of the alley, away from the lights of the main road, until I reach the bottom of a grimy stairwell. I can see the silhouette of Mo's bulky frame, ambling towards the same pre-arranged spot from the opposite direction, I greet him.

'As-salāmu 'alaykum.'

'Wa'alaykumu s-salām.' Mo replies as we keep our voices to a whisper. No one could be listening to us here. But there's a reason neither of us has ever been arrested or even spoken to by the police. We are always careful, always following the rules we have made for ourselves.

'Mo, the two brothers I told you about yesterday, I believe they are ready. It is time.'

'And we trust them? We must assume they are being followed.'

'I gave instructions to them at first prayers this morning how to disappear. They've been trained well.'

'And you're sure they are capable of executing the plan?'

'I'm controlling what they do at each stage. Only we know the full plan. But they will do their part. Then we can move to the caliphate.'

'Then proceed, brother.'

I embrace Mohammed quickly before we go our separate ways. Our meeting has lasted less than a minute. Now I need to get to work, to fulfil my part in society, hiding in plain sight. It's only a two-minute walk from here, but I don't take the fastest route. Instead I start off in the opposite direction, turning back on myself to make sure I am still not being followed. Finally, I see my place of work, shining brightly, a picture of Western opulence.

Walking through the entrance, I'm met with the familiar face of the receptionist. The way she flaunts herself is degrading, the usual garish red lipstick as familiar as her greeting.

'Doctor Khan, how are you?'

I don't show my disgust. 'I'm very well, thank you.'

'I hope you're ready for the night shift. We're short-staffed again.'

'I'm always ready,' I reply, waving a hand as I walk past her.

I smile to myself. She has no idea how ready I am.

1

Stumbling, a junkie badly in need of a fix. It's raining and my filthy jeans and ripped parka are already soaked through. Rainwater squeezes in through the holes in my trainers, and I start coughing – a nasty rattling that makes me sound as if I'm properly sick. Through half-closed eyes I can see the abandoned building, but I don't head straight for it. Instead I lurch into a corner of the disused park opposite and collapse under a tree that gives at least some protection from the downpour. Surrounded by bits of old tinfoil that glint in the passing lights of the odd car, I catch sight of a broken syringe and an old burned spoon. Under the penetrating smell of cat shit, I can detect the faint but distinct odour of heroin, like rancid vinegar burning its way into my nose. Flipping the hood of my parka up with a grimy hand, I fix my gaze on the door of the building opposite.

'From Zero Three, I have direct on the house, I can give them away, but can't go with.'

Talking into my radio, my voice is hushed but clear.

Now my team knows I'm in position. The targets are inside, and as soon as they move, we can keep control of them. All I have to do now is what junkies do best: wait. My cover is good – no one would believe the foul-smelling, dishevelled wreck slouched under the tree, surrounded by syringes and other junkie paraphernalia, could be an under-cover surveillance officer. Which is fortunate, as in this run-down area of Birmingham, the drug gangs pretty much own the streets, and if they made you as police, you'd be dead. And the truth is, most surveillance officers wouldn't be capable of doing it in a convincing way. It's one thing look-ing and smelling the part: anyone can put on piss-soaked jeans and a grimy T-shirt, leave off shaving or washing for a few days, get some nicotine stains on their fingers and dirt under their nails. It's another thing to walk and talk like a down and out, to think like someone who survives on the streets. To really *live* the part.

For me, though, it comes naturally. I grew up on streets like this. I learned the hard way how to survive. And though, thank God, I never became an addict, I spent a lot of time with people who did. Which made me a unique asset within the intelligence services. I wasn't comfortable working in posh areas like Chelsea, trying to blend in with the upper classes, but out here, getting into the mindset of a hardcore junkie, was no problem at all. Which might have explained my nickname during training: 'Tramp'.

They didn't call me that for long, though.

'Roger that Zero Three, you have Zero Eight in close to support you and Charlie Seven Seven has taken note of all the vehicle registration numbers in the area, base acknowledge.'

The team leader, Lee, already had control of this operation, making sure the operations officers back at Thames House were in the loop but also responding instantly to us.

'Base roger, we've checked those VRNs, no results showing on the grid, For information Iron Sword last seen dark jacket, light blue jeans and Stone Fist green jacket, black bottoms. And for information we don't have any technical assistance on this, no tracking at all.'

Those were the code names for the brothers, and having no other way of tracking these two other than our team following them, it meant if we didn't keep hold of them, they'd disappear. As a surveillance officer, that was your worst nightmare. Especially since we suspected that was exactly what they were planning to do. But right now, I knew the rest of the team would be finding all sorts of places to conceal themselves, waiting for me to send the stand-by signal over the radio. The brothers would have to show capabilities we hadn't seen before to escape our iron grip. It was only the bosses, the people who gave us our orders, I sometimes worried about. The police are already becoming accountable for their actions in open courts. I just hope we have enough protection higher up so the same thing doesn't start happening to us.

Keeping my eyes on the front door, I shuffle over as a group of half a dozen locals appears, parking themselves under my tree. This is when I need to keep playing my part for all its worth; if one of them gets the idea I'm not who I'm pretending to be, it's game over. But they seem too drunk or wasted to take much notice, and fortunately they have plenty of pills, and a plastic bottle of cheap cider they're passing around, so hopefully they're not going to bother me. My attention is still focused on the door, and these lowlifes are not my concern. They could start murdering each other and I wouldn't budge. But we're trained to notice everything when we're on a job, to take in every detail, in case something is out of place, something isn't right, and we need to change our plans immediately to avoid being compromised. So while most people would just try to shut them out and pretend they weren't there, I find myself noting every detail about them.

From the state of their hair and fingernails, they're clearly living on the streets and have been for some time, stuck in the vicious cycle of searching for their next fix and then finding somewhere relatively safe to come back round. The woman in this group of six addicts, in her early twenties I'd guess, though you could be forgiven for thinking she was twice that from her gaunt and haggard features, is so off her face her ripped tracksuit bottoms have slipped halfway down her arse, showing off a ragged thong which clearly hasn't been washed in a while. She stumbles over and collapses in a heap next to me as one of the men starts urinating behind our tree.

A small voice inside my head asks me what the fuck I'm doing sitting under a tree in the rain, getting splashback from a homeless drug addict, but suddenly I can see a blade of light creeping from behind the door of the house as it slowly opens, and I focus my mind on what I'm here for. Wasted as they are, my new friends are too close for me to risk talking on my radio, so I'll have to use the covert messaging method instead.

The door opens fully, and I can see the side profile of a male coming out. He's talking to someone still inside the house and is being handed something that looks at this distance like the pistol grip of a small weapon, I can't be sure, and I can't yet see if they're our targets. I catch myself frowning in concentration as I try to make out who they are, and tell myself to relax my body position, to not give away that I'm interested in the house. Then a second figure leaves the house and turns to face in my direction.

It's one of the brothers. I have to alert the team but can't talk. Using the covert message system, I give the stand-by signal.

'STANDBY STANDBY heard! Zero Three, are both Iron Sword and Stone Fist out?'

My team leader knows the right questions to ask me, but I need to alert the team to this small unknown item that looked dark and small enough to be a pistol.

Responding, I use our covert message to tell the team leader yes.

'Roger that Zero Three, both out. Are they walking away from you south?'

I message back a negative, as I can see the brothers and they're walking fast, directly towards me on the other side of the road. Even with the rain and the crappy street lighting I can tell it's them because of the distinctive scars on their faces, mementos of their last prison stay. Something's definitely different about them, though, since the last time we deployed on them. They've suddenly become super-vigilant, looking at everything, complete three-sixty awareness. I tell myself not to react, not to tense up. Just live your cover.

There's some tension showing back at base, though.

'Stations from Base, we have nothing on this at all, no eavesdropping or electronic.'

'Base roger from Team Leader, we're on it. Zero Three, are they walking north?'

Still unable to talk, I reply with a yes, 'Roger that, Iron Sword and Stone Fist are walking north, north on Lozells Street towards Wills Street. Zero Eight acknowledge?'

'Zero Eight roger and in position.'

Shit. I've got to find a way of transmitting openly here. My team needs to know how aware both targets are, and if they are armed we could do with some police backup. But I sure as hell can't do it now; the brothers are getting closer to my position, walking faster in the rain. As they hurry past, one of the addicts hauls himself to his feet and shouts out. The brothers both turn instantly, and the addict gestures to the woman, now halfway decent again and slumped against the tree. He mumbles something, most of it complete garbage. It's got the word 'fuck' in it. He's trying to sell her for sex. The brothers have other things on their mind and start moving on, but not before their eyes briefly lock onto me. I know I'm good, there's nothing about my appearance or behaviour that can give away the fact that I'm not who I'm pretending to be, but all the same I feel a small surge of adrenaline. This is where it could all go wrong. This is where I could let down the team and fuck the entire operation.

One of the brothers pulls the other by the arm and they're gone. Now I just have to wait until both targets are under someone else's control and I can get out of here. But right now, I can only get the team leader to interrogate me using the covert messaging system, in the world's deadliest game of yes or no.

Sending a message out onto the net, I'm hoping the team leader is on the ball and starts asking the right questions, quickly.

'Zero Three is that you?'

Perfect, now I've got to get this going and quickly.

'Roger, have the targets stopped prior to the junction?'

Fuck. This was going to take too long, time we didn't have. I needed to get the message across right now.

'Yeah. From Zero Eight, I have control of Iron Sword and Stone Fist, both extremely vigilant, Team Leader, this is what Zero Three might have been trying to say. I'd like to give these guys some room.'

Thank God Dexter had taken control of the two brothers, and had already spotted that they were acting differently.

Now I could get away from here and change my profile, get out of these piss-stained clothes. My van was parked a few streets away, so it wasn't going to take me long. Hearing the team was in control of the targets and aware of their new behaviour was a huge relief. If we gave them some room, maybe everything was going to be all right.

As long as we didn't give them *too* much room.

'Base, permission?'

The operations officers at Thames House know they have to ask permission from the person in control of the targets, in this case, Dexter, to get onto the net to ask questions or give updates.

'Go ahead, both walking west on Wills Street towards the food market, still very aware and now walking very slowly.'

Their initial brisk walking pace could have been to get them away from Lozells Street, a risky place to be at night even for them, but I couldn't help thinking this was classic operational behaviour, speeding up, then rounding a corner and slowing down, trying to catch out any surveillance.

'Thanks, crews for information, we'd like you to keep a tight control of the brothers, intelligence from G Branch is suggesting they are going to try and drop off the grid. Base out.'

'Roger that, crews close in and we'll rotate it around as much as we can. Back to you Zero Eight.'

Slowly getting to my feet, using the trunk of the tree to slide up, I listen to Dexter as he gives a running commentary on what the brothers are doing, their appearance, their alertness levels. I step over the wannabe pimp, whose got a stillness about him I know well. His rigid breathing corpse, complete with a small bag of bright-yellow pills poking out of the top of his socks, is waiting to metabolize the chemicals that has incapacitated all of the group. The woman is out of it, curled up in a pool of her own piss under the tree. Now that the brothers are gone, I can afford to see them as fellow human beings rather than bit-part players in a drama of my own creation. I hated seeing people like that. I know from experience it was probably one wrong decision years ago that led them to being here in this state, that what they needed was a helping hand to haul them out of the shit. But although I could sympathize more than most, I was no social worker. My job was to stop terrorists killing civilians. If the civilians chose to kill themselves by putting a needle in their arm, there was nothing I could do about it.

Ducking under the low branches and out into the rain, now easing to fine drizzle, I shuffle across the street and along the path, heading south past the house the brothers had left a few minutes ago. My van was only around the next two corners, but I had to keep living my cover. Head down, shoulders dropped, I manage a quick glance at the house. In complete darkness, it looks like any other derelict building in the neighbourhood. Until you clock the steel sheeting over the boarded-up windows. And while the door is covered in graffiti just like the others on the street, underneath it is solid steel too.

I slow down, pretending to have a good cough. But the

truth is, I'm using the moment to gain as much useful information as I can. What's missing? What should be here but isn't? What's here but shouldn't be? I only have a few seconds before I'll start to look suspicious. Think! Nothing ground level. Nothing—Bingo! That's it. A very small CCTV camera high up near the roof line, tucked away under the guttering on the church on the opposite side of the road.

The fact it's clearly an off-the-shelf type of camera you can buy anywhere, powered by a battery, instantly tells me it's not an official part of the CCTV network installed by the council. It's pointing directly at one house in this row, which means it was highly likely put there by whoever is operating out of this house. A small wireless aerial at the top suggests it's probably transmitting wirelessly.

A massive amount of effort has gone into making it look like a regular derelict building, but with added features designed to keep squatters out, meaning there were only two plausible explanations: either this was a drug-money house, or some sort of weapons stash. Given the brothers' history of drug dealing, it could be either, but I'm betting on the latter. All the more reason not to let these guys fall off the grid. Rounding the corner, resisting the urge to speed my shuffle into a fast walk, I'm keen to get back to the van and send a message to Base about the CCTV. Most people in my situation would think I'd gotten lucky here, but the truth is our teams always live our cover no matter what the circumstances. You'll always be caught on camera, but if you are living your cover properly then it doesn't matter. Anyone watching this camera feed would see another druggy. Not an MI5 operator.

'All stations Zero Eight, hold back hold back, that's both IN IN to a takeaway chicken shop on the corner of Church Street, any vehicle call sign get this?'

Dexter's right, asking for vehicle support. When any target goes into a building it becomes easier for them to sit and watch people outside, and identify people like us.

'Charlie Four Seven has the front door.'

'Stations from Team Leader, I don't want anyone to go inside. Let them breathe for a while.'

We know this chicken shop well. It's a nightmare to cover properly, not in the worst part of the neighbourhood but right on a busy junction with floor-to-ceiling glass windows. In his car, Charlie Four Seven – Imran – has sight of the front door and a clear view inside because of the lighting, but I know he'll be struggling for cover. No one in their right mind sits in a stationary car for long around here.

I have some time to change my profile and get with the follow. I unzip my jacket as I approach the last corner, glancing behind me as I cross the road, as if I'm checking for traffic. I'm still clean, no one following, but anyone watching my van would question a homeless guy getting into it. So, turning the corner, I slip my parka off quickly, straighten the way I walk, take my keys out and walk confidently towards the driver's side, get straight in and pull away. The brothers might not be watching, but surveillance teams always try and leave as little sign as possible when entering and leaving an area. You never know, we could be working here for the next few years. The last thing you want to do is ruin that by wheel-spinning away or sitting there with the engine running right outside someone's house. No one knows better than us: you *never* know who's watching.

'Direct, Charlie Nine permission quick message?'

By switching from my foot call sign to my vehicle call sign, the team will know I'm not pretending to be a drug addict anymore and am in the safety of my van.

'Charlie Four Seven, go ahead no change, still inside facing the counter. Looks like they're ordering.'

'Roger, thanks, Base, the house the brothers left, number 158 Lozells Street, has the appearance of a derelict building with security sheeting on the windows and the door, but there is a CCTV camera tucked under the roofline of the church directly opposite. It's pointing at the front door of the target address. On leaving it looked like Iron Sword was handed a small dark object, couldn't confirm but it looked similar to a pistol grip. Charlie Nine out.'

'Base, roger, all stations acknowledge that the targets could potentially be armed. Thank you.'

As the team all respond to the Ops officer's call from Thames House, confirming they understand the targets could have a weapon on them, the team leader will have got straight on the phone to Base to ask for armed police support.

'From Charlie Four Seven, that's both Iron Sword and Stone Fist now sitting down inside the takeaway with food.

Iron Sword has a view straight out of the window for information.'

Driving round in a big circle, I move into a position where I can potentially help my team without being too close in. There's no point in saturating the area, especially when one of the brothers can see directly onto the street, and I know the rest of the team will be holding key routes out of the area too. So far, so good.

'Stations, while we have a lull, security checks please, down the list.'

I know why the team leader is checking on the other operators in the team. In this area, the brothers aren't the only threats we have to worry about. The only people in their cars at this time of night will be dealers or police, and because we've taken great pains not to look like police, we are obvious targets for gangs defending their patch. I can tell by the team's responses as they confirm their positions that the control around the brothers is as tight as can be, and no one is in any bother from the locals.

I keep running my memory back to when the brothers came out of the door. Could the object have just been a big phone, or something else more innocuous than a pistol? It was too hard to tell at that distance, in the rain, at night, but it had still been worth putting it out to the team.

'Charlie Nine, holding the park to the west on Villa Street.'

'Thanks stations, Direct, back to you.'

There is barely a second between transmissions; Imran is clearly desperate to get a message out on the radio.

'STANDBY STANDBY, SPLIT SPLIT! From Charlie Four Seven, that's Iron Sword OUT OUT and walking westbound towards St George's Park and Villa Street, Stone Fist is northbound, north on Church Street. Team Leader, just before they split, Stone Fist pointed in my direction, looking aggressive. I'm going to have to front this out and hope it wasn't me he was pointing at. If I move away now I'll be bang to rights for sure.'

'Charlie Nine, roger.'

The lull is well and truly over. The brothers are definitely not behaving normally. It could just be drugs paranoia, or it could be they are getting close to their endgame. The trouble is, neither us on the ground nor the intelligence officers back at Thames House have the faintest idea what that endgame is. They had both been serving long prison sentences for firearms offences when they got involved in a fight, which seemed like a deliberate ploy to get them moved to the wing where all the extremists were. Once we knew they had been converted, the agent handlers from G Branch showed massive interest, but in the six months since they'd got out we hadn't been able to figure out what they were doing. All we could be sure of was that they could have done a hell of a lot of planning and preparation in that time.

'From Charlie Nine, I have control of Iron Sword walking westbound on Wills Street, now at the junction of Villa

Street. Stations be aware he's just stood at the junction look-ing slowly at everything in front of him.'

Sat in the van, I can see Iron Sword now. He's calmed down, isn't looking as paranoid, but even at this distance I can see him studying everything; vehicles, houses, the odd pedestrian. The rain isn't bothering him either. He looks as if he knows what he's doing. This is new. The suspicion has gone, replaced by calm certainty, almost as if the brothers have been told they're being watched and it's just a case of finding us. If that's true, things have progressed much fur-ther than we thought. And, more to the point, we'll need to be at the top of our game to avoid being compromised.

'Aargh, shit, Charlie Four Seven! Stone Fist has just thrown a brick through my back window. Driving out of the area now.'

2

I can hear the engine bouncing off the rev limiter as Imran desperately tries to get to safety.

'Team Leader, roger that. Are you OK to drive? Do you need medical?'

'Yeah, yeah, yeah, fine. He shouted "pigs" and made a gun with his hand. Then he ran away northbound.'

'Roger that, Charlie Four Seven, get back to the garages and change the car.'

The high pitch of Imran's normally deep voice shows he's been taken totally by surprise. Stone Fist must have spotted him watching the takeaway. Targets don't pull stunts like this unless someone's done something fucking stupid to compromise the team, and I can't see what we've done wrong. Which makes me even more certain they've had a tip-off. But how?

'Roger, stations be aware please, we want everyone to get home tonight. Base, anything to suggest we've been blown here?'

'Team Leader from Base, when the targets were arrested

nine years ago, it was on Barker Street, which is just to the north.'

OK, so Stone Fist might have good reason to be paranoid. He might still not realize it's MI5 that have him under surveillance.

I feel a bit more confident. But I fucking hate it when someone in charge reminds us of getting home. I don't need that clouding my head out here, I don't need to be thinking about my wife and little boy. I tell myself my family are safe at home because I'm out here protecting them, but the truth is I feel like shit spending so much time away from them, never sure when I'm going to be back, never sure when the call is going to come to hit the streets again.

'Base, Team Leader, with Stone Fist acting like this I'm going to drop him and stay on Iron Sword, as he may be the one that is potentially armed too. Any update on the armed support we requested?'

What? We're dropping Stone Fist? I stop short of banging my fist against the steering wheel and just glare at the radio speaker in the van as if it could give me an explanation. I'm about to transmit to question the decision, but base beats me to it, just as Iron Sword starts to cross the road towards my position.

'Base, roger that. Understood. There are no police CTU teams available tonight, I've tried the Special Forces strike teams too, but we don't meet their response criteria and they are currently on standby for another live operation in East London. But we still need as much actionable intelligence as possible. G Branch are confident that the brothers are going to try and go completely dark within the next few hours.'

The operations officer, Jeremy Leyton-Hughes back at Thames House, is passing the buck. Slimy bastard. Yes, the situation is risky; there are no armed Counterterrorism Units on the ground to help us out if things go tits-up; he wants to keep the public and the team safe. But these guys are clearly about to try and evade our surveillance. That means they must be planning something big, and if we lose control of them now, we might never pick them up again.

Until it was too late.

By backing off Stone Fist because he's acting aggressively, we're playing into the brothers' hands. Fuck, these are *our* streets. If they push back, we should be stepping up our game, not running for cover. I knew I wasn't being a good team player, but I had to try and push the team leader into making the right decision.

'From Charlie Nine, can we have a separate channel for Iron Sword please, he's static at the entrance to St George's Park on Wills Street.'

'Negative, stay on channel seven, we're dropping Stone Fist, just be aware of him providing counter-surveillance for his brother – and I want everyone inside their vehicles until we can confirm if he's armed or not.'

Bollocks. It sounds like the team leader is scared. I know he's thinking of everyone's safety, but for fuck's sake. We're

MI5 Surveillance Officers. We're meant to be able to do things the police and Special Forces can't.

'Roger that, sorry, must have missed that. Thought we were keeping hold of them so they don't manage to drop off the grid. Iron Sword has taken a phone out of his pocket, checked the screen and placed it back in his left jacket pocket.'

No response from the team leader. I've pissed him off.

'From Charlie Nine, is there anyone who can get imagery of Iron Sword at the north-west corner of St George's Park on the south side of Wills Street? Base, I've GPS'd the site for you if you don't have his phone already.'

'Roger that, thanks. No, we don't have this phone. Still nothing on the technical assets.'

'Charlie Six Six could come round and try to get imagery.'

'From Team Leader, negative, we'll spook the target. Keep control of Iron Sword but don't get too close, we have NO armed support in the area.'

Fucking hell, it's like the team leader is determined to not get any intelligence at all. Have I fucked up by pushing him? So far, the only bit of intelligence we have is that the brothers are trying to slip the net. We've lost one car due to Stone Fist putting a brick through it and we've GPS'd a phone location, which is pointless if Iron Sword ditches the phone. Damn it, we need more than this if we're going to stop their attack.

'Stations from Charlie Nine, that's Iron Sword checking

the screen of his phone again and now walking fast west on Wills Street.'

I bet he's had a message. Not knowing what Stone Fist is doing is worrying me. It's obvious the brothers are working on a plan together. Iron Sword has become totally focused. He isn't looking around him at all as he continues to walk in my direction. My van radio sparks up with a transmission from one of the team, Alex.

'From Bravo Two, Stone Fist is walking east towards Iron Sword's location now on Wills Street.'

Good work. On her motorbike, Alex can hide her profile behind cars, and thankfully she's spotted the other brother walking behind my van. I catch him now in my mirrors, on the other side of the street. Stone Fist also looks more focused now, less edgy. My gut tells me they have a plan and are about to execute it. We have them back under control, but I've got a feeling it's not going to last for long.

'Thanks, Bravo Two, and from Charlie Nine, that's Stone Fist now back with Iron Sword and both walking west on Wills Street . . . Stations, that's a STOP STOP STOP at an address on the north side. I've been blocked. Bravo Two, can you?'

'Yes, yes, now both IN IN to a derelict-looking building, unsure what it is.'

Trying not to give away my position, I slowly turn my head and catch sight of the brothers slipping into the building just as the door swings shut behind them.

My phone vibrates in my pocket. Alex. There must be a problem.

'You OK?'

'Logan, did you see the guy who opened the metal door? Looked like he was holding a pistol, trying to hide it. I'm not putting it out on the net – we'll get pulled off this straight away without armed support.'

Fuck. This was fast becoming a health and safety mine-field. I had to think fast or the team leader would have us backing off once again.

'Mate, I didn't see that, are you *sure* you did?'

'Second thoughts, I have to move out of the area, so can't see anything either.'

Just in time.

'From Team Leader, what type of property is this, any house number?'

'Bravo Two has had to change position, couldn't see it from my position.'

Me and Alex are doing a good job of muddying the waters.

'Charlie Nine, can't see from this position, it's roughly two-five metres east of the junction with Hunter's Road. On the north side; derelict building with a steel door.'

'Stations from Base, we have a text message from the phone GPS'd by Charlie Nine belonging to Iron Sword. Message sent to unknown number reads: *I'm outside, let us in. Need a Henry.* Message ends.'

Henry as in Henry the Eighth, as in an eighth of cannabis

most likely. They're buying drugs, using burner phones and are potentially armed? Criminal activity often funds terrorist activity, so our surveillance is justified, but this is already falling under police remit, not MI5 counterterrorism. I know that's how Base will see it anyway.

The radios go quiet. It's probably only for a few seconds, but it feels like an eternity as I wait for the inevitable. The team leader breaks the silence.

'All stations, I'm going to drive past the address now. If the brothers are dealing drugs tonight, and given they could be armed, we'll have to rethink. We've got no armed support, as you know. Give me one minute.'

I feel the seconds tick by before my mirrors fill with headlights turning into the street. Without slowing down, Lee, Team Leader, drives past the address and keeps going. It doesn't take long before he's on the net.

'Base, do you read Team Leader?'

'Go ahead.'

'We can't be sure exactly which door the targets went into, due to the compact nature of the addresses. However, there is a large steel door on a derelict-looking house similar in style to the one they left on Lozells Street.'

'Roger, from the searches we've done there is a known drugs den in that exact area.'

'Roger that, base. It's your call.'

Lee had passed the decision back to Thames House. He knows dropping these two is a massive mistake, but what comes next is still no surprise.

'Stations, we have G Branch assets in play. We're confident we can pick the brothers up again quickly. I don't want
to risk your team without armed support if all these two are
doing is drugs. All stations CEASE and WITHDRAW. Back
to you, Team Leader.'

I start the engine, listening to the other operators confirming they're pulling out. I can feel my anger building, but
I make sure it doesn't show in the way I drive the van as I
head out of the area and back towards the garages. As I drive
slowly past the park, I glance towards the tree where I'd
been sitting in the rain. No one there. I hope my fellow
addicts have found somewhere better, but experience tells
me that any comfort they find will only be temporary. In the
long run, things will only get worse, and all too often there's
only one way out of their situation: an early grave. I wonder
how they'd feel if they knew they'd been sharing a bit of
shelter from the elements with an MI5 surveillance officer.

Once I'm clear of the area, I put my foot down. Focusing
on driving safely at speed usually calms my mind, but tonight
I can't get the vision of the brothers disappearing into that
drugs den out of my head. What are they doing right now?
Will we really be able to pick them up again? The truth is,
whatever happens to the brothers, my frustration is about
more than just this operation. Even if we arrest them, suc-
cessfully prosecute them and send them to jail, it's really just
like sending them to terrorism school. All the extremists
together in one place, with all the time in the world to com-
pare notes on how they were caught and what got said in

each of their secret court cases. Pretty soon, they've got a detailed guide on how we operate, making catching the next lot twice as hard.

My job is keeping people safe, but sometimes it seems like playing by the rules just means letting the other guy win.

Pulling into the garages, I can see Alex taking her helmet off and unzipping her leathers, while the others lean on their vehicles. I can tell the whole team feel deflated. No one is talking; they're just stood around inspecting Imran's car, watching Lee kneeling on the back seat and sealing the brick in an evidence bag, on the off-chance Stone Fist left any DNA on it.

As Lee backs out of the car and stands upright, Dexter shouts, 'Done that before?'

'What?'

'Bent over the back seat of a car, bagging up . . .'

Alex is laughing so much she snorts. However stressful the situation, you could always rely on Dexter to take the piss. Sometimes it's just what the team needs. But right now, I find it hard to see the funny side. The operations officer, Jeremy Leyton-Hughes, walks up to the car, looking out of place in his suit and tie. He might as well have a sign round his neck saying, 'I just sit at a desk.' He waits until the smirking has subsided.

'Right, quick update before I'll let you go. From the agent handlers in G Branch, the brothers are definitely involved in some sort of drugs activity, and whoever they are dealing with is more than likely armed. Intelligence is suggesting a criminal family originally from Belarus. GCHQ have inter-cepted text messages from targets currently unrelated to Iron Sword or Stone Fist, using known code words for weapons and ammunition. Those messages have been tracked back to the vicinity of the derelict building you had the brothers leaving out of. At the moment, it looks like you need to be back here in roughly seven hours for an early start for a Russian pick-up job at the airport. I'll brief you on it tomorrow, but it's the usual foreign intelligence officer from their SVR, posing as a diplomat.'

So that's it. An hour up the motorway to get home, and I won't even get to talk to my wife before I have to turn round and come back again. And then on to the next job. And the brothers? Well, we'll just wait for them to turn up again, won't we?

'Sorry, bear with me.' Breaking off to answer his phone, Jeremy turns his back to us, but we all study his body language as he gives one-word answers. It takes all of ten seconds for him to finish the call. I can tell from his face he's just been given bad news.

'That was the assistant director of G Branch.'

This wasn't good. The AD of any branch doesn't get involved in operations unless it's a massive fuck-up.

'The phone you GPS'd belonging to Iron Sword is still pinging up at the derelict address.'

So his phone was still there. But where is he? Jeremy's next words confirm my worst fears.

'Both of the brothers withdrew two hundred pounds in

cash, their daily limit at a cash point, a few miles north, near Walsall, confirmed by CCTV. They have since gone to ground and we have no technical tracking, no location or eavesdropping on them, no phones, email. Nothing.'

The whole team start to shake their heads, Alex muttering under her breath as she looks at me.

'Fucking bullshit. What's the point?'

She puts her helmet on with her visor up and walks straight over to her bike. Following her lead, Dexter walks to his car as the intelligence officer tries to reassert his position.

'I haven't finished yet, team!'

Jeremy shouting only highlights his superiority complex. Ignoring him, I turn to Lee.

'For fuck's sake, we've bent the rules before. All we had to do is stay on them. It's not as if we haven't all sat next to armed terrorists before, is it?'

'You know we have to follow procedure, even if we don't like it. It became a health and safety issue because we hadn't requested armed support in time. Otherwise—'

I carry on, not listening to this pathetic bullshit.

'Two of the biggest threats to the public, doing everything they can to shake us. We still don't know what their fucking plan is and we let them walk because of health and fucking safety? We're MI5!'

Jeremy looks on but stays silent as Lee counters my anger with a level of authority I'm not ready to receive.

'Hold on Logan, you're out of order here. I understand

your frustration, but if we're patient, G Branch are confident we'll be seeing those two again.'

Suddenly an image flashes into my mind. A street filled with smoke, the noise of sirens, children screaming.

My anger has gone. I just feel cold. 'Yeah, and I'm sure they're right. But it'll be on the fucking news.'

Without waiting for a reply, I climb into my car and drive away.

3

Even seasoned operators like us fall into a deep sleep sometimes; for me it only happens when I'm at home. I'm woken by my phone vibrating noisily against my car keys on the bedside table. Surely it can't be time to sneak back out of the door already? In my confused state, I feel like I've only just got home. Pressing my knuckles into my eyes, I take a deep breath and look at my phone.

New time: 1600hrs Garage A

Thank fuck for that. I can get another hour's sleep before little Joseph wakes up. I'll actually see my wife while we're both awake, can even do the nursery run. I feel a weight slip off my shoulders. Dropping the phone to the floor, I collapse back under the duvet. I can hear Sarah breathing softly next to me, asleep. That's what I need. Sleep. I hadn't realized how exhausted I'd become. I close my eyes and breathe in slowly, trying to get my heart rate back to normal. Seconds pass and my eyes flick open. Through the doorway, I can see the nightlight in Joseph's room start to dim.

It's no good. My phone vibrating has automatically put me in full operator mode, and however tired I am, I know I'm not going to get back to sleep now. It's like my body has aged forty years overnight. But there's an upside: I can sneak downstairs and have a quiet tidy up, get breakfast ready for Joseph and Sarah, put some washing on. By the time I've done all that they'll be awake and I can switch the coffee machine on. I smile to myself. It isn't much, but at least I'll be making a contribution.

I've always been good at moving around a house quietly. As a kid, I quickly learned how to sneak past my dad to avoid setting off his hair-trigger temper. I shake the memory away as I carefully plant one foot on the floor, then the other. Moving towards the stairs, I poke my head round Joseph's door. I can't believe how small he looks in his cot, lying on his side still holding his elephant teddy, as he does every night. Man, what I wouldn't give to be his age again. Absolutely nothing to worry about; everything new and exciting. And a mum and dad who would do anything for him.

Smiling, I carry on downstairs to the kitchen, careful not to walk on the steps that creak. Bloody hell – the place is immaculate. There's a toy dinosaur under one of the chairs, but that's it. Everything else clean, tidied away and in its place. I don't know how she does it. Looking after Joseph is a full-time job – *more* than most full-time jobs: it's eighteen hours a day every day, with no time off except when you're asleep. And even then, as a parent, you never really allow yourself to slip into a deep sleep in case your child needs you. Looking around the living room, I realize there's nothing for me to do. I sit down at the table and put my head in my hands. What am I actually contributing to this family? When I first became a dad, I really looked forward to reading to my kid at night, but I hardly ever do it. I'm never here. And Sarah; what she needs is a husband who takes the slack, maybe even takes her out for a nice meal once in a while. I feel like grabbing one of the mugs on the draining board and smashing it against the wall. But that would only make things worse. *Come on, get a grip.* Stop feeling sorry for yourself and *do* something. Anything.

The house might be spotless, but I could make us all breakfast and we could sit down like a proper family. Then I could run Sarah a bath and take Joseph to his nursery. Porridge for Joseph; blueberries on some little pancakes and a nice strong coffee for Sarah. Easy.

A few minutes later, I can hear Joseph starting to stir upstairs, so I turn the heat down on his porridge and try and get to his room before Sarah gets out of bed. It takes him a second to adjust when he sees it's Daddy rather than Mummy coming to lift him out of his cot, but then he smiles and kicks his legs excitedly. Is this the best feeling in the world? Still holding on tightly to his elephant, he holds his arms up, ready for me to lift him out.

'Morning, little man.'

I carry him through to Sarah and she greets me with a huge, sleepy smile. I sit on the edge of the bed with Joseph on my knee; he starts wriggling uncontrollably, bumping his head against my shoulders. Sarah starts tickling his foot.

'You love Daddy, don't you?'

I'm grinning like an idiot, but I can feel the tears beginning to well up. Do I really deserve this?

'Want some breakfast, you two?'

We go downstairs, Joseph still wriggling for all he's worth. I settle him in his high chair and start making Sarah some coffee. Then I remember something.

'Shit, one second, left my work phone upstairs.'

I go upstairs, grab the phone and sprint back down. Sarah's poured herself a mug of coffee and looks at me. She's not smiling any more.

'What time have you got to leave?'

'Don't worry, not till two-ish. The job got pushed back, so I'll take Joseph to nursery while you have a bath if you want?'

'*Yes!*' Now she's smiling again.

I grab a coffee and we sit down. Together. A family.

I don't want this to end.

'Tell you what, why don't we go to the zoo today? It's time Joseph saw a real elephant, don't you think? Otherwise he's going to grow up thinking they're all pink with button eyes. And I know how you feel about meerkats.'

At first she doesn't believe it. 'But what about . . .?'

'Don't worry. We've got time. You know what he's like. He'll go nuts for an hour then spark out and I can bring you both back before I have to leave. It'll be perfect.'

She pushes her dark hair out of her eyes and gives me a big grin. 'All right! Let's do it.'

The bliss of family life is interrupted again as my team phone goes.

Her grin disappears as if a cloud had just moved across the sun. She hands me the phone without looking at me.

'Don't worry, it'll just be some sort of admin, I'm not due in till later on.'

Sarah smiles but there's no longer any warmth in it. 'Sure. Whatever.' She gets up and starts putting porridge in a plastic bowl while I swipe the screen to answer. The voice that responds isn't the one I'm expecting. In fact, it's one I've never heard before.

'Logan, it's the DG. I'd like you to come to a meeting.'

What? The director general of MI5 is calling me at home. The man in charge of the entire Security Service. I've never even met the assistant DG, let alone his boss. What the fuck could he want? Did I overstep the mark so badly yesterday he wants to haul me in for a bollocking? Or worse: am I going to be fired? Surely Lee wouldn't have been petty enough to take his beef with me upstairs. Or was it barking at Jeremy Leyton-Hughes the way I did? Maybe they realize we've lost the brothers for good and they need a scapegoat. I know there are one or two people at Thames House who think my background will always make me suspect, including privately educated Jeremy. However good an operator I am, they'd be happy to see the back of me. But the DG?

'I . . . er . . . I'm due in at sixteen hundred hours. I could come in a bit earlier, sir, if you want me to come to your office . . .'

He must pick up on the hesitation in my voice, and his tone softens. 'Listen, Logan, you're not in trouble. But I need to meet you earlier than that, I'm afraid. Eleven hundred hours. And not in the office. At one of our garages. Zulu. You remember the location?'

I clear my throat and try to put my paranoid thoughts out of my mind.

'Yes, no problem, sir. I haven't been there in a while but I know how to get there.'

Zulu Garages are completely off-site, within a military compound. I've only ever been there once, to change a team car. I thought we'd abandoned them years ago. I do a quick calculation in my head. If the meeting isn't too long, I can get there and back and still have time to take Joseph and Sarah to the zoo before the team meeting at 1600 hours. It would take some nifty driving, but it would be worth it.

'Good, Logan, good. When you get to the garages, make your way down to the basement level. I'll meet you there.' He pauses, and when he speaks again, there's an edge of steel in his voice. 'And Logan, make sure you're not followed, tell no one. This is strictly need to know.'

'OK, sir, but—' I want to ask him who else is going to be at the meeting. Why isn't it going to be at Thames House? Why can't I tell anyone? But the line is already dead.

I quickly wipe the bewildered expression from my face and turn to Sarah, who's spooning porridge into Joseph's mouth with total concentration, as if she hasn't been paying attention to the conversation. But I know she's been processing every word, trying to figure out if our plans for the day have just gone out the window.

'Fuck me if that wasn't the director general . . .'

She throws me a quick frown. Little Joseph can't understand a word, but I know I shouldn't swear in front of him. He still only says a handful of words, but neither of us want him picking up that sort of language.

'Sorry, look, I've got to go and see him . . .'

Another disappointed face. Worried this time. She knows my reputation at Thames House as well as I do.

'Nah, nah, nothing serious. I think he probably wants to give me a medal. And it's not too far away.' I glance at my watch. 'I'll be back in plenty of time. We can always leave a little bit later to get to the zoo. The elephants aren't going anywhere.'

She looks into my eyes, a spoonful of porridge hovering in mid-air, just out of Joseph's reach. He makes a complaining sound and slaps his hand on the top of his seat. Maintaining your cover and fronting things out when you're under pressure is all part of the job, and I like to think there's no one better at it, but Sarah's the one person I can't lie to. She instantly knows when I'm trying to pull the wool over her eyes, and right now they're like laser beams, searing into me.

'I don't believe that. Why can't he see you when you're in the office? Why does it have to be today?'

She goes back to feeding Joseph.

I feel a surge of frustration. I'm doing my best here. 'Look, I wouldn't normally get this much time with you and Joseph during the week. This afternoon is a bonus . . .'

As soon as the words are out of my mouth I want to snatch them back. Sarah swivels in her chair, knocking the pot of porridge to the floor. 'A *bonus*? This is what normal people do, what normal *families* do. It shouldn't be a special treat I'm supposed to be grateful for. If we can't do things like this then what's the point?'

'The point?' I can feel my anger rising. All the frustrations about my own failings are coming to the surface. 'In case you've forgotten, I'm trying to keep us safe, to keep you and Joseph safe, to stop those bastards—'

Joseph lets out a wail and puts out his little hands, fingers reaching out to his mum. My raised voice has scared him. Oh, God, this is the last thing I want. I don't want to be this person. Unbuckling his safety clip, I lift him gently out of his high chair and pull him to my chest.

'I'm sorry, baba. Daddy's sorry. I didn't mean to scare you.'

I smother him in kisses and he stops crying as quickly as he started. I let out a breath and gently rock him, then reach an arm out and gently squeeze Sarah's shoulder.

'I'm sorry. I didn't mean to snap at you. It's just—'

She shrugs my hand away. 'Logan, I married *you*, not your team, not the director fucking general, *you*. But I feel I don't really have you to myself any more. Of course I know it's important, what you do, and I'm proud of that. But Logan, Joseph and I need you too.'

'Look, I know it's hard. You know I want more time with you both. And if it was just a team meeting, you know, I could turn up late for once . . .' She purses her lips, not believing it for a moment. 'But it's the director general, and you know I can't say no. But it'll be quick, I know it will. And we can still go to the zoo.'

Joseph makes a gurgling sound against my chest, almost as if he understands the word 'zoo'. Sarah's still angry, though. She won't look me in the eye. I cup her chin with my hand and gently turn her face towards me.

'I promise!'

She sighs and holds her arms out for Joseph. It's like she's given up; resigned herself to the fate of being a single mum. Her voice doesn't sound angry, just sad.

'Logan, go. Get ready, or you're going to be late.'

Passing Joseph over, I look at my watch and quickly work out how long I've got to get ready. Shit, it's going be tight. I go back upstairs, resisting the urge to sprint. The last thing I want to do is freak Joseph out again now he's calm. Three minutes later, I'm all set. Sarah's standing by the door with Joseph. I give her a peck on the cheek and kiss Joseph's forehead.

'I'll be back soon.'

She opens the door. 'Just go!'

* * *

As I pull away from the house, I have to clamp my hands tight on the steering wheel to stop them from shaking. After the screw-up with the brothers, all I wanted to do was get home to Sarah and Joseph, to spend some quality time with my little family. Instead, I ended up having a row with my wife and making my son cry. Why was it so fucking hard?

I dodge and weave my way through the traffic, driving at the limit, daring any copper to pull me over. As I overtake a startled Porsche driver on the inside, a thought strikes me and suddenly I laugh out loud. I slap my hand on the steering wheel. Of course! What if the DG *has* summoned me to this secret meeting to fire me? That would solve all my problems at a stroke. No more frustration because I wasn't being allowed to do my job properly. And no more rows with Sarah. We could spend as much time together as we liked, go to the zoo every day of the week until we're sick of the fucking sight of elephants! Of course, that was leaving out the question of how I was going to earn any money to support my family, but what the hell, I'd think of something. I laugh like an insane man. Zookeeper maybe? How about looking after the elephants? I'm good at clearing up shit.

After another ten minutes of slightly calmer driving, the idea of losing my job doesn't seem so hysterically funny anymore. I don't want some crappy job that anyone could do. I want to make a difference. But I'll just have to see what the DG has in mind. What will be will be.

I hear my phone vibrating on the passenger seat and pull over to check it. A text from Sarah:

Don't worry about rushing back. Going to zoo this morning
with Janie and Leo. Take your time. Love S.

Damn! After all that, they're going without me. That is
typical Sarah: now her anger has cooled, she's trying to do
what's best for everyone else – for me, for Joseph – without
thinking of herself. She knows how hard it is for me to balance work and family, and she doesn't want me to feel guilty.
For the millionth time, I tell myself I don't deserve her.

The barracks come into sight and I scan the fence, trying
to see how many guards there are on the perimeter. The
place was only manned by a skeleton force the last time I was
here, and even they were really only there for our benefit.
Being a Tuesday, there are also no weekend warriors about
today, so the place looks practically deserted. The DG obviously wanted somewhere that was secure but where the chances
of us being observed were practically zero.

I follow the fence line to the main gates. There's a Military
Provost Guard Service guy on the gate, and I can see from
his spotless uniform and the way he moves and holds his rifle
that he's keen as mustard, even though he won't have a clue
about the garages he's guarding. No chance of just cruising
through the gates then. I'll have to show my civilian cover
ID. Slowly coming to a stop, I morph into a slightly stumbling civil servant.

'Hello, sorry, bear with me. I have my identification card
here somewhere . . .'

'No problem, sir. You're a civilian I take it?'

'For my sins, yes. Civil Service. I think my office have left some files in one of the buildings over there. Ah, here it is.'

As he checks the photo ID, he clearly recognizes the type; a Civilian All Access card that has just the basics: photo, hologram crest and expiry date. Defence contractors and ex-military advisors use ID cards like this to get onto military bases. I have a lanyard attached to mine that has 'Defence Contractor' printed on it, so I should be able to slide in without creating a fuss. Internet forums are full of geeks speculating about what these sorts of barracks are for, so the last thing you want is to march in like you own the place, shouting 'We're MI5!'

'Thank you, sir.' The MPGS man hands the card back to me with a courteous smile. 'I take it you know which building you're going to?'

'Yes, I won't be long, I'm sure.'

He raises the barrier and I give him a wave and drive through, nice and slow, the way an anonymous pen-pusher would drive. It takes a full minute to cross the camp to the garages, an unmanned, windowless block with two massive shutter doors covering the entrance and exit. I enter my pass code into the keypad and the shutters roll up smoothly, revealing a pitch-dark interior. I can feel my heart rate starting to climb.

I creep into the garages in first gear, then wait for the roller door to shut behind me. Standard practice. We used to keep a lot of specialist vehicles here, and I don't want to be responsible for letting a curious guard or squaddie in to have a look around. Flicking my lights on, I move slowly down to the first lower level. I recognize some of the older vehicles from old boys' descriptions; some of these look like the ones they used back in the day. On the next level down I spot an old situation awareness car we used during our training with Special Forces, its windows still broken. The deeper I go, the more evident it is that this place hasn't seen any life for a long time, almost like I was driving back in time. Vehicles getting older, filled with technology I've never used, probably dating back to the Cold War. I just hope I'm not about to be consigned to the history books too.

Finally, I reach the deepest level. A dusty sign tells me I'm in the basement, eight floors underground. There's just one vehicle down here, its engine on, vapour pouring out of the exhausts. I pull alongside and I can see the DG behind the wheel. There's no one else in the car. This isn't right. As far as I'm aware, he never goes anywhere without a protection detail, one of whom would always be doing the driving. I kill the lights and get out. Trying to appear professional, I walk round towards his passenger door before I realize he's already climbing out, holding out a hand.

'Logan, thanks for making the time to meet. You recognize me, I take it?'

'Of course, sir. Your face is all over the walls of Thames House, talking about equal opportunities and health and safety . . .'

My attempt to lighten the tension washes over him. He doesn't smile.

'You'll have to excuse the setting, Logan. This is the first time we've met, but it needs to be the last, too.'

I nod as if I understand, but I don't. I can't believe the DG would be taking all these operational risks just to tell me I'm out. So what the fuck *is* going on?

I wait for him to speak. He maintains eye contact, and his steady gaze starts to make me uncomfortable. It's as if he's weighing me up, deciding whether he can trust me. You don't get to be in his position without having years of operational experience. After what seems like minutes, he clears his throat.

'Logan, how would you say we were doing in the war against terror, if I can use that media phrase? Are we winning?'

I reply without hesitation. 'Look at how many attacks we've stopped. I'd say we're the best in the world at what we're doing.'

'I dare say we are. I'd certainly like to think so. But that doesn't answer my question, does it? Maybe we've just been lucky up to now. What if our luck runs out?'

Instinctively I want to defend my team, assure him that we can do it. 'We can win, sir, I'm sure of it. If we can just—' I stop myself, realizing I'm about to stray into dangerous territory.

The DG smiles thinly as his eyes sharpen. 'If we can just be allowed to do our job properly? Is that what you were going to say?'

'Well, I . . .'

'Look, Logan, I know what happened yesterday. I know you weren't too happy we let two important targets slip out of our grasp. And frankly I'm not happy about it, either. It's not the first time we've let rules and regulations get in the way of our work, and I'm sorry to say it won't be the last.'

I don't know what to say. I'd openly criticized the team leader for not bending the rules. Now the DG seems to be encouraging me to go even further. Is it a trap? Is he trying to get me to incriminate myself even further?

He keeps looking at me with those steely eyes. I know he can see through any attempt I make to cover up what I really think.

'Yes, sir. I think we screwed up. Those two could be planning to kill hundreds of innocent people, but either lack of planning – like failing to request armed police – or not having the balls to keep us on the ground has let us down. We *are* good enough to beat these guys, but if we have our hands tied behind our backs, we can't do it.'

The DG nods. 'So what's the answer? How can we give ourselves the best chance of winning the game?'

The tension in my body starts to ease off. He's giving me the green light to tell him what I really think. The floodgates are opening. 'What we need is the freedom to do whatever's needed in the circumstances, to make the call on the ground. Not having to worry about conflicting operations, support from the police. I don't care about someone back at Thames House shitting their pants over health and safety. We need the ability to do exactly what's needed within the confines of our own team.' I swallow hard. I've already gone too far. Now I'm about to put the cherry on the top. 'And, if there's no other way, then a hard stop. Take the bastards out.'

I wait. The earth doesn't swallow me up. A gang of military police fail to rush out from behind a pillar to arrest me. Instead, the DG grins broadly.

'A deniable team. Not bound by the usual rules. You decide how far you need to go to counter the threat. Is that what you mean?'

'Yes, sir. That's exactly what I'm saying. But obviously that wouldn't be—'

He holds up a gloved hand. 'Don't try to sugar-coat it. We both know exactly what we're talking about. What if I was to say that I propose setting up just such a team, and I'm inviting you to join it?'

Shit. So that's what all the cloak and dagger's about. No wonder the DG didn't want anyone knowing about this meeting, let alone being within earshot. What we're talking about is way outside our legal framework.

'It would still be MI5; still surveillance, with some added skill sets according to your background. But you'd be in a completely deniable team. You wouldn't set foot in Thames House. You'd be working harder and for the same pay, but when it came down to it, you'd have the freedom to do what's needed. With your military background, I believe you'd be perfect for the team. What do you say?'

My mind is spinning. On one hand, this is exactly what I wanted. A chance to even out the playing field. To maximize our chances of stopping every terrorist plot that we could uncover. Stopping them hard. I've dreamed about something like this, never thinking it would actually happen. And now the director general of MI5 is offering it to me on a plate.

But what about Sarah and Joseph? I'm barely managing to keep my family together as it is. If I take on this new job, I know exactly what will happen. They'd see me even less than they did now. We'd fall apart.

'Boss, we need this, this absolutely needs to happen, but—'

'*But?*' The DG's face changes, his encouraging expression replaced by a look of icy determination. This isn't a man who people say 'no' to. 'A surveillance team of people like you, stopping the ones the normal teams struggle with. Look how long it took to get that hate preacher Green Moss out of the country. Without this new team, the bad ones, the really dangerous ones, will continue to use our own justice system against us. We can't afford to let that fucking happen.'

Hearing him swear is shocking. It's like the first time you see a teacher out of school, having a drink or going into a bookies. But it makes the point.

'Boss, I can't. My family. I already don't see them enough.' A knot in my stomach tightens. This might be the first time I've genuinely put my family first. I feel sick, but I know it's the right thing to do.

The DG looks like he's going to explode, but after a moment he just nods, like he understands. 'Logan, I've made the same sacrifices. I had a son. Have. I have a son. All grown up now, I suppose. I haven't seen or heard from him in years.' He reaches into the pocket of his coat and pulls out a card. It's blank except for a handwritten phone number. 'People like us, Logan, make sacrifices. So no one else has to. Think about it. Give me an answer by the end of the week. This is my personal number, active until this coming Friday.' He leans closer. 'Obviously, this discussion goes no further.'

I've got three days to change my mind. Fuck, he's clever. The DG had done his homework, and knows that with my personality I will obsess over this decision. I stare blankly at the card as he gets into his car and drives up the ramp to the higher levels. I get into mine and sit behind the wheel, waiting for my heart rate to slow and giving the DG enough time to clear the building. I slide the card into my wallet and drive slowly back up to the exit.

As the shutters roll down behind me and the first spots of rain start to hit the windscreen, it feels like an exciting new part of my life is being closed off before I have the chance to explore it. But my family comes first. It has to. I put my foot on the brake and the car comes to a complete stop. I take my phone out of my coat pocket and start typing out a text message.

Hope you guys are having fun at the zoo. I'm on my way home. Love you both.

I press send, then take a moment to change back into civil servant mode again before driving slowly towards the guard on the gate, who waves me through without a thought. The DG's car is nowhere to be seen.

Back on the road, I have to stop myself from driving too fast. I know I've got plenty of time to get back now, but I'm desperate to see Sarah and Joseph. I know as soon as I hold them both in my arms, the temptation of the DG's offer will lose its power over me. The job is all about protecting people just like them, but what's the point if you have to sacrifice your own loved ones to do it? I just need to see, feel, smell and touch them, then I'll know for sure.

I drive on through the rain, through anonymous city streets, then out into gently rolling countryside, everything grey and wet under dark clouds. I wonder if Joseph and Sarah got caught in the rain at the zoo. Would she have remembered to bring the rain cover for the buggy? I smile to myself. Of course she would. Sarah remembers everything. She's the best. And I'm not going to lose her.

Checking the time on the dashboard clock, I figure they might not be home yet when I get back. I've got time to stop off at the shops and get some flowers for Sarah. Maybe find a cuddly toy for Joseph. Not that he needs any more. And he only really likes his toy elephant anyway. I wonder what he made of the real elephants. Did he even know they were the same thing? At that age, it's hard to know what they can understand. I smile to myself. He has so many amazing things to learn. So many experiences to look forward to.

I turn on the radio, looking for some music to carry me home. Instead I get the middle of a newsflash.

'. . . *so far, we have two confirmed dead and at least six people severely injured in the frenzied attack. Unverified eyewitness reports from the scene suggest that two of the victims are a mother and her young child. We can confirm that a man was arrested at the scene, and a weapon has been recovered, believed to be a knife. Eyewitness reports have suggested the man, who's believed to be local and known to the police, was under the influence of drugs. Police have sealed off the area around the zoo but it's believed to be an isolated incident . . .'*

For a moment, everything goes black. I can't breathe. A horn blares as I veer into the next lane.

I hear a voice screaming. It's my own. 'No, *no*! Please God, don't let it be them.'

4

Move! As I make my way through traffic, I still can't get through on the phone. *Come on, Sarah, pick up, answer your phone!*

It rings out again, switching to voicemail for the seventh time. It's probably on silent in her bag, I tell myself. It doesn't necessarily mean . . . Dropping down from fourth gear to third, I swing onto the hard shoulder to accelerate past a long line of traffic, then suddenly realize I don't know whether to go home or to the zoo. Shit – which? Fuck, you're panicking, calm yourself. Ring Lee.

After what seems like an age, the call connects.

'Lee, the attack at the zoo on the news. My wife and son are there. Can you find out who the mother and child were that got injured? I can't get hold of Sarah.'

Lee's answer is rock-steady, professional. 'Yeah, mate, let me ring Ops now. I'll ring you back straight away. Head home, don't worry, I'm sure they'll be fine.'

I'm not that far away from either the zoo or home, maybe thirty minutes to either if I can keep picking my way through traffic. I just need Sarah to answer her phone. *Jesus*, what's the point of having a mobile phone if you don't answer it? I remember the tracking app on my phone; I can see where she is through the family locator we have. I snatch up the handset. *Come on, come on, find Sarah's phone.*

As I wait for the app to finish its buffering cycle and provide a result, I get clear of traffic and put my foot down. Then the dash screen flashes with another call.

'Logan, it's Lee.' His voice isn't quite so steady this time. 'Mate, go to Luton and Dunstable Hospital. Intelligence coming in so far is suggesting your wife and son could have been injured. I don't have any other details yet. I'll meet you there.'

'What? Are they injured or not? Is Joseph OK?'

'I don't have any more information. Don't go home, though. The Ops officers are taking precautions to protect you just in case this was a specific attack on your family. Until we know more, we need to keep you safe. Thames House have sent armed police and Special Branch to the hospital, too. Go to the main entrance. Me and Special Branch will meet you there. I'll be twenty minutes.'

While one part of my brain is desperately trying to digest what all this means, another part is just focusing on getting me to the hospital. Spotting signs for Luton, I pile on the revs, flashing the headlights constantly to force the traffic on the other side of the road out of the way.

Doing surveillance work, your mind can be the worst enemy you'll ever have. Sometimes you'll spend hours at a time sitting still, with nothing to do but think. So you learn to shut your mind down, just focus on your cover. But right now, my thoughts are racing as fast as my driving. And I can't stop them.

A specific attack on your family. Meaning what? What sort of an attack? I have to know what's happened to Sarah and Joseph. I don't give a damn about the who or the why. Then another thought hits me. Lee said they could be targeting me, which means I'm doubly responsible. Not only was I not there to protect them, but it was because of *me* they were attacked. *Attacked?* Fuck. Visions of Sarah and Joseph, screaming, covered in blood, fill my head.

The sign for the hospital, thank God. Pulling off the main road, I follow signs for the entrance. I hit the brakes hard, the tyres skidding to a complete stop. I ditch the car in a reserved spot and barrel through the doors, almost knocking over a smartly dressed woman who must have been waiting for me. She quickly regains her composure and puts a hand on my arm. I realize I'm shaking.

'Hello, sir. If you'd like to follow me, we have a room just down here.'

'A fucking room? Where's my family? Who the fuck are you?'

'I'm Special Branch. We can explain everything. Please, come with me.'

She purses her lips, trying not to show any emotion, but her eyes have already told me the worst. The surrounding voices of the doctors and nurses all blend into one another as we make our way down the corridor to a room with an armed police officer standing outside, the butt of his specially modified Heckler & Koch MP5 resting against his right shoulder.

The Special Branch officer opens the door. My team leader is standing by an empty chair. He greets me with that same look.

'FUCK YOU! Stop looking at me like that. Where's my family? I know they've been hurt, I want to see them. Joseph will want to see me, he'll be scared.'

'Logan, please take a seat. Please.'

'*No!* If no one's going to tell me anything, then either take me to my wife and son or I'll find them myself.'

He stands there next to the Special Branch woman, saying nothing. A couple of shop-window dummies. A wave of anger washes over me and my instinct takes over as I fire back towards the door. I need to see Sarah and Joseph. I grab the handle and rip the door open, but the police officer is standing in the way. He turns towards me, clearly not expecting the door to open so quickly after I entered.

'MOVE!' I shout into his face.

He doesn't react, just puts one arm out with his palm towards me in a 'calm down' gesture. I don't have time for this. 'Fucking MOVE!' I stiff-arm him out of the way and, despite the fact that he's well over six foot and built like a heavyweight boxer, he staggers back against the wall.

I turn left down the corridor, looking for the sign to A&E. That must be where they are. But all the signs just have names of wards on them. Everything starts to get blurred as my head swings left, right and back again. Where the fuck is A&E? I go right. If I keep going in one direction I'm bound to find it.

'Logan!'

Lee is right behind me. I step out in front of a nurse, blocking her path. Seeing her panicked look, I try to sound calm and sane.

'Excuse me, my wife and son have been brought here. I think they could be in A&E. My wife is Sarah Logan, my son is Joseph. He's eighteen months old.'

She wants to help but I can see from her vacant expression that the names mean nothing to her. Hundreds of patients come through A&E every day. 'They were both attacked at the zoo earlier, it's been on the news?' I add, hoping that will help her.

She puts a hand to her mouth to stifle her horror. She knows. *Everyone knows.* Lee steps in front of her and fills my field of vision. He grips my shoulder firmly, but not aggressively. The rage inside me drops to my feet like I've just let go of the world's heaviest weight, leaving me light-headed. The need to tear this hospital down brick by brick until I found them was protecting me; my aggression, my need to retaliate, was shielding me from the awful truth. A truth I cannot bear to admit. My family. My little Joseph.

No, I won't believe it.

'Logan, please. Please come back into the room and sit down.'

I can't focus. Details move in and out, like someone is

adjusting a camera lens. A sign reminding people to wash their hands; the safety catch of the police officer's rifle; a yellow strip light in a ceiling of otherwise white lights. It feels as if I'm standing still and the world around me is moving as I'm led back into the little side room. The police officer, still expressionless, takes a step back to allow us in. I can't see Lee's face as he gently pushes me forwards, but by the reaction of the Special Branch woman, a look has passed between them.

Weirdly, I feel calmer back in this room, as if the terrible reality only exists across the threshold. Back in here, Sarah and Joseph could still be OK. I sit.

A new hand squeezes my shoulder.

'Mr Logan?'

A doctor, in clean scrubs. Beside him a man in a dark suit with a gentle expression, who I instantly know is one of the family liaison types who try to rationalize death with a leaflet. Sitting on a grey sofa, sandwiched between Lee and the Special Branch officer, I feel boxed in, claustrophobic. I take a deep breath. Focus. Front this feeling out. Sarah and Joseph are fine, just hurt. They'll be recovering. That's all. Recovering.

I just need someone to tell me that. But no one is talking. Why the fuck doesn't anyone say anything? Somebody. Anybody. TALK!

Lee breaks the silence.

'Doctor, I'm Mr Logan's team leader. You've been briefed

by Special Branch about the potential security threat we're investigating, correct?'

'Yes, of course. My primary concern, though, is Mr Logan.'

The doctor looks at me. His expression cuts through the thin veneer of hope and exposes the well of darkness below. He knows that, deep down, I already know the truth.

'We did everything we could. I want you to know, they both fought hard. But . . . the injuries they sustained . . .'

He breaks eye contact as he tries to clear his throat. I know he's thinking about the injuries to my wife and son. I want to know what he's seeing, but at the same time I'm terrified of what it might be.

'I'm sorry. We're all sorry. We couldn't save them.'

Now that someone has actually put it into words, I can feel the tension in the room easing. It's as if everyone was holding their breath. And I feel different, too. A moment ago, I was a jumbled mass of emotions: hope, fear, anger. Now it's as if all my insides, all my feelings, have been ripped out, and I'm just an empty shell. For what seems like an eternity, I just sit there. I can see my hands, placed flat on my knees to stop them shaking, but they seem to belong to someone else. I'm not here. I'm nowhere.

And then a small flicker of feeling, like a spark in the darkness. It grows into a flame and I start to feel it burning inside me.

'I want to see them. Now. Right now.'

I stand up. I need to remove myself from the compassionate sandwich of this sofa.

'Tell me everything or I'm going to fucking lose it.'

'Matt . . .' Lee never uses my first name, ever. I realize he's holding a brown folder, and I instantly know what's inside. 'It's not advisable for you to see them because of their injuries, but you can ID them. We still don't know if this was a specific attack to get to you. We're making arrangements to get you out of here. Right now, we're just not sure if this was a lone wolf attack or a larger cell.'

Nothing he's saying makes any sense. All I know is that he's about to show me pictures of Sarah and Joseph. That's the closest I can get to them. I can't hug them. Kiss them. I won't be able to touch them ever again.

The liaison officer stands up, preparing himself to be a shoulder to cry on while I look at pictures of my dead family. The thought of it fans the flame inside me into an inferno.

'Don't you dare try and offer me comfort.'

I lurch towards him, hands clenched into fists. Lee's hand slams against my chest as the hospital's liaison officer stumbles back towards his chair. He's terrified.

As quickly as it had erupted, my fury is replaced by shame.

'I didn't mean . . . I shouldn't have . . .'

The doctor tries to take control. 'Mr Logan. Matt. I was in charge when your wife and son arrived with the other victims from the zoo. I treated them personally.'

Taking the folder from Lee, he pulls the first picture out, then another. He holds the two pictures against his chest.

Moving to stand alongside me, he puts his free arm around my shoulder. He holds the pictures in front of me, one behind the other, as if he's about to demonstrate a card trick.

Sarah. She's sleeping, her head to one side. Eyes closed. I feel my hand moving towards her to touch her cheek. To gently wake her up. But I know now why no one wants me to actually see them. The photograph is cropped close, only showing her face, but I can see the beginning of gashes where her hair should be.

'Sarah . . .' My voice is barely a whisper.

The doctor removes his arm briefly from around my shoulder and pulls the second picture out from behind the first.

'Baba . . . my little man.' This time I can't stop myself from reaching out to touch my son. There is a piece of gauze hiding one cheek and his left eye. I want to pull it away.

Then the pictures are gone. The doctor quickly passes them back to Lee, who puts them back in the folder. The magic trick is finished.

My eyes fill with tears and my chest tightens. I want to be sick, but I can't swallow. I have to move. I hear voices but I can't hear what they're saying. Arms claw at me but I don't feel them.

I'm nearly at the hospital exit. How did I get here? More voices, shouting now. *Just get away, Logan. Run.*

'Logan, wait!'

I'm not waiting for anyone. I have no idea where I'm going, but I can't stay here. It's dark outside, cold and starting to rain. My team car's still where I parked it. I jump in, reverse out, then floor it, turning onto the main road without bothering about oncoming traffic. *Drive, Logan. Go somewhere, anywhere.* The radio's still on, the music interrupted by the warning alarm telling me I haven't put my seat belt on and the beeping horns of cars swerving to avoid me. I slam into third gear. Speedo jumps to eighty. *Drive faster, just get away.*

But I can't outrun reality. The music stops for a newsflash. *'Breaking news tonight, a drug-fuelled knife attack in broad daylight leaves a mother and son dead and half a dozen more fighting for their lives . . .'*

Bile surges from the bottom of my stomach, my abdominals are suddenly in full spasm and I start to lose control of the car. Instinctively, I hit the brakes and clutch at the same time, turning my head as vomit spews out onto the passenger seat and down into the foot well. The screech of the tyres drowns out the rest of the news report. I push my body back upright, bracing myself for a collision as I bring the car to a halt.

But the crunch of twisted metal and broken glass doesn't come. Instead, my headlights pick out a row of dark, dilapidated buildings in front of me. I've slid off the main road onto a disused access to an industrial estate.

The screen on the dash lights up again with an incoming call. And another. The stream of calls is endless as I stare out of the windscreen at a rusting metal fence protecting an old abandoned warehouse. In front of it there's a lamp post, its bulb long broken, providing no light at all in this dark corner of nowhere. My phone is receiving text messages; voicemail from the missed calls. But I don't want to talk to anyone. Except for the two people whose voices I'll never hear again. I'm desperate to see Sarah and Joseph, to hear their voices one more time, but my work phone is sanitized – no personal photos or videos. All I can hear is the ticking of the engine as it cools.

They're gone. And I should have been at the zoo to protect them. If I'd chosen my family instead of this fucking job I could have stopped that cunt hurting them. My fist flies out, my knuckles banging the window, but it's too late. My anger has missed its target. They died because of me, because of what I do and because I wasn't there. The most important job in the world, being a father and a husband, and I failed.

Suddenly I'm retching again, but I don't have anything left in my stomach. Whatever my pathetic body is trying to achieve, it's futile, like me. Pathetic and futile.

My family is the only thing that makes me whole. Without them there is no point in existing. We had so many plans. Now I'll never see Joseph's first school nativity, Sarah and me holding hands in the audience, glowing with pride. Or pretend to be the tooth fairy, sneaking a coin under his pillow. We'll never play football in the park.

An animalistic cry comes out of me. I can't bear this.

I've never believed in an afterlife, heaven and hell and all that. When you're gone you're gone, I've always said. But maybe I was wrong. Maybe they're in some sort of afterlife, not clouds and angels with harps, but . . . something. Life's mysterious. After all, energy can never be lost, right? Only transferred into a different state. Wherever they are, I could join them right now. We'd be together forever. And this time I'd never leave them. Never let anything bad happen to them ever again.

I breathe out slowly and an icy calm settles over me.

OK, let's do this in a way that doesn't hurt or kill anyone else. I can't drive flat out into oncoming traffic. Can't slit my wrists in case someone finds me and tries to save my life. Has to be quick.

I look out of the window and there it is. My salvation.

I turn the car around and reverse back towards the lamp post, ignoring the beeps of the parking sensors. I walk round to the back of the car and open the boot. Searching through the operational kit bags, I find the breakdown kit and its two long, heavy tow ropes. I nod to myself. They'll do.

The car's beeps are now telling me that I've got the boot and driver's door open while the engine is still running. Their rhythm oddly matches the thumping of my heart against my chest.

I wrap one of the two ropes around the base of the lamp post, looping it onto itself to create an unbreakable anchor point. I'll have to feed the loose end into the back seat of the car through the boot space. Grabbing the second tow rope, which is longer and a fair bit heavier, I move round to the back doors of the car and lean inside. I join the second tow rope to the first, make a second anchor loop, then feed this loop through the headrest of the driver's seat, leaving most of the slack on the back seat directly behind the driver's position. More than enough. I walk round to the driver's side and get in, shutting the door behind me.

I've got just enough tow rope to slip over my head and around my neck.

Bong, bong, bong, bong, bong . . .

It seems like the car's warning bongs are speeding up along with my heart rate now. The cold air from the open boot is like the touch of the grim reaper, waiting to escort me to my family.

I'm ready.

I should be able to get up to 20 miles per hour before the slack runs out and the lamp post tightens this makeshift noose. The break should be instant. I don't give a fuck if it pulls my head clean from my shoulders. The quicker this is done the quicker I'll be with my family again.

I keep the clutch down, slip into first gear and pile the revs on. My left foot is sliding off the clutch, seconds to go and it'll be done. No more pain. Closing my eyes, I can picture Joseph holding his elephant teddy, a smile growing across his face. Daddy's coming!

There's a bright light and my eyes open instinctively. It's the information screen on the dash.

Not a call this time. A text message from Alex. From anyone else, I'd ignore it.

Logan, the guy responsible was acting alone. It's early in the investigation but it looks like he'll be tried for manslaughter and will get away with diminished responsibility because he was hallucinating. I'm sorry. So sorry. Ring, text or come meet me if you need anything. Day or night. A

Until now, I'd managed not to think much about the man who'd killed my family. I didn't give a fuck about him. All that mattered was that my family was dead. Now, suddenly, he's real. Alex's words lodge in my brain and I can't get them out. *Diminished responsibility*. I could see how it would play out now. He won't even be tried as a murderer. I can see him sitting in court, smiling to himself.

The revs on the engine come down as my foot comes off the accelerator. My hand instinctively slides the gearstick into neutral again. I take my foot off the clutch.

This bullshit system of arresting people for murder and letting them off, blaming it on the drugs that warped their minds. He's a killer. He murdered my family! I'm not cold anymore, I'm boiling hot, ready to erupt. If that fucker wants to play the human-rights card or pretend he's mentally ill, I'll make him wish he was never born. I'll rip him apart with my bare hands.

In this moment of rage, it hits me that I can't commit suicide. It would be so easy, just forgetting about the injustice of the world so I can be at peace with Sarah and Joseph. But I know now that would be betraying them.

Letting the murderers escape justice. Letting them win. Letting them have this world.

I can't just shrug off the pain of losing them by taking my own life. I don't deserve to have that peace. I need to keep fighting. And I'll be a tougher opponent this time round. I'm stronger now, because I have nothing to lose.

And there's another reason too.

My wallet's on the passenger seat. I pull out the director general's card, pick up my phone and punch in the number. As it rings, I force the tow rope back over my head and throw it behind me.

I wonder if the DG will tell me how sorry he is; ask me if there's anything he can do. But when he answers, his voice is steely.

'Logan.'

I pause, like a diver on a high board, working up the nerve to jump.

'I'm in.'

5

I'm lying in a coffin, wearing my best – my only – suit. Hands are by my sides like I'm stood to attention back in the army. Waiting. The smoothness of the silk lining is like nothing I've felt before. It's pitch-black but I'm calm, knowing I'm dead, absorbing the non-judgemental ease of it. There's one more thing I have to do before I can be completely at peace; I just have to let them push the coffin into the flames. There'll be a few seconds of pain, as the excruciating brightness overwhelms me, then I'll quickly turn to ash and blow away in the wind. Wait, I'm dead. So why will there be pain? How am I talking to myself? There's something else; another thing I have to do, and I can't quite remember what it is. Not knowing starts to gnaw away at my sense of calm. I start shifting around; it's no longer comfortable inside the coffin. It's suddenly become harsh and strong, not soft to ease my journey. It's been made to keep me in here, a prison to keep me locked in the guilt of failing my family. God, please no. I'm still alive.

Suddenly there's a loud rapping on the lid of the coffin, right over my head. I jolt upwards and bang my head on the wood. The knocking continues – *bang! bang! bang!* – and now I can hear a voice, pleading from the other side.

'Logan! Logan! Open up!'

It's Sarah.

Of course! How could I have been such an idiot? That's what my sense of unease was all about. Sarah and Joseph are outside. They need to be in here with me; we need to be buried together, as a family. I raise my hands awkwardly and push against the coffin lid as hard as I can but it doesn't budge, and the knocking's getting louder and Sarah's sounding even more desperate.

'Logan! Come on, it's time!'

I make another huge effort to push my way out, but my arms somehow get tangled up in the lining, and then suddenly I'm free and falling and I land on something hard with a crunching sound. I feel a stab of pain in my hand, and as I open my eyes a wave of nausea wells up inside me and the light coming through the partially opened curtains stabs into my retinas. I'm lying on the floor, next to the bed. I've smashed an empty bottle of vodka, and blood is running through my fingers and into the carpet.

My brain finally registers the bad news.

I'm not dead. It's Monday morning. Sarah and Joseph's funeral is tomorrow.

So who the hell is banging on the front door? As if in answer to my question, the knocking starts up again.

'Come on Logan, open up!'

I recognize Alex's voice. Tough, no nonsense, but with a

layer of tenderness behind it. I haul myself to my feet, sending another empty bottle skittering under the bed. My jeans are in a crumpled heap on the floor and I put them on, despite the mingled smell of piss and vodka they're giving off. I grab a tissue from the bedside table, which is at a slight angle – that must have been what I hit my head on. I close my fist around the tissue to stop the blood dripping as I stumble down the stairs and open the door.

Alex is wearing a dark skirt and jacket over a white blouse. Her blonde hair is pulled back into a tight ponytail and her eyes are hidden by dark glasses. Her right hand is raised as if I caught her just as she was about to start another round of knocking. She drops it to her side.

'Christ, Logan. You look like shit. What've you done to your hand?'

'I . . . I don't . . .' I can't think; don't know what to say. I'm still half in the dream, the other half numb with the realization that another day has dawned, another day I have to somehow get through, and my head feels as if someone's buried a hatchet in the back of my skull.

'Right.' Alex pushes past me and turns to slam the door. It's like she's gone into operator mode: all business. 'I'll put the coffee on. You're going to need gallons. Get into the shower. Can you do that on your own? No, let me look at that hand first. Where's your first aid kit?'

As she starts pushing me back up the stairs, I finally find my voice.

'What are you doing here? I know it's all a fucking mess, but the funeral's not until Tuesday.'

The disappointed half-noise she makes says it all. 'It *is* Tuesday, Logan. The car's coming to pick you up in an hour.'

Jesus. I've lost a day. If it wasn't for Alex I'd have missed the funeral. The thought makes me feel even sicker than I already am. Sick and ashamed. It's been six – no, seven – days since Sarah and Joseph died, since they were *killed*. At first there were things to do: death certificates, paperwork, organizing the funeral, deciding on the coffins, what Sarah and Joseph should be wearing, what flowers would she like? I stumbled through it like a zombie and every decision seemed to take forever, but focusing on all the different tasks kept me from falling into the abyss. Once it was all done I had nothing to block off the pain, nothing to keep the memories, the regrets, the guilt from overwhelming me.

So I hit the bottle. I didn't want to sleep, because then the dreams would come. Sarah and Joseph holding out their arms, covered in blood and crying, 'Help me! Please, why won't you help me?' And I didn't want to be conscious either, because everything in the house, everything I saw and touched and smelled, had the power to stab me through the heart, from the bed Sarah and I shared, to the rows of baby food lined up in the kitchen cupboard. Only when I was so smashed that I couldn't think or feel was there any relief from the pain. My dad was an alcoholic. Which is probably why I never drank as a teenager, and had contempt for people who did. But maybe the craving was in my blood all along, just waiting for the right trigger to bring it to the surface. In a matter of days, I'd become someone who couldn't imagine how it was possible to get through the day without a bottle by his side, how to even get out of bed in the morning – that's if I'd managed to get to bed before passing out – without a couple of stiff ones.

And right now, despite the hammering in my head and the sickness in my guts, what I really want is a drink. As if she can read my thoughts, Alex steers me away from the bedroom and into the bathroom, where she sits me down on the toilet seat and uncurls my right hand, still clutching the blood-soaked wad of tissues.

'OK, not too bad. I reckon if we can just get the bits of glass out you'll be fine with a bandage – no need for stitches.' She rummages in the cabinet above the sink until she finds a pair of tweezers – Sarah's, of course – puts my hand under the tap to wash the blood off and starts to pick shards of glass out of my palm. 'Right, that's most of it anyway. Get in the shower. I'll sort out your clothes and get this place tidied up.' I don't move. I'm mesmerized by the blood spatters against the whiteness of the sink. 'Logan.'

'Yeah, right. Thanks, Alex. I don't know what I . . . I'm sorry about all this.'

She waves that off, points at the shower cubicle and leaves me to it. As I stand under the scalding hot spray, I can hear her in the kitchen, dropping empty bottles into a bin bag.

Thirty minutes later I'm shaved, dressed and looking as

human as I'm going to after several days of non-stop drink-ing, with my hand discreetly bandaged so you wouldn't notice anything if I kept my fist clenched. We sit at the kitchen table, a pot of coffee and two full, steaming mugs between us. I'm not going to risk a sip until I'm sure the handful of painkillers I'd taken with a gulp of water aren't going to come back up, but at least I'm starting to feel that I can get through the funeral without pissing myself or having a shaking fit. Two bulging black refuse sacks stand accusingly by the back door.

'Look, Alex—'

'Fuck sake, Logan, stop saying sorry, all right? I can't imagine what sort of a state I'd be in if . . . you know. And I know today is going to be probably the hardest day yet. But you're going to get through it, and then Sarah and Joseph will be at rest.'

I nod. Yes, I need to do this for them. I can't be at their funeral looking like a wreck, however destroyed I am inside. And I can't go with them on their last journey, as much as I'd wanted to. I've already made that promise. I need to stay alive. I need to be strong. I have work to do.

There's a knock on the door, a tentative rat-a-tat-tat unlike the furious banging of earlier.

I stand up, take a gulp of coffee, straighten my tie and close my hand over my injured palm.

'OK, I'm good to go. Let's do this.'

Outside, two gleaming black vehicles are waiting, and we drive slowly down to the end of the road before turning right towards the local golf club. The road is slick with rain, but the sun is just emerging from behind the clouds and the fields are a sparkling green. Planes are coming into land at Luton Airport in the distance, as we weave our way through winding roads in the direction of the crematorium. With Alex beside me, gripping my good hand tightly, all I can see is the hearse in front, with its two pale coffins, one normal size and one just big enough for a child. I feel a surge of irrational anger: why is someone else driving Sarah and Joseph? Why am I not behind the wheel, looking after them? What if there's an accident? What if some crazy Porsche driver comes round the next bend and loses control on the wet road? The driver of the hearse won't know how to take evasive action. He won't have the training. Or what if there's a petrol tanker jackknifed across the road over the next hill and the hearse smashes into it and there's an explosion, and Sarah and Joseph—

Jesus, I might be sober, but I am definitely not in my right mind. I shake my head, like a dog shaking the rain from its fur, trying to rid myself of these crazy thoughts. Here we are, on the way to the crematorium, where Sarah and Joseph's bodies will be put in a furnace and burned to ashes, and I'm worried we might have an accident on the way. Well, I'd had my chance to look after them, and I'd blown it. Today, I suddenly realized, was all about finally facing up to that. I relax my fingers and open my injured hand. Today is about letting go.

By the time we arrive at the crematorium I feel steadier,

confident that I won't break down and throw myself on the coffins or start smashing the place up in a fit of rage. I almost lose it when the hearse is opened and the coffins are brought out. Six of Sarah's friends shoulder her coffin, but before anyone can touch the other, I reach in and gently pull out Joseph's smaller coffin and cradle it in my arms. No one else is going to take my little boy. It feels as if I'm carrying him up to bed as I walk slowly towards the group of people gathered round the entrance to the crematorium. I don't know if this is the way you're supposed to do it, but I don't care.

I look straight ahead, avoiding eye contact. I don't want to see those desperate looks of sympathy. But in my peripheral vision I recognize a couple of team members, discreetly positioned on the fringes of the main group. Instinct makes me glance to my left and I spot Graeme, parked up in a highway maintenance van. Despite acting on his own, my team are obviously taking no chances. I shake my head, almost laughing at the absurdity of it. Sarah and Joseph are dead. What could another terrorist attack possibly achieve? What could anyone do to make it any worse? But the presence of the team reminds me that there is a world outside of my all-consuming grief, that the terrorists are still out there, and if they aren't planning to attack this little funeral, they're planning to attack somewhere else. Threat levels might go up and down, but that was just for public consumption. For us, the threat level was always the same, and you could never afford to relax.

I get through the service somehow. I sit in the front row

of the little chapel, my eyes fixed on the two coffins, each with a wreath of white flowers resting on top. I try to stop thinking about Sarah and Joseph's mangled bodies lying just feet away from me, and remember them as my living, laughing, loving family. While the priest says some consoling words about two people he's never met, my head fills with memories: Sarah and I walking on a beach at sunrise on our first holiday together; the look on her face when she walked down the aisle at our wedding and I turned and caught her eye; the whoops of joy as she waved the pregnancy test in front of me; Joseph's birth – all that pain, all that joy; his first cry; his first laugh; rocking him to sleep in my arms.

'Goodbye, sweetheart. Goodbye, my son,' I whisper.

And for me it was over. There are some readings. The Bible. Some poems I've never heard of. People crying. But I don't take any of it in. They are gone. I don't stay to watch the coffins on their conveyer belt, passing through the curtains. Sarah and Joseph's remains – their real remains – are tucked away safely in my heart where the fire can't touch them.

I walk out into the day. As the rest of the mourners file out too, they make space around me, nobody quite knowing what to do, what to say. I take advantage of the moment, before anybody plucks up the courage to talk to me, and carry on walking, out of the gates and down the road, towards the sun. I can't remember if there is some sort of wake organized, or where it is. It doesn't matter: they are better off without me; I'd only make people feel more awkward.

I don't know where I'm going, only that I'm not going home. I can't face that empty house. I've had my last drink. That is finished. When I do go home, it will be to pack things away, decide what to keep, what I can bear to put in the bin. But not yet.

I don't know how long I've been walking for but I'm starting to notice pain in my feet where my smart shoes are pinching my toes. I'm so used to wearing scruffy trainers that my feet don't fit into proper shoes anymore. I take them off. I'm thinking about throwing them over a hedge into someone's garden and carrying on barefoot, when I remember the last – the only – time I'd worn them. At our wedding.

I'm still standing there with my shoes in my hand when a black Volvo S60 pulls up next to me. It's come from nowhere, so must have been driving fast, but there's no screech of tyres as it comes to a halt. Without looking at the driver, I know it's one of my team.

The passenger window lowers, and Alex leans across from the driver's seat. I open the door and get in. As soon as my door closes she drives away without saying a word. She turns the car back towards town, and a few minutes go by as her progressive driving cuts through the traffic, before she breaks the silence.

'You OK?'

I nod. 'Yeah. That was the hardest thing I've ever done, but yeah.'

Alex glances over at me. 'What people said, about Sarah – and Joseph. It was beautiful.'

'Good.'

I let her drive some more. Usually I'm a terrible passenger. I always need to be in the driving seat. But being driven by a real professional like Alex, fast but with total control, feels oddly calming. For once I am letting someone take charge, and I feel some of the tension of the last six days easing. We are back in open country now, leaving other drivers in our wake on an A road, heading north.

'Where're we going?'

'I thought you wouldn't want to go back home just yet.'

'Yeah, thanks. But what about—?'

She nods towards the back seat. 'I've got your grab bag in the boot and some extra clothes and other bits I thought you'd need.'

I turn and look at her with a puzzled expression. 'Need for what?'

'For when you meet the rest of the team.'

'I'm not with you. What team?'

She drops a gear and powers past a lorry, smoothly tucking back into the left-hand lane before a Mercedes shoots past us heading the other way.

'You got a call from the DG, didn't you? Secret meeting, secure location, no driver, no bodyguard.'

'Yes, but how did you know?'

Alex doesn't say anything. But there's a hint of a smile. Then the penny drops.

'You got a call too. He asked you to join.' She nods. 'So . . . what did you tell him?'

'What do you think, Logan? We've been working with one hand tied behind our backs for years. Losing the brothers in Birmingham wasn't a one-off. We need to get back in front of this thing. The DG is saying we can have free rein. Do it our way. What do you think I fucking told him?'

I let go half a laugh and a smile breaks briefly on my face. The first time I've laughed in days. It's so refreshing to hear someone speaking bluntly to me instead of mewing like a kitten, so afraid of saying the wrong thing to the grieving husband and father.

'That's awesome. He couldn't have picked anyone better. I really mean that. But you didn't answer my question. Where *are* we going?'

'There's an RAF base. Totally secure. And we've got our own little corner. No one will question us coming and going. And no one will know what we're really doing. It sounds perfect.'

It does sound perfect. And the thought of it sends a surge of adrenaline through my veins. Suddenly I can't wait to get there.

'OK, sounds good. So, who else is on the team?'

She shrugs. 'I guess that's what we're about to find out.'

6

Eventually, Alex turns down a narrow road with fields on either side, and a mass of dark buildings come into view behind an intimidating razor-wire perimeter; the only things discernible from this distance are the huge radar dishes. I've never been to this particular base, but I know what it is. Everything about it is low-key – just another RAF barracks – but in fact it's one of the key defence installations in the country, the base used for the early warning systems against missile attacks. If a country went rogue and launched an attack on us from the other side of the planet, this anonymous-looking place is where the threat would be identified and the necessary counter-measures launched. Not only will security be as good as it gets in the UK, but most of the defence-systems personnel will hold top-level military clearance, meaning everyone on camp is used to not asking questions. In a nutshell, it is the perfect hiding place for an intelligence unit that's not supposed to exist. Smart move.

As we pull up to the gates, armed guards approach the car. We slow to a stop. From the passenger seat, I admire the guards' professionalism. As one eyes our number plate and walks towards Alex's side, the other provides overwatch, his rifle butt secure against his right shoulder, index finger running alongside the trigger guard, keeping both me and Alex in his natural firing line without pointing his weapon directly at us. Staying natural, we both have a role to play even at these gates; you can't role into places like this as if you're big time, bragging about who you are, making it mega obvious you're not regular military or even normal civilians. That would defeat the object of the place, and the point of being a highly sensitive counterterrorism unit. A covert operator operates for life. It's clear the people protecting this camp are switched on without being twitchy. This is another good sign our new team is in the right place.

'Afternoon, ma'am, can I see some ID and your car pass, please.'

As Alex pulls out her civilian cover ID and laminated car pass, I can see, printed on the blue lanyard, the words 'Fraud Prevention'. It's obvious Alex has already been briefed on her cover and who knows what else while I've been drinking myself into oblivion. I feel a twitch of annoyance that I've been out of the loop, even though I was in no fit state to be briefed on anything. But now I want in. I don't want anyone treating me like I'm not quite up to it. I'm anxious to get where we're going and get started, and I'm starting to get pre-emptively pissed off with anyone treating me like a second-class member of the team, even though we haven't actually met anyone else yet and less than twenty-four hours ago any sane person would have written me off as a drunken fuck-up.

Alex can see the dark look on my face. 'Are you all right?'

'Yeah, I'm good. Just want to get stuck in, you know?'

She nods. 'That's good. Me too.'

As we wind our way slowly through the camp, past what look like the barracks stores and two huge block buildings that I guess house the electrical substations needed to power the huge early warning radars, I realize I haven't given any thought to how I am going to interact with my new team members, or – maybe more importantly – how they are going to interact with me. I might not know anything about them, but they'll know all about me, and about what happened to Sarah and Joseph. They'll be expecting a wreck, a broken man. Some of them might be full of sympathy. Others might not want to work alongside an emotional basket case. I have to make sure I put both groups straight, right from the off. At the funeral, I'd put my feelings about Sarah and Joseph in a box and sealed it up tight. From that moment, no one else was ever going to see that side of me. Ever. What they'll see is the old Logan. The operator. Switched on to the environment, unflappable and now, because my heart went with my family, with absolutely no emotional weakness. Anyone who dares question my ability to operate on the ground will fucking regret it.

'Yeah, just fucking try it,' I mumble under my breath.

Alex puts a foot on the brake. 'Sorry?'

'Nothing. Nothing. Carry on. Where the hell is our new place, anyway? You sure you know where you're going?'

She frowns, but there's a hint of a smile in it. I guess Alex is pleased the Logan she's known for years is starting to make a reappearance. As if on cue, we round a bend and the smooth tarmac we've been driving on gives way to rough concrete. There are weeds growing from between the slabs and it looks like we're the first people to drive to this part of the camp for some time. Bending around the back of the substations, we bump along towards a pair of grimy roller-shutter doors.

'Well, it's not Thames House, that's for sure.'

Our new home doesn't look new at all. The roof is mostly covered in moss, which is starting to creep up the overly large chimney, the gutters are completely blocked and about to drop off the building any minute, and there isn't a single window. It's just a brick box, about fifty metres by about thirty wide, and looks as if it might cave in at any minute. The only clue that it might be a bit more robust than it looks is the discreet camera pointing down towards the roller doors and a new, very clean matt-black keypad stand.

'I like it,' I say.

Alex winds down the window and taps a six-digit code into the keypad. The shutters start to wind up with a smoothness that doesn't fit with the building's grimy exterior, and we enter what at first glance looks like a regular garage or work-shop, with several cars parked along the far wall. Alex backs in alongside them. We always reverse park unless we're on the ground operationally, where it's better to blend in. There are a ton of reasons why we do it this way, but the main one is that the front of a vehicle is stronger than the back, so it's much easier to drive your way out of an ambush facing forwards. Even though we are in relatively safe surroundings here, Alex's decision shows how the manoeuvre becomes almost like muscle memory.

Killing the engine, we survey the ground floor of our new home. Most of the floor space is taken up by the parking area. Along one wall there's a row of brand-new storage lockers, just like the ones at Thames House, and two doors marked 'WC'. In the far corner is what looks like an incinerator – a big industrial-looking thing that I assume is there for burning sensitive material rather than heating the building. On the other side of the cars is a set of wrought-iron stairs leading to the upper level, where a gantry walkway runs around the building and gives access to numerous rooms around the outside. Alex and I glance at each other, clearly having the same thought: just like a prison. The only thing missing is the anti-suicide cargo net to catch you if you jumped – or were pushed – off the walkway. I feel lightheaded for a moment, flashing back to the moment I almost decapitated myself.

Alex doesn't notice and is already beckoning me out of the car with a brusque 'Right, come on.' We walk up the narrow stairs and onto the top floor. Following the sound of voices, we enter a low-ceilinged room which still smells of the plaster on the recently erected stud walls. A dozen white plastic garden chairs – four of them occupied – are ranged in a rough half-circle in front of a white formica table where a man in a dark suit, crisp white shirt and a military tie is sorting documents into neat piles. Jeremy Leyton-Hughes, the intelligence officer on the brothers' case, with a direct line to the DG. Even if this unit was the DG's baby, there was no way he could be directly tied to it; he needed to keep his hands clean, so it made sense that Leyton-Hughes would be heading it up. But that doesn't necessarily mean I'm pleased to see him. I've always hated his arrogance towards us grunts on the ground. It feels like he sees operators as disposable objects, like a wet wipe he's used to clean up a mess before discarding. Without looking up, he indicates two empty chairs. The talking abruptly stops, and as we make our way to sit down I give the other team members the once-over.

Three men. One woman. A couple of them look vaguely familiar, but I've definitely not met them properly before today. With me and Alex that makes six. Is this everybody or are the extra chairs waiting to be filled? My old team was way bigger than this. I wonder how we'll be able to mount proper surveillance ops, let alone execute any of the more hands-on stuff. I give each person a nod out of courtesy, trying to pack as much meaning into the gesture as I can. They're all used to evaluating body language, making instant risk assessments based on the way people carry themselves, so hopefully they'll get the message loud and clear: expressions of sympathy not required. I wish we'd stopped off at a service station so I could have changed out of my funeral suit into my normal clothes. I might as well have a sign around my neck saying 'Just Been to a Funeral'. As I sit down I unknot my tie and stuff it in my jacket pocket, just to hammer the message home.

Clearly no one is going to introduce themselves, but they look like an interesting bunch. Immediately on my left is a guy in his late thirties or early forties, wearing jeans and a black T-shirt and lounging so far back in his chair it's in danger of tipping over. With his long black hair and a colour-ful tattoo of a Japanese koi carp that I can see disappearing under the sleeve of his T-shirt, he gives off a very different vibe to Leyton-Hughes's military correctness. Next to him is the second woman in the group: early thirties, dressed like a mum running late on the school run. Despite her relaxed nature, her eyes suggest she is extremely aware of her sur-roundings. The type of look I'm increasingly used to seeing from worried mums on the streets. Then, at the opposite end of the row, there's the two other men: an Asian guy dressed in grey shalwar kameez with black Nike Air Max trainers has a broad, open face that seems perpetually on the point of breaking into a grin; and a sharp-faced guy with short blond hair who meets my challenging look with an unreadable one of his own.

Leyton-Hughes finally stops shuffling his papers and straightens. A lean six-foot with a narrow face and close-cropped dark hair, he taps a pen sharply on the table to get our attention.

'Right, everybody's finally here.'

Did I imagine the slight emphasis on 'finally'? I give him a hard stare, but he doesn't blink and carries on.

'Each of you was personally recruited into this unit by the director general, so I don't need to tell you why we're here or what our purpose is. And that's the last time the DG will be mentioned within these walls. We have his full support, of course, but his position cannot be compromised. None of you will have any further direct communication with him, or with anyone else at Thames House. I will be the sole point of contact there. I will also be your operations officer.'

In my opinion, individuals who have risen through the ranks from being an operator within the surveillance teams make the best ops officers; they understand the challenges of being on the ground and what information you need and when. The intelligence officers who dual-role as operations officers normally lack the field experience that's needed to make sure everything runs smoothly for us.

That is one problem with Jeremy Leyton-Hughes, but the other is that he is a complete twat.

He pauses to see if there are any dissenting voices. In practical terms, what he said made sense, but I don't like the heavy-handed way he's trying to establish his authority. Isn't the whole point of the unit that it does away with all that hierarchical bollocks and just gets on with the job? Alex can sense I'm bristling and gives me a nudge. I get the message: calm down and give him a chance. I give her a little nod without turning. Fair enough. No point getting riled up before we've even started.

Leyton-Hughes continues. 'Let me be absolutely clear. Officially we do not exist. As far as Thames House is concerned, we do not exist. What we, or you, will be doing, is not legal. Collectively and as individuals, we are totally deniable. If we need to refer to the unit among ourselves, we will call it Blindeye.'

Well, that made it crystal clear. I haven't heard anyone use that phrase for a while, but some of the old boys talk about an operation being given a 'blind eye' during the Cold War days, when MI5 and MI6's ops were still deniable. The term meant the operation was deemed illegal but necessary. No one would stop you, but if you got caught you were on your own. Sink or swim.

'OK, good. Now, what are we supposed to be doing here? What's our cover story? Obviously we're on a military base, and you are all Fraud Prevention Officers with the DVLA, looking for untaxed vehicles all over the country. Hence the need for coming and going at all hours, in different vehicles. Hopefully no one will ask any questions, or poke their noses in here, but over the next few weeks and months it'd be just as well if a few of you occasionally use the RAF canteen and gym so you can start sowing the seeds of our cover story. Dropping "work-related" terms into conversation when they're in earshot of you, mentioning DVLA, tax, fraud, that sort of thing. That way no one gets too interested in what we are doing.' He grins. 'Unless they're driving an untaxed vehicle, of course.'

The Asian guy smiles dutifully.

On the face of it, it sounds a little far-fetched. Tax inspectors holed up in a secure military base? But I have to admit it's actually totally plausible, as well as being nice and simple. Real estate is expensive and the British taxpayers are sick of their hard-earned money going into over-funded agencies, especially when those agencies are supposed to be collecting even more taxes. Plus, with the reduction in our military's size over the past few years, there's more space within camps like this. It won't be a difficult cover to maintain.

'Living your cover begins now. Which means your old identity goes in the bin – now. All your Security Service ID badges need to be handed in – to me. From this moment, you can NOT deploy with them or go back to Thames House.' He taps a pile of manila folders. 'And your new identities are all in here: cover IDs and addresses, fuel cards, credit cards, phones and keys to new team vehicles. Needless to say, the admin team who set all this up are off-site and have no knowledge of the use to which all this is going to be put.'

That must have been a tricky one to pull off, I think: new cars, bikes and vans; radios, new driving licenses with cover names to match our addresses; new passports. And even harder to hide all this activity within the Security Service. Just explaining why A4 surveillance teams had suddenly lost half a dozen or so experienced operators would require robust cover stories. Redundancies, medical retirements, private-sector job offers – whatever the reasons given for people leaving the teams, it would all have to look legit in order to pull this level of deniability off properly and allow us to operate long-term. We're all nosey bastards by profession, and most MI5 employees, whether it be admin staff or operators on the ground, notice little things like staff being moved around.

'Before you introduce yourselves to each other, I should mention one member of the team who isn't here. Alan Woodburn is our tech. He'll sort anything, from comms in here to your personal kit, and he's currently working to make this place absolutely secure. This is one of two rooms in this building where your phones or radios won't work, for instance.'

We all take our phones out to confirm that we don't have a signal. I'd already noticed the metal mesh-work in between the plasterboard panels, making the room into a do-it-yourself Faraday cage, which would remove the threat of our phones being turned into mobile microphones for anyone trying to listen in to our briefings.

'Communications and voice procedure will be as it was in your old A4 teams. You have a radio system that was bought by the service specifically for entry teams when they went out to install eavesdropping devices, but they ended up with the A4 surveillance radios and the kit was just lying around in a locker until Alan borrowed it. No one else on the planet has these radios or access to the encryption they use.'

I'd worked with Alan, and it's good to know he has our backs tech-wise. There's nothing he doesn't know or can't do with our operational kit. He designed some of the earliest versions of the technical kit we use today. I've always thought that if he'd gone into the private sector he'd be the billionaire CEO of some revolutionary tech company, but for whatever reason, he never has. The best thing about Alan is that he doesn't just try and bodge something with bits of batteries and tape and see if it works, he'll design it, think it through. He's quick and always keeps in mind that the people using his stuff will be under pressure in challenging conditions, so he tries to keep it simple. It's easy to fuck up a complicated piece of tech when surrounded by terrorists, unless it's as simple as possible.

'Alan's tech bay is on the ground floor. As I said, his first priority is getting the building's security up to scratch, but tomorrow he'll be handing out some more bits of kit. Before your first briefing at 0900 hours.' Leyton-Hughes sees the raised eyebrows among the team. 'I don't need to tell you, we don't have time for the usual protocols. We have to hit the ground running. I'm going to hand out your new IDs etcetera, everything you'll need, then I suggest you get to know each other. Tomorrow morning you'll be back on the ground.' With that he scoops up the folders, dumps them on the nearest empty chair, straightens his tie and walks out.

For a moment, no one says anything. If they have questions, Leyton-Hughes is no longer here to answer them. Better get used to it, I think. That's his style.

Alex leans across and starts sorting through the folders. She takes one for herself and hands me mine. The others find their own.

I dump the contents on my lap. One completely genuine British passport in the name of Anthony Davies, a driving license to match, with cover address. Credit card in the same name, Audi car keys, presumably to the grey S3 parked downstairs, a phone and charger. My civilian ID card to get onto the base is in my bag, in Alex's car. Good to go then. I just need whatever goodies Alan is going to hand out. I drop everything back in the folder, place it on the floor and sit back while everyone else finishes sorting through their stuff. There is an awkward silence as everyone waits for someone else to kick things off. I decide to seize the moment.

'Right, I'm Logan. Before A4, I was Military Special Operations. Before that, regular army.' I pause. What else is there to say? As far as I'm concerned, when I handed in my Thames House ID, my old identity would be incinerated along with it. There is no point in telling them personal details about someone who no longer exists. I might as well just make a clean break. I realize it's different for them. They'll be living two identities from now on, as they shuttle between home and the alternative world of Blindeye. For me it will be a lot simpler. I only have one identity now and one home: this soulless warehouse on a windswept RAF base in the middle of nowhere.

And this little group of strangers is my new family.

They collectively realize I'm not going to say any more, and some of the tension leaves the room. I can tell they're relieved not to have to confront what happened to me.

The Asian guy takes up the baton. 'OK. Good to meet

you, Logan. My name's Riaz. I'm currently – I should say I *was* until five minutes ago – A4, same as you. The Navy before that, but for some reason they thought I'd do better sitting in a van all day and pissing in a bottle than commanding a nuclear destroyer. Go figure.'

That gets a laugh and the atmosphere lightens even further. Alex is next to step up to the plate. 'I'm Alex. Background, Royal Signals. Mostly ride bikes with A4. I hope they've given me a good one.'

The other woman grins. 'Claire. I was an avionics technician before joining A4. Army. Nice to meet you.'

'And I'm Craig,' says the blond guy. 'I went straight into the Service after . . . university. Found my niche in A4. Good to be here.'

'Which just leaves me,' says the long-haired guy with the tattoo. 'Ryan. I was in the Intelligence Corps, running agents in Iraq. Thought I'd come home before someone cut my head off.'

Well, there we are, I think. Odd to think that these strangers are now the only people I'll be able to trust.

'Bloody hell,' says Claire. 'This is like an AA meeting. "My name's Claire and I'm a surveillance officer. It's been three days since I last followed someone."'

Riaz grins. 'Not too much, I hope – a drink seems like a good idea. I've got a bottle somewhere. There's a kitchen, I think. Let's see if there's anything to drink out of.'

He goes downstairs to the parking area and by the time he comes back with a litre bottle of vodka, Claire has found some paper cups in the kitchen, two doors along the gantry. Riaz pours the drinks and hands them round. Alex glances anxiously at me but I smile to let her know it's OK, I can handle it.

Ryan looks at his cup thoughtfully. 'I suppose we should drink a toast.'

'Here's tae us,' says Craig.

'To Blindeye,' adds Claire.

There's pause, and we form a circle with our raised cups.

'To finding the fuckers . . . every last one of them.' Everyone cheers and laughs as our cups bump together, except Alex. She knows my toast isn't a smart little joke. I'm deadly serious. I want to find everyone who is thinking about causing us harm and kill them. All of them.

7

Joseph's small coffin, in my arms, feels empty. Maybe it is. If it's empty then where is he? I can see Sarah standing at the altar in her wedding dress. Fuck. What will I tell her? I've lost Joseph. I'm still walking towards her but feel like I need to slow down, to buy some time. But I can't.

The look on Sarah's face, confused at the coffin I'm carrying. I don't understand it either. It still feels empty, I can't see any signs or names on the top. Sarah crying. Distraught, gut-wrenching tears with a howling cry that erupts instantly. I want to rush towards her but my legs refuse to move any quicker. I feel heavy, lethargic. The coffin. It's not empty.

Like someone is piling weights on top of my cradled arms, I can't hold onto the coffin for much longer. Refusing to let go I drop to a knee, then both, the weight becoming unbearable as it pushes my arms to the ground. Sarah still screaming as the coffin, Joseph's bed, digs into the tarmac, carving deeper into the ground, pulling my arms into the darkness. Sarah's screams become louder, higher pitched, brutal.

* * *

There's ringing in my ears, then my eyes snap open and suddenly I'm awake. It's pitch-black. I have no idea where I am or how I came to be here. My heart starts hammering and a rising tide of panic threatens to engulf me. My brain starts to register the smell of plaster dust and it all comes back in a rush. I fumble for the light-switch above the bed and a bare bulb hanging from the ceiling flickers into life, revealing the outlines of my new home. Not that there's anything homely about it. It's more like a monk's cell, with a bed, a stainless-steel sink against one wall, and a flimsy-looking wardrobe on the other side. There's nothing else apart from my kit bag and a plastic bottle of water on the floor by the bed. My mouth is bone dry and I take a long pull from the bottle.

I unlock my door and the cold air of this vast open-plan building rushes in to replace the staleness of my temporary home. It's eerily quiet without anyone else here. I can just about hear the dull whines of the fans keeping the servers cool on the opposite side of the building as I step onto the metal gantry walkway. The cold metal against my bare feet makes me shiver. *Right*, I tell myself, *get yourself sorted out before the rest of the team arrive*.

I quickly wash, dress and head down the stairs. Poking my head into the tech room, I find I'm not quite alone. Alan's sitting hunched over his work bench, doing something with a circuit board. The last time we worked together was in Northern Ireland against the Irish paramilitaries. But he hasn't changed much – still the same big bear of a man with an unkempt beard and thick glasses. I take a seat opposite him and watch him work. His quietly methodical way of doing things instantly has a calming effect on me, and I remember why I used to enjoy being around him. In a world of unbelievable stress, with people often at – or beyond – breaking point, Alan always remains unflappable, however much pressure people are putting on him to produce miracles in double-quick time. After a couple of minutes, he looks up. 'Pass me that thin-gauge solder, will you, mate?'

'Sure.' I hand it over and he nods his thanks. We've made eye contact for about a second and hardly had what you'd call a conversation, but somehow in that brief, trivial exchange we've communicated something important. He understands my pain, but he knows talking about it won't help.

'There's coffee if you want it.' He points with a screw-driver to a sink unit with a coffee-maker alongside. I grab a mug and sit down again to watch. It looks like he's assembling a normal iPhone. I'm so absorbed trying to work out what he's doing I lose track of time, and when Alan finally looks up from his work my coffee's gone cold.

'Guessed what it is yet?'

'A . . . phone?'

He grins. 'Well, don't take it back to Apple, because they'll tell you it's proper fucked! No, it's a very small incendiary device. Generates enough rapid heat to combust and burn for around thirty seconds.'

'Incendiary? Why—?' Before I can finish asking why, all

of a sudden, we might need something like this, Alan's face changes. He looks cagey.

'Probably best we wait for the briefing. All I do is make the kit, you know.'

I nod. 'No problem. I guess we'll find out soon enough.'

We both hear the shutter motors kicking in at the entrance. I get up and walk over to see several team cars come in and park up. Alex is first out, carrying a McDonald's takeaway bag and a cardboard coffee cup.

'Thought you could do with some sugar and fat this morning.'

I grab the bag with a grin. 'You're a fucking legend, Alex. Alan, you want some of this mate?'

'No thanks, Logan. Gotta keep an eye on my figure.'

'Good point, Alan,' Alex says, grabbing the hash browns out of the bag before I can stop her. I pull out the sausage and egg McMuffin before she can steal anything else back.

We stand there, stuffing our faces and grinning at each other, when Leyton-Hughes walks in. He strides past the team without a word and starts walking up the stairs, obviously expecting us to follow him. Halfway up, he turns. 'Briefing room, please.'

We walk up the stairs like a bunch of schoolkids who've been caught shoplifting and file into the briefing room. Leyton-Hughes is standing in front of a whiteboard, arms folded.

'OK, first Blindeye briefing. In an ideal world, we would have had more time before our first job, but it's become a matter of extreme urgency, so we're going to have to hit the ground running. The DG believes he picked the right people for the job. This is where you prove him right. I know all of you at some point have been deployed on Stone Fist and Iron Sword, the two brothers who recently fell off the grid. These two are our targets. They've been classed as priority-one targets. The guys in the office at Thames are still working to get control of them and get some actionable intelligence, but not to put too fine a point on it, we fucked up. They're smarter and better trained than we thought, and the chances are we've lost them for good. But the DG has asked me to put a stop to them. It's imperative that they don't get back into the system or, worse, get to their endgame.'

We still didn't know what their endgame was. The intelligence we had up to this point was that they're hell-bent on mass murder. Whether that be a car bomb at a busy school fair, opening fire on a packed tube in rush-hour London or targeting specific people, like high-ranking soldiers, these two brothers are about to kill. They need to be caught.

I can feel the adrenaline start to surge through my veins. Losing control of the brothers had been the last straw for me. Stopping them would prove that Blindeye can really make a difference. But something isn't adding up.

'Boss, you said we have to put a stop to them? Does that mean we have new intelligence?'

'No, Logan. That's the point. They've gone dark, and the

DG doesn't believe that we can find them again with . . . traditional methods.'

'So how are we going to get in front of this?'

'The white Muslim convert turned cleric who radicalized them in prison is the target today. Khalid Nasir; target name Stormy Weather.'

There are puzzled looks around the room. Claire puts a hand up. 'But he was interviewed. They didn't get anything useful out of him.'

Leyton-Hughes smiles thinly. 'Well, you're going to interview him again. But in a slightly different way.'

I run through the possibilities in my head. What is he thinking? That we'll send someone into jail posing as a prisoner to try and get his confidence? Maybe pose as someone ripe for radicalization and hope he takes the bait? I've taken on some difficult and dangerous roles, but that was a suicide mission. It would take too long, surely? How the hell would you pull it off?

Alex obviously has the same thought. 'So he's out, then?'

Leyton-Hughes shakes his head. 'Day release. Thames are running Operation Cloud to gain access to his financial trails. He's a big recruiter and facilitator. Sends a huge amount of cash to overseas cells. But he only does it once, then the accounts lie dormant. We think he's about to transfer a huge amount of money to Algeria via Western Union.'

That means there's a window of opportunity. But something still doesn't add up. Claire is the first to put it into words.

'Sorry, I must have missed something really obvious here. If A4 teams are on Stormy Weather, then why are we being used? I thought the whole point of Blindeye and the reason we were recruited was to go where they can't.'

She's right; A4 teams are the best in the world at what they do, not much misses their control.

Like a crowd watching a tennis match, our heads swivel from Claire back to Leyton-Hughes, waiting for the thing we've all missed. For the first time, he doesn't look entirely comfortable.

'OK, an A4 team will be deployed on Stormy Weather today. I don't have direct access to the team's comms or the ops room any more, for live feeds. However, our job is to get to Stormy Weather without A4 seeing us and find out where the brothers might have gone. It's highly likely he will have given them safe places around the UK to drop off the grid.'

Claire sits back in astonishment. It's one thing to operate outside of the normal constraints of MI5, but this is asking us to deploy *against* an A4 team to achieve our goal. We could normally outwit suspected terrorists, but our own intelligence service, when the stakes are so high? For the first time, I wonder if the DG has actually lost it.

'How the hell do we get a target off the street who is being followed by an A4 team without them seeing us do it? It's like trying to make an elephant disappear on stage. Apart from anything else, we've all been recruited from A4 – there's a big chance at least one of us will be recognized.'

We all look at Leyton-Hughes. He glares back like a teacher sorely disappointed in his pupils. '*Quis custodiet ipsos custodes*, eh? Who watches the watchers.'

What the fuck is he talking about? He's briefing us in Latin? Somehow I'd never picked it up, growing up on the streets, but it had never been a problem until now. He catches my hostile look.

'Come on. Who better than you to defeat a surveillance team? If anyone knows how to do it, you do. But you'll have an edge; Alan's got some new kit that should cause enough of a diversion, if you're quick.'

With that, maybe we have a chance. I stop being pissed off with Leyton-Hughes and his Latin phrases and start to try and figure out the logistics.

'Have we got any maps of the prison? The pick-up is where we need to disrupt the team.'

I'm thinking that getting control of Stormy Weather quickly is our best chance of pulling this off. Leyton-Hughes points to a table behind us, where there's a pile of maps and two laptops. 'Ordnance survey and Google Street View and some other bits and pieces.'

We crowd round the maps and laptops, trying to identify likely positions for a surveillance team near the exit of the prison and surrounding streets. Alex grabs a pen and pin-points places on the OS map.

'Here you'll likely have the direct position, allowing you to see Stormy Weather leaving the prison. Here, someone close in for a foot or bus move. Vehicle here and here, watching for a vehicle move on a stand-by. Biker probably waiting out of the area here, in the services. We've got to have someone close in to get a grip of Stormy Weather the minute he comes into view and try and get the jump on any A4 team that might be there.'

We all agree with Alex's quick analysis. We're all used to doing this sort of stuff on a daily basis, often while driving at high speed towards a target's location. The only difference here is we are looking at it from an aggressive point of view. So much for the surveillance team. But what are we going to do?

While we all scratch our heads, Riaz jumps in. 'Once we see Stormy Weather come out, we can't take him off the streets there and then. Too many cameras, right? What about if we had two high-sided vans? We use one travelling westbound, here, to block the cameras, then the second van travelling east to pick him up with the side door open as he crosses the road. Ryan, I bet you've done similar pick-ups in Iraq and Northern Ireland, right?'

Ryan nods. 'Yeah, that's what I was going to suggest. Although the chances of fucking it up are massive in confines like this. Why don't we wait until he's rounded a corner, presuming he's on foot? The direct position for the surveillance team won't move, we know that. Assuming Stormy Weather has to walk onto the south side to get a bus or for a vehicle pick-up, we can wait until he's done this first corner, to the north. There will be an A4 vehicle or foot call-sign in this area, but again we can block that with the vans.'

Riaz turns to me. 'Logan, what do you think?'

'I like it. It's simple, which means it's harder to fuck it up. We need to assume that he's not going to come along willingly. I'll get close in, then once he's in position near the pick-up van I'll nudge him in, then Ryan and Riaz – I'm assuming you'll be inside?'

'Yeah that makes sense. I'll be in full traditional dress to try and ease his cooperation with Ryan.'

A few minutes ago, I thought it was mad to try and snatch a target from under the noses of an A4 team. Now I can see how it can be done, with a little help from Alan. But I can tell from her body language that Alex isn't convinced.

'Guys, there's only six of us. We need someone driving the pick-up van. That's three people straightaway. Someone direct on the prison exit when Stormy Weather leaves and to disrupt the A4 team. Logan close in. That leaves one person to drive a second blocking vehicle . . .'

Claire now adds her own doubts. 'We need to get down for a recce, to plan this properly. We don't have enough time. This isn't just a normal lift off the streets. He'll be wearing a GPS tag on his ankle too and those things are monitored.'

So far, Leyton-Hughes has been letting the team figure things out for themselves, but now he steps in.

'Iron Sword and Stone Fist are planning a major attack. They've dropped off the grid and we need to find them now. This cleric is our only realistic means, and we have a twenty-four-hour window. It might all look like a shower of shit but we have no alternative. This is the hand we've been dealt. We can't just wait for something better to turn up, I'm afraid. So figure out how we're going to do this. Alan's waiting downstairs to brief you on your kit.'

No one speaks. The realization of what we've all gotten ourselves into really hits home for the first time as we make our way sullenly down to Alan's tech room. The big man is waiting with three phones lined up on his workbench.

'OK, I've got three incendiaries for you. To all intents and purposes they look like broken iPhones, and don't take long to get up to temperature at all. Around ten seconds and it will be at full burn, giving off a good-size flame, then a huge amount of smoke, so be aware of that. To switch it on, just flick the volume switch on the side of the phone. The safety switch, if you like, is the mode it's in now; volume switch on silent. Once you've flicked the switch to loud, there's no turning back – it'll trigger the chemical reaction inside. The good thing is, it's silent while getting to temperature and then at the start of the burn, so it should give you time to get enough distance to not be associated with it.'

Then Alan pulls out what looks like a really bad kid's arts-and-crafts blanket from beneath the bench.

'Excuse the patchwork, but this will work. It's absolutely state of the art, something I designed personally. Stormy Weather will have a tracking tag around his ankle as part of his day release. Wrap this around the tag and it eliminates the problem. No more tracking.'

He dumps more kit onto the workbench, including two yellow DeWalt cordless cutting discs, rolls of duct tape and plastic zip-ties.

'Once you've wrapped the blanket around his GPS anklet, it should block the tag's signal while you cut it off.'

I can tell from the expressions on the faces of the rest of the team that they are beginning to see how we could pull this off. But I'm thinking a step ahead. The guys running the A4 surveillance operation on Stormy Weather, both on the ground and at Thames House, aren't stupid. They'll know within minutes of losing sight of Stormy Weather that something completely unnatural has happened. And that means they'll come after us.

'One more thing.'

Alan places a small stack of number plates on the workbench. They instantly topple over like an unstable tower of dominoes.

'Put these on your respective vehicles. The registration plates are clones of identical vehicles elsewhere in the country.'

Once the A4 surveillance teams realize what's happened and Stormy Weather is nowhere to be seen, the operations centre will pull all the feeds from any local assets they have. We have to assume most of the operators on the ground will remember some if not all of the registration numbers on the vehicles in the area, so we'll have to obscure our number plates. We need to stay ahead by any means possible, but I can't shake the feeling that even dirtying fake plates won't put us enough steps ahead.

'Stick them on now and when you get close to the area I'd obscure the plates however you can – mud, black markers or a seemingly badly placed sign covering the plate – anything like that.' Sometimes the easiest methods are the best ones to use.

As we look through the registration plates, I can see the eyes of the team darting at the figures: with a marker pen a number 3 becomes an 8, E becomes a B at distance, and so on. It's a crude method and one that won't hold up to much scrutiny, but we won't need to pass a police stop, just change the profiles of the vans enough to snatch this guy away from MI5 and get out of there.

Claire flicks her wrist and holds up her watch. 'If we leave now we should be on the ground before the A4 team starts plotting-up around the exit to the prison. We'll have to just figure this out once we get there.'

She's right. To have any chance of pulling this off we need to get going. Then we're going to have to pretty much make it up as we go along. Improvising and adapting to evolving situations – making split-second decisions that could mean the difference between success and total disaster – was all part of the job. But this is taking flying by the seat of your pants to another level. I'm confident Alex and I can hack it – but the rest of them? Well, I'm about to find out.

Scooping up the various items from the bench, we move towards the vehicles. Alex nods at me, showing me the keys to her van. 'We'll go in the blocking vehicle.' Craig takes a boy-racer Seat Leon FR, Riaz and Ryan walk over to their pick-up van – the one I'll be hoping to push Stormy Weather into – and Claire jumps into a people carrier that looks like a stereotypical mum taxi, complete with baby-on-board sticker in the back window and a baby seat covered in biscuit crumbs. We might be about to walk into a giant clusterfuck, but I have to admit the level of detail is pretty impressive. You'd never guess this vehicle was about to play a massive part in a deniable MI5 operation.

We file out of the base in a loose convoy – no need to try and disguise the fact that we are a team on an operation; it just isn't an operation to track down a few people who haven't paid their road tax. As soon as we're rolling, we sort out our comms. In A4 we only refer to each other's operational numbers, but we haven't discussed that for Blindeye yet. I don't know anyone else's number apart from Alex's.

'Anyone give Ryan a test call on channel eight?'

'Loud and clear to Claire, how me?'

'Loud and clear to Riaz . . .'

'Roger, Riaz, likewise to Logan.'

'Logan you're loud and clear to Craig, bro.'

'And everyone is loud and clear to Alex.'

'Roger, Alex, That's Ops on, too,' Leyton-Hughes adds from the base. 'Just to update you all, Stormy Weather is due out shortly after 1300 hours.'

The next few hours, driving south-east towards the area of the prison, is straightforward. Alex and I enjoy the calm before the carnage that is about to take place, not feeling awkward. Alex takes a detour down a wooded track, disappearing into some trees to allow me to change the look of our van – amber flashing lights on the roof, magnetic highway maintenance signs on the sides and back – before accelerating hard towards the area of the prison so we can get ahead of the A4 team.

We'd spotted Craig blasting past us a while ago, so it's no surprise he's first to our target. 'Craig, in the area now, no sign of another team yet. I'll hold close in to the west until everyone's here.'

Leyton-Hughes responds. 'Ops, roger that. For information, the closest Western Union transfer point is to the west of your position, in Gillingham.'

That confirms what we thought. The A4 team will be set up with the assumption that Stormy Weather will likely be travelling west towards Gillingham to make his money transfer. The prison is actually on an island, separated from the mainland by a thin stretch of water with only one route in and out, which I'm hoping will provide an advantage later on.

'Guys, from Craig, there is a bus route just to the southwest of the prison exit, within walking distance on Brabazon Road. Ryan and Riaz, when you get to the area give me a shout and I'll come to you, so you guys can jump in the back of your van ready for the pick-up. I'll just need dropping off later to pick my vehicle up.'

'Roger, thanks Craig. We'll be in the area in figures four.'

There is so much said on the net between team members that we usually precede any time references with 'figures', to make them clear and distinct from any other messages flying around. So far, so good. Everybody seems to understand their part in our improvised plan. But I know from studying the map that finding a gap the A4 team had left for us to exploit is still going to be massively difficult. 'Just pull over for a minute, Alex.' Alex stops at the side of the road. I get out and open the sliding side door of the van, grab some kit from the back and pass it over the seats before sliding the door shut again.

'Hard hat, glasses, wig and hi-vis jacket in there, mate. Just don't throw me about too much with your rally driving, yeah.'

The disguises aren't designed for long-term deployment, but soon we look the part of road workers here to assess some repairs, complete with paperwork and clipboards in the dash of the van. With our amber lights and signs, we're good to go, and I see we even have cones in the back if we need to push our cover deeper.

Five minutes later, we're getting close. Claire shouts up on the radio that she's in the area now, and Craig lets us know he's with Ryan and Riaz, driving their van. 'How we looking, Alex?'

'Yeah, all good, just coming past that bus stop to our offside now. Prison is up in front, two hundred metres away . . .'

Just as I'm about to reply through the gap in the seats from the back of the van, Alex speaks again.

'Fuck. Logan . . . A4 surveillance team is already here.'

8

The stress is obvious in Alex's voice as she passes on the bad news on the net.

'All stations be aware, the A4 surveillance team is already here. They have one on foot on his own at the bus stop, and a grey BMW 3 Series close in to the south on the junction of Alexandra Way.'

I'm not surprised Alex has managed to spot them so quickly. It was just a case of looking at the location and figuring out where we would have put people – then seeing if we could recognize anybody. I was mentally prepared to find them already in place. It's what I would have done. A4 teams are extremely good at getting things like this right, we do this day in day out. No point in losing the game before the kick-off.

Even though I trust Alex's observational skills, it's frustrating not being able to check them out myself, but my field of view from behind the seats is not ideal, and the fact that I'm bouncing around like a pinball doesn't help. We pass the bus stop but I can't verify her identification.

'Did you see what team they're from, mate?'

'Not sure. I think the guy at the bus stop is from Green Team. The BMW driver I've seen in Thames House before. They're fucking quick off the blocks, aren't they?'

'Yeah, if they already have one direct at the bus stop we might have to put this blocking vehicle in between him and Stormy Weather and get Claire to fire off one of the incendiary devices. I hope she finds the right cover to make it work. But look on the bright side – at least they're taking the exact positions we reckoned they would.'

Leyton-Hughes agrees with my assessment. 'Ops, roger the last.'

As the last of the team make it into the area, we start to spot more of the opposing operators. What makes MI5 surveillance teams the best in the world is the constant anti- and counter-surveillance methods used to avoid being seen and to prevent a target slipping the net. And yet here we are, trying to defeat the very people we learned our craft with.

On any other day, we'd be classed as traitors. But everyone in Blindeye knows the bigger picture.

'From Craig, we're holding out to the north-east. There's an A4 surveillance car in front of us, facing towards the prison exit about two hundred metres from the junction. Black Toyota Avensis, one up only, male driver. Don't recognize him but caught him whispering into comms.'

Even if all the members of the A4 team weren't known to us, if we're very sharp we'll be able to spot those telltale signs. We just have to make sure we don't replicate them and get made in turn. And the best way we can do that is to stay on the outside of the surveillance ring, leaving one person inside, close in – which would be Claire – to tell us when Stormy Weather is out in the open. When he is, we'll try and move in quickly before the A4 team has a chance to organize themselves . . .

Luckily Claire chimes in, bringing me back to the task at hand.

'Guys, I'm going to get out on foot, close to this direct position.'

'Roger that, Claire,' Alex responds. 'I'm dropping Logan in close by, then I'll be holding further north-east towards Craig's van. May as well have cover in numbers.'

She's right. We have to hide in plain sight. One van might stand out on its own, especially covered in highway maintenance signs. But park it next to another van disguised the same way and it blends into the environment. As Alex rounds a corner to pull in behind Craig's van, with Ryan and Riaz in the back, I slide out the back doors in full work gear. Hard hat, hi-visibility jacket, carrying some spray paint, ready to do some on-site inspections.

I know I can't hide from the A4 team in this area. There's no point in even trying. But the hard hat and sunglasses will hopefully prevent any of them recognizing me. And me being out in the open gives us another advantage. I can help identify other team positions in support of Claire, just before we go in for the kill.

I walk away from the vans, inspecting potholes in the pavements and spraying a few red circles around the ones deep enough to need repairing. It looks like I'm intent in the task, but I'm actually sweeping my surroundings for anything that makes my antennae twitch. I quickly spot another surveillance car nestled in between other vehicles, but facing away from the road junction. This was one of the close-in cars for sure, the telltale sign being the wing mirror pointed at a slightly different angle from normal, suggesting the operator in the driving seat is using the mirror to keep a keen eye on this junction. He or she isn't being sloppy. In fact, I like the way they are hiding their profile with the high seat. Even if the target has been properly trained, they probably wouldn't notice the detail with the mirror. Russians might be the exception, but the A4 don't have to worry about them on this operation.

The sun is high and the day is getting hotter – luckily a perfect day for wearing shades, but with all my layers, I'm already starting to sweat like a fat man in a sauna. I cross over to the other side of the junction as if I'm looking for more potholes. I glance at the squat grey concrete mass of the prison, looming to my left, but I can't see the exit clearly because of the glare bouncing off the security signs. I figure it must be something like 150 metres away. Hopefully Claire's got it covered. Then, as I lean down to spray paint a hole in the pavement, I hear her whispered tones over the radio.

'Standby, standby. That's Stormy Weather out, out and walking south-east towards the bus stop now.'

Something isn't right. It feels like everything's happening too quickly. I suppress my instinct to look towards the prison. Instead, I take my phone out and start casually taking snaps of my potholes. It's 1245 hours. Fucking typical, he's out early. Putting my phone back in my pocket, I keep my movements smooth and unhurried, but I know I need to get a shift on to be alongside the prison exit in time for our vans turning up. I decide I'm going to deploy Alan's incendiary device, still not completely sure how strong this thing is, and need to make sure I'm not going to cause a massive fire, just enough to cause a distraction. Hopefully the A4 team will pass it around there is a fire and if we get the timing right they'll be too busy talking about that and give us the seconds we need. I need to ditch it. Spotting a bin, I know this is the perfect place. If I drop it in here it should be close enough to draw the attention of that surveillance car I identified.

Taking a napkin left over from my McDonald's breakfast, I cross the junction again and walk towards the bin. Holding the napkin, I reach inside my pocket, neatly wrapping the dummy iPhone while flicking the mute button to on. I know I have about ten seconds before this thing starts burning.

Dropping the napkin-wrapped phone into the bin on the corner of the junction, I pray Alan's device is strong enough to turn this bin into a big smoking mess, but not so strong that it sets the whole place alight. With a bit of luck, the local residents will call the fire brigade too. By the time we lift Stormy Weather, the place will be swamped. Well, it's done now. Make or break. I smile to myself as I think back to my setting fires in bins as a kid. The bin starts to smoke heavily, with the odd flicker of a low flame, and soon there's a very obvious plume of smoke charging higher into the sky. This needs to work; either we lift Stormy Weather or we all end up in the same jail he's just come out of.

For surveillance operatives like us, total silence is our worst nightmare, especially after a stand-by is given out. Normally the net would be exploding with acknowledgements and constant movement updates of the target, but the lack of information pouring into my radio is unnerving. I move away from the bin and start walking purposefully towards the prison while still looking as casual as possible. In my peripheral vision, I see the flashing amber lights of Craig's van flicker on as it passes me on the other side of the road. Fuck, I have to speed up, however conspicuous it makes me. Still nothing on the comms. Maybe Claire is in a black spot too.

Rounding a slight bend in the road, I can see Craig's van half-mounting the pavement, keeping the back end on the road, as a single-decker rolls past me. This could be our chance.

'Anyone read Logan?'

No one's answering me.

For fuck's sake, please let the comms be back on!

'Yeah, loud to Alex, I'm going past you now. Craig, I'm going to block the view to the north from behind you. I can see Stormy Weather crossing the road now west to east, continuing south towards the bus stop.'

'Yeah, roger that, seen too,' Craig responds calmly. 'Stormy Weather walking solo, full dark-grey shalwar kameez, relaxed.'

Hearing their voices does wonders for my heart rate. I've managed to close the gap to thirty metres from Storm Weather, and can see the bus slowing to a stop behind Craig's van. But we still need more time. I see Craig get out of the van and start placing cones across the road. I smile to myself. Smart move. That could buy us the time we need. No word from Claire, though. I guess she must be staying close to the A4 foot surveillance. But Alex has driven past Stormy Weather to create a sandwich, and with the bus blocking the view from north and south, the prison to the west and tall hedges lining this pavement on the east side, once Stormy Weather makes it into our little box, we'll have our opportunity.

'Alex is in position.'

Just as Alex finishes transmitting, I hear the low rumble of a motorbike. Taking a moment to bend down and mark another bit of damaged pavement with my spray paint, I see the black bike cruise past and pull up on the other side of the bus, presumably to check if Stormy Weather is about to get on board.

'Guys, we have a biker, offside of the bus.'

'Roger that, Logan,' Alex came back. 'I can see their

helmet through the bus windows; he's stopped on the other side of the bus now.'

Fuck. This surveillance biker could be the thing that fucks us up – A4 surveillance bikers are normally the cream of the crop of operators.

Craig comes back on. 'I'll sort this out.'

From my angle, I can just see him in his hard hat and high-vis jacket, moving some of the cones, holding his hand out to the bus and beckoning with his other hand to the biker. 'Come on mate, you first. Come on, come on!'

I'm starting to like the way this guy operates. Craig knows this will put the biker in a difficult position. Basically, he has to ride out the area now, otherwise he'll draw too much attention to himself. We're using the very things we used to try and avoid like the plague against this surveillance team. He revs past Craig and accelerates down the road, no doubt cursing all the way.

'Thanks, Craig. Biker is forced pass,' Alex acknowledges.

'Ryan and Riaz, roger that, we're ready for Logan to pass Stormy Weather to us when he's ready.'

Perfect. I can see him now, a white male in a dark-grey shalwar kameez, checking his surroundings exactly like someone who's been in a cell for a while and isn't used to open spaces with people and traffic. I let the team know. 'Logan, roger that. I'm fifteen metres behind him now, he's almost at Alex's van, about to walk past.'

Both vans have their orange lights flashing on the roof. Craig is playing his part well, apologizing to the bus driver as he painstakingly moves the cones to let him through. This is it. Our perfect opportunity. If we snatch him now, while we have a normal-looking situation of highway vans about to do some road work, we can totally confuse the A4 surveillance team. Stormy Weather would have briefly been out of their sight as he walked in front of Alex's van, and the operators will have seen the bus sitting there for just long enough to think that their target could have got on. If we get the next bit right, they could be checking the bus long enough for us to get out of the area.

Every step I move closer to Stormy Weather, I feel more confident that we'll be able to snatch him away cleanly.

'Riaz, Ryan, I'm closing in,' I let them know. 'Get ready with the doors.'

'Roger that.'

'Craig, roger.'

I close in, five steps behind Stormy Weather, now it's only us in this box as the bus creeps away. It has to be now. The can of spray paint goes into the deep pockets of my jacket, both hands now free to control him. Craig walks back towards the van with the cones in his hand. Stormy Weather stops dead. He may not be used to being on the street, but prison has made him wary, and suddenly he doesn't like the situation he's in. Fuck, we need to grab him now before he panics and takes off, putting him back in the A4 team's vision. But it has to be done smoothly. If he shouts or struggles it will fuck everything. We'll have the police and MI5 all over us in seconds. I can see that Craig's aware of Stormy

Weather's discomfort, but he doesn't know what to do. His van is too far away for him to risk bundling the target in.

Taking advantage of the fact that Stormy Weather is still focusing on Craig and hasn't clocked me, I move in fast. I nod at Craig, hoping he'll understand instantly that I'm changing the plan – the target's coming with me, in Alex's van. Switching my body position so I'm side on to his back, I reach out with my left hand, grab his mouth and lift up underneath his nose, controlling his head. At the same time, I dig my hip into the small of his back and lift him off his feet, his wiry ginger beard scraping against my strengthening grip.

As his hands come up against my left arm in a vain effort to defend himself, I'm already opening the side door of Alex's van with my right hand. Throwing him in face down, I pile on top of him, slamming the door behind me. I can feel his panic.

I shout to Alex, 'Change of plan. *Drive.*'

I catch her eye in the rear-view mirror, calm and focused. No point discussing why the hell Stormy Weather is in our van instead of Craig's.

I relax the pressure on him a little. 'Sssh, my brother. Khalid, I'm not here to hurt you. We're rescuing you. You don't have to go back to jail. I need to get the GPS tag off your ankle, so the police can't track you, OK?'

His head turns and his eyes are wide with fear as I take my hand from his mouth and start to wrap the blanket round his anklet to block the signal.

I need to keep talking so he can focus on what I'm saying and not on the physical situation he's in. 'I've been sent by friends.'

It's a risk, momentarily loosening my grip on him, but we have to make sure he can't be tracked by the surveillance team. If he goes full-on apeshit now I'm going to struggle to get control of him again without doing him some serious damage, but luckily now my weight is off him and he can breathe freely, he begins to calm.

'I . . . don't . . . who?'

He's still in fight or flight mode, adrenaline coursing through his veins, and he's finding it hard to talk as well as breathe.

Alex can hear the commotion. 'All good?'

I know Alex is on top of this, driving quickly but without making it obvious. The whole team need to get out of the area before the A4 team leader organizes the search. I just hope Claire was close enough to get the message that she too should pull out.

'Yep, all fine, we'll be safe soon,' I respond, as much for Stormy Weather's benefit as for Alex's.

Confident that she knows how to improvise her part now, giving me the information I need while reassuring Stormy Weather that she's part of his rescue team, I pause to take off my hard hat and high-vis jacket. Placing my hand over Stormy Weather's, I look him directly in the eye.

'I need to cut this tag off, OK? Don't worry, I've done this many times and it won't hurt, but you need to be still, OK?

It'll make a loud noise, but don't be alarmed. It shouldn't take long.'

He holds my gaze, trying to work out if I'm really friend or foe, and grips my hand tightly. The moment seems to go on a long time. I realize I'm holding my breath.

'OK, I trust you.'

Bingo.

He smiles and nods, his fear turning to relief that he won't have to go back to prison, that he's finally safe. Sliding my hand out of his grasp, I reach round and grab the disc-cutter, catching Alex looking at me in the rear-view mirror before her eyes return to the road. As the disc spins into life, I lift the blanket and Khalid's shalwar kameez just enough so I can see the band of the locating tag without uncovering it completely. I don't want a signal leaking out. Alex is keeping the van steady as I start cutting into the hardened plastic, and she takes the opportunity to brief the rest of the team, knowing that Stormy Weather won't be able to hear her over the noise of the machine. The cutter breaks through the tag strap and it drops onto the blanket. Job done.

'Sit tight, my friend, we'll be safe soon.' Brushing away the plastic shards, I stand up to talk to Alex from behind the seats. I tell her the tag is off 'our friend', just loud enough for Stormy Weather to hear, then lower my tone to add, 'We could do with Ryan in here to get the info.'

'Agreed, Claire is just behind the vans, the bus is in front of us. She's going to fake a breakdown behind us, blocking the road going over the bridge. After that we'll pick Ryan up and take the lights and signs off, then split up from the other vehicles. We'll be there in one minute.'

I sit back down with Stormy Weather, smiling to reassure him that what he's just heard is all part of the rescue plan. I need to start adding some more detail to bolster his belief and make sure he doesn't start wondering if we're actually from British Intelligence.

'Me and my crew, we work for a lot of different people, yeah? This is our thing. My mate is going to help us stay hidden from the police and we'll get you to a safe place. The guy who paid us told us to get you to Hamburg. We've got a boat we can get you onto not far away, in Gravesend. It'll be cramped, but you'll have food and water. It's only for a couple of days.'

I knew he would see through me right away if I pretended to be a fellow jihadi, but I could play a people-smuggler with total confidence.

The change of gears and climbing engine revs tell me we are on the bridge now, just as we hear the sirens of a fire engine screaming past us. I briefly catch sight of the blue flashing lights bouncing around Alex in the driver's seat before they speed into the distance, presumably to deal with the small but smoky bin fire I started. With Claire behind us providing the block, we need to push further ahead and away from the A4 team. They're probably still checking the bus for Stormy Weather, but we have to assume they are switched-on enough to be pursuing the vans, too. We need to put some distance between us so we can stop to remove all the highway maintenance signs and lights. And we need to do it quick, so Ryan can get the intelligence we desperately need about the brothers before Stormy Weather decides we're not actually a bunch of people-smugglers trying to get him out of the country.

'But I don't know anyone in Hamburg . . .' He looks quizzical, and I realize I need Ryan in here quickly. I may be pretty good at improvising, but he's an experienced agent-handler.

I shrug. 'I don't get told anything, my friend. Just your name, what you look like and where to take you. That's it. I don't even know your last name, Khalid. We get paid to move people around, nothing else.'

The van veers left and there's a crunch of gravel under the tyres, and before we've come to a halt, Alex is shouting, 'Let's go. All change, lights and signs.'

I put my hand on his arm. 'Wait here, Khalid. We need to change the look of the van to stop the police finding us.' I wait for his answering nod before I jump out, leaving the side door open. Ryan and Riaz have finished stripping the other van and are walking towards ours as Craig drives off. I intercept them, giving Ryan a muttered heads-up and quick covers for them both before they approach.

I usher them into the van. 'Khalid, these are my friends, Aaron and Omar. They'll help get you to the ship in Gravesend, and on to Hamburg.'

Ryan steps confidently into the van and shakes Stormy Weather's hand.

'Good to meet you, Khalid. We'll be on our way in just a few seconds.'

I rip the signs and amber lights off the van and quickly put on some rental-company stickers. Now we're just another white van. I jump in the back, and Riaz is holding Khalid's hand and kissing him on both cheeks, before saying 'As-Salāmu Alaykum,' in a comforting tone, playing his part to the hilt. Alex guns the engine and slips back into the traffic. She's ditched the hard hat and jacket but is now wearing a dark-brown wig, brushed forward over her shoulders. I should be the last person to be taken in by a simple disguise, but she looks totally different.

I lean over the passenger seat. 'Route?'

'Dual carriageway heading south.'

I nod. Away from the prison, but also the opposite direction from base camp.

'Craig's gone north straight away. Alan's arranging the pick-up of Craig's car. I'll do a big loop and head north soon.'

I turn to see Riaz giving Khalid a sandwich and a bottle of water. 'Khalid, we'll be at the boat soon, but we've been asked to get two brothers out of the country too. The police are looking for them and I think they're in hiding. They need to be on the same boat as you, otherwise we can't help them.'

Khalid looks dubious. 'What brothers? I know many people. When I get to Hamburg where will I go next, Aaron?'

Ryan isn't fazed. Clearly he's done his homework. 'I'll meet you in Hamburg with the two people who are paying us. I believe they are going to get you across the borders into Turkey then into Iran, but they want the brothers that were in prison with you. The ones with the scars? Masood and Hamza?'

I've only ever referred to the brothers by their birth names or their code names, Iron Sword and Stone Fist, but Ryan is on the ball enough to use their prison convert names. It seems to do the trick.

'Ah, yes. They will be with my cousin in Liverpool, 170 Mill . . .' He pauses, an element of doubt obviously creeping into his mind. Ryan decides not to press him, but instead takes his phone out and pretends to make a call.

'Yeah, it's Aaron. Have a car pick the brothers up and bring them to the boat. Yeah, I'm with Khalid now. We'll have to pay the guard at the port an extra grand to look the other way. Yeah, yeah. Hold on.' Holding the phone away from his mouth, Ryan moves in closer. 'Khalid, sorry, I missed it. 170 Mill . . . what?'

There's just a brief hesitation before Khalid answers. 'Road. Mill Road. Knock on the door, ring the bell once, then knock on the door again. My cousin, Ali, will answer. Tell Masood and Hamza that their teacher sent for them.'

'Got it.' Ryan puts his phone back to his ear. 'One-seventy Mill Road, Liverpool. Be quick – we don't want the pigs to get them first. Knock on the door, ring the bell *once*, knock on the door again. Tell the brothers that their teacher has sent for them. Yeah, that's right, mate. Be quick.' He turns back to Khalid. 'OK, that's sorted. We're heading to the boat now. I can't travel with you to Hamburg, but I'll be waiting for you over there and I'll have the clean passports for you and the other two, OK?'

'OK, thank you. But tell me, who is paying you?'

It's the obvious question. Ryan frowns, like he's thinking on the spot. 'Please, Khalid, don't ask questions, OK? It's how we stay out of prison and how you don't get taken back there.' He pauses to read a text message on his phone. I can't see what it says, but it obviously gives him some information to feed into the role playing. 'It will take us a while to get someone to pick them up, Khalid. We'll try and have everyone together around the same time, about five-ish tonight to get you on the boat. If not, don't worry, we'll get them out a few hours after you. I'm just being honest with you, Khalid. We don't have any helicopters I'm afraid, and if we get caught speeding, everyone goes to jail.'

Khalid smiles at Ryan's joke about the helicopters and looks more relaxed now. His doubts are gone. But Riaz and Ryan keep him talking just to make sure he doesn't start thinking any more bad thoughts, while Alex keeps an eye out for other surveillance vehicles or police. My phone vibrates in my pocket. I pull it out to see a text message:

Go to channel 10.

Switching my covert radio to the different channel, I realize this is a specific message for me from Ops, which means Leyton-Hughes. But I can't talk openly in front of Khalid. I signal that I'm on channel ten with our covert messaging system – Khalid has no chance of hearing or seeing this. I'm hoping Leyton-Hughes has been around operational teams enough to know this means I'm on the net but can't talk.

'Roger, the address Stormy Weather gave us checks out. He has a cousin, Light Rain, who lives at the address given. Thames House have a camera on that street. Alan is searching the footage now. It's actually on the extraction list, ready to be removed, as no intelligence was ever recorded and Light Rain hasn't been live-monitored for nearly a year. He's no longer a priority. We are NOT passing this intelligence on to A4. We need to get you guys up there, and quick.'

A thought strikes me. Khalid's intelligence has paid out. So why the secrecy? Why am I being spoken to on a private channel no one else on the team can hear? Jeremy continues his message to me:

'Logan, Stormy Weather is now Blindeye disposable. He cannot be allowed to identify you and the team, or reveal how we got him out of the area and that he gave up the brothers' location.'

I don't respond, just replay his words in my head. *Disposable*.

'So I'm being clear, he cannot be allowed to leave that van. Logan, acknowledge what I'm saying to confirm.'

I reply back with the covert acknowledgement. Fuck.

'Do it. Now! Ops out.'

Time slows down, even though I can feel my heart rate going through the roof. I look at Khalid. He's smiling and nodding at Ryan and Riaz. I guess even when you've preached a doctrine of hatred, when you've ordered people to blow themselves up, taking as many innocent lives as possible with them, there's still a part of you that responds to kindness, that craves friendship instead of violence and death. Maybe if you strip away all the madness, that's what's left. Just an ordinary man, with the same desire for belonging as the rest of us.

I wrench my gaze away and take a deep breath, trying to focus on the bigger picture outside of this van and its occupants. What do we matter, as individuals, after all – any of us? After switching my radio back to the team channel, I turn away so I'm facing into the corner of the van, away from Khalid's eyeline. I take a roll of duct tape and four of the industrial-sized zip-ties, and start making two big loops.

A message comes through the team channel. 'This is Ops, Stormy Weather is now disposable. Logan has green light to start clean-up. Ops out.'

Catching Alex's eye as she looks in the rear-view mirror, I try to read her expression. Is it shock or just apprehension? I move behind Khalid with the zip-ties in my left hand, leaving my right hand to pull the nooses tight. Riaz is focused on keeping Khalid's attention off me, chatting about the daily prison routine and the lack of respect from the guards, but I can see he's drying up. The horror of what Leyton-Hughes has just whispered over the net to us is sinking in. Ryan is looking at his boots. Either he just doesn't want to watch what's going to happen, or he's trying to avoid giving Khalid any clues about what's coming.

Let's make this quick. Looping the zip-ties over Khalid's head, I slam my bodyweight into his back and force his chest into his legs. His lungs are brutally squeezed, instantly expelling all the air. With my right hand, I grab the loose end of the bottom zip-tie and pull it tight. It digs into his skin, taking his ginger beard with it. He starts to squeal, gasping for air; I block out the sound and tighten the second one underneath his chin, back and forth, pulling them tighter in turn.

I've lost the roll of tape in the struggle, so I wrap my left hand over his mouth, pinching his nose at the same time, as hard as I can. He's starting to fight for his life. The mucus streaming from his nose makes it difficult to close his nostrils, and I can feel a surge of adrenaline pumping through him, legs and arms pulling and kicking furiously. A foot flies out and hits Ryan square in the chest, knocking him to the floor, while Riaz looks frozen, unable to move. I realize I need to get more purchase. I walk my feet up high on the van's side and onto the roof, the metal panels bulging with the pressure I'm exerting. There's no more air coming out of his mouth. The zip-ties are so tight they've cut through the skin of his neck, taking his beard with them. I put everything into maintaining my grip. I don't know how much longer I can keep it up.

'Die,' I hiss into his ear as my head is forced into his. Letting go of his face, I grab his hands and force them down so he can't make contact with his final thrashings. Pushing onto my toes, further increasing the leverage, I apply more pressure on top of him. Then, thank God, the twitching starts, signalling he's near the end. His body, desperate for oxygen, goes into one final convulsion.

'*Fucking die.*' I wrench myself away and his eyes – red with burst capillaries and almost coming out of their sockets – tell me it's done. The smell of urine and shit mingles with the sour smell of fear and fills the van.

I walk my feet down from the roof and take a few moments to get my breath back. Riaz and Ryan are staring at me in horror and I feel a surge of anger. I'm the one who killed him, but they're just as responsible. We all are. What did they think we were getting in to? 'Come on, grab his feet, let's stick him in this corner.' Looking pale, they do as I tell them. I grab the ankle tag, still wrapped in the signal-blocking blanket. 'If we pass some deep water we can ditch this, away from cameras, yeah?'

Alex isn't responding. I don't think she knew I was capable of this. *I* wasn't sure I was. But what did I have to lose anymore? This fucker deserved it. I'm going after everyone who tries to hurt people in this country. I couldn't protect my family, but that gave birth to something inside me. A darkness that has consumed me and will be used to destroy fuckers like this.

I touch Alex on her shoulder and she flinches. She's always been good at masking her emotions during an operation, and she quickly regains her composure. 'Sorry, what? Oh, the tag – what about the train line?' She nods to the left of the road. 'No cameras on there.'

Perfect. Hard for anyone to search the tracks unless they stop all the trains. 'Pull up here, mate. I'll toss it over the fence. Any road cameras?'

'Negative. Not for the past mile or so, and there's loads of routes in and out of this village back to the motorway.'

Grabbing the anklet, I throw it high over the fence and can hear it hitting the stones surrounding the railway track. Riaz has jumped in the front with Alex, possibly trying to get as far away from what's just happened as he can, leaving me and Ryan with Khalid's body.

Leyton-Hughes's voice breaks in. 'From Ops, is it complete?'

Ryan gives me a look I can't read, then gets straight back on the net. 'Yeah. It's done. Back towards you now.'

I start to feel pain in my fingers, see the outlines of the zip-ties embedded in my skin like a brand. I look down and there's further evidence of what I've done. Hairs from his beard, mixed with blood and snot. Suddenly I feel like I'm covered in dirty guilt. I need a shower – the chance to wash myself clean of these traces of a dead man that cling to me. To wash myself clean of his death.

It had to be done, I tell myself. It had to be done. But the words seem hollow. I lean back against the side of the van and close my eyes, wondering what I've become.

9

We drive back to the camp in silence, each cocooned in our own thoughts. But it's painfully obvious we're all thinking about the same thing. Khalid's lifeless body might be hidden by a blanket, but there's no hiding from what we've done – what *I've* done. At least I'm not alone in the back with him. Ryan is sitting opposite me, leaning back against the side of the van, and I feel a desperate need for him to say something, anything, to tell me he's OK with what's happened. I close my eyes for a moment, beginning to feel dizzy, the adrenaline now washed out of me, no fuel left in the tank, just totally drained and empty. It's a familiar feeling to anyone who's seen combat. Your mind and body have been in overdrive, doing everything to make sure you survive and the other guy doesn't, but now the action's over and you've come out the other side, everything just starts to shut down.

Ryan nudges my arm. 'You OK, mate?'

Focusing on his eyes, I think I see genuine sympathy rather than disgust.

'Yeah. It had to be done. This team and the impact we're going to make is bigger than one nutjob cleric . . . right?'

He nods, like he understands.

'Have you . . .?'

He shakes his head. 'No. Never been in that situation myself. Trained for it, of course, but I went pretty much straight into intelligence.'

'So you never got your hands dirty.' Bollocks, I'm no good at all this sharing stuff. 'Sorry, that came out wrong.'

He waves it away. 'No offence taken. And in a way, you're right. I've never had to kill someone with my bare hands. Don't know if I could do it, to be honest. But have I killed people? Sentenced someone to death because of a decision I've made? Knowingly put someone in harm's way and let them be killed? Yep, I've done that.'

'So you don't have a problem with what just happened?'

'A problem? Mate, I do have a problem with it. I wish it was something we didn't have to do. I wish there was an alternative. But as soon as the boss told us the plan, I could see where it was all going to end up. What we'd have to do. I've seen enough bad guys we let go, because legally we couldn't touch them. I've spent too many nights lying awake thinking about the consequences of that, whether we were putting other people – innocent people – at risk. There's no perfect solution, no way of stopping these bastards and keeping our hands clean. So, we do what we have to do. And sometimes –' he flicks his eyes at the bundle beneath the blanket – 'it isn't pretty.'

Knowing I wasn't on my own in this was a relief and slightly comforting. I let out a breath I hadn't realized I was holding. 'Thanks, mate. I'm not so sure Riaz feels the same way, though. I don't think he was expecting anything like that.'

He's unable to hear me talking slightly quieter in the back, but I want to make sure he is OK. I need Ryan's point of view again, he's good at reading people.

Ryan nods and lowers his tone to match mine. 'Maybe not up close and personal, no. But he knew what he was getting into, like we all did. He's probably a bit in shock. Give him a bit of time and he'll come round.' He gives my shoulder a squeeze then settles back and closes his eyes. 'I reckon we'll be back in action as soon as the boss has briefed us on that address, so I'm going to try and shut my eyes for a bit.'

'Sounds good.'

You can tell he's been in the military. It was the first rule of army life. Sleep when you can, eat when you can. But I knew I wouldn't be able to sleep yet, however exhausted I was. Ryan had reassured me that the rest of the Blindeye team would come to terms with the execution of Khalid. We'd all take collective responsibility for it and move on. But there was someone else I needed to talk to before I could relax. Someone else who needed to understand why I did what I had just done.

Sarah.

I close my eyes and instantly there she is, sitting at the kitchen table with her arms folded and a questioning expression on her face. A strand of blonde hair is over one eye, and

I just resist the temptation to reach out and smooth it behind her ear.

Hello, Logan.

Hello, I murmur, hoping my lips aren't moving. But a quick check reveals that Ryan has his head on his chest and seems sound asleep.

Sarah looks at me. I know she knows everything that's happened in the van.

I had to do it. You do understand, don't you?

She just keeps looking at me, her eyes narrowing, like she's trying to see inside my head.

Tell me you understand, Sarah. Please! I need to know. I'm doing this to keep people safe. Innocent people, like you and Joseph. And I'll do whatever it takes. Even if it means killing people.

She frowns.

Please say something. Please! I feel like I'm about to explode.

Logan?

Yes!

Just tell me one thing.

Yes! Anything!

Tell me you didn't enjoy it.

The van hits a bump and I'm jerked back into reality.

'Almost home,' Alex shouts from the front.

I try to get a grip on reality, but Sarah's words are still echoing in my head. She was the person who knew me best, who could see deep inside me. There was nothing I could hide from her. Had I enjoyed it? Had I wanted to make him suffer? To be honest, I don't really know. I've managed to put a lid on my emotions, so I no longer consciously feel anything. But they're still there, bubbling away out of sight. Better make sure the lid stays slammed on tight, then.

'Ops, do you read, Riaz?'

'Go ahead.'

'We're ten minutes out.'

'Roger that, you're deploying straight out once you get back here. Craig is back already. Alan is out recovering Craig's car. Claire, what's your ETA?'

'About twenty minutes. A4 got blocked behind me on the bridge. Haven't seen them since.'

'Roger that. I've spoken to the DG. A Branch are monitoring the police investigation into Stormy Weather escaping prison and ditching his ankle tag. A4 aren't involved in the search yet. Ops out.'

We all exchange relieved looks. At least we aren't being chased by the police or a surveillance team from MI5. We seem to have got away with it.

Riaz and I make eye contact. 'Riaz, you OK?'

'Yeah, mate. We're stopping the public getting hurt, right? It's why we were brought together. No different than dropping a five-hundred pound JDAM on a compound in Afghanistan, right?'

A smile grows across my face. 'Yeah, the only difference is this bomb was delivered with my bare hands.'

He grins back. We're good.

'OK,' Alex chimes in. 'No traffic cameras for the past few

miles. Let's change the look of the van and we can get home. We're about two miles away now.'

As Alex turns down a side road and brings the car to a stop, Ryan jumps out of the side door and we hear Alan pop up on the net.

'From Alan, I've got Craig's car now. Out of interest, did anyone use a dummy phone out here?'

'Yeah, Alan, I did,' I respond. 'I dumped it in a rubbish bin, it definitely started burning.'

'No worries. It's probably destroyed itself now with the burn rate.'

Normally we would never leave operational kit out, especially as police will be checking the area, but we were lucky to have got out clean. We can't afford to risk going back when there is an active police presence. It definitely feels like we have been fortunate rather than skilful, though. Next time we deploy on the ground we need to be more prepared.

As Ryan jumps back in, I can tell from his face that the smell has really hit him, and for the first time I realize how badly it stinks of death in here. We need to deal with the body and get the van cleaned up as soon as we get back to camp, but first we've got to get through the gates. Ryan stands up and pulls a black roller shutter down to separate the cab from the back of the van – hopefully this will prevent the guards seeing into the back.

A few minutes later, Alex winds down her window and shows the car pass that matches the plates. We all hold our breath, hoping the guard hasn't got a keen sense of smell, but he waves her straight through and we roll slowly through the camp to our building. As we wait for the roller doors of our building to open, I release the shutter blind and ask Alex to reverse the van up to the incinerator at the far end. She locks eyes with me again in her rear-view mirror. 'Roger that,' she whispers hoarsely. She's compartmentalizing what's just happened and maybe preparing herself for what's coming next.

As the van swings round then reverses, I make my way to the back to open the doors. Swinging one door open, I shout, 'Keep coming, mate, keep coming. That'll do ya.' Alex smoothly brings the van to a standstill. I step down out of the back and walk over to the huge incinerator door, pulling the big lever handle down with a grunt. Shit, this thing is old, and it looks like it hasn't been used in a while, but I reckon it'll still do the job OK. In the past it must have been used to destroy not just documents but also military equipment or maybe hazardous waste, judging by all the different inlet and outlet pipes, so it must be capable of getting hot enough to take care of a body.

I exchange glances with Ryan and Riaz. They understand what we have to do. I duck back inside the van, pull off the blanket and grab Khalid's shoulders. Ryan joins me and helps push his lower body out, then he and Riaz each take hold of a leg while I get my hands under the armpits. I notice Khalid's lost a shoe in the struggle. We'll need to find that and make sure it goes in the incinerator, along with the blanket. He's surprisingly heavy, and all three of us are quickly sweating.

Leyton-Hughes sticks his head around the van doors, but is stopped in his tracks by the sight of Khalid's head hanging down, tongue swollen and hanging out of his mouth. Whatever he was about to say sticks in his throat, and he just nods like a meek little schoolboy before disappearing again.

With one quick heave, I manage to get Khalid's head and one shoulder onto the short roller system that leads into a steel grate inside the burner. I can see why Leyton-Hughes didn't want to stick around. On the journey back, Khalid's face hasn't got any prettier; his skin tone, the way his eyes have almost been forced out of his face, and the distortion of the zip-ties still biting into his beard and neck like some unrelenting beast, tell the story of what I did to him. Refocusing my gaze, I make use of the rollers and shove his body along, and all three of us push his feet and legs until he's all the way in. I go back to the van, find the shoe and toss it in the burner along with the blanket. I close the heavy door with a dull clang and push the lever back into the closed position.

Ryan and Riaz stand either side of me. I turn to my left and Alex is there too, along with Craig and Claire. I make eye contact with each in turn. They don't need to speak. We're doing this together. As a team. This wasn't fucking Hollywood, it was our life, no high fives and beers in a bar surrounded by beautiful people with chiselled bodies. No staring into the sunset, receiving medals. No matter how fucked-up the work our team did today, it bonded us, like a chemical reaction. Different materials fused together, creating one new substance. That was us. We've been together less than twenty-four hours, and I already feel closer to these guys than any surveillance team I've ever been on.

There are two red buttons on the side of the burner. I press the top one and there's a whoosh that sounds like gas starting to flow, followed by a thud as it ignites. I can see a flame showing in the little window at the bottom. Over the next few hours the temperature will rise to 1,900°C, at least according to the operating guide just to the side of the door. After the incinerator is finished, the diagram on the guide shows any material that remains being passed through a crusher of some sort. All the evidence of what we did today will be gone. Apart from the DNA in the van – we'll have to let Alan know about that.

Leyton-Hughes reappears, looking fresh in a suit and tie, his hair neatly combed. 'Briefing room when you're ready, please.'

I realize that, compared to him, I must look and smell like a tramp. 'Gimme five, yeah?' I say, heading for the toilets. There's no time to get properly cleaned up, but I just need to wash my hands and splash some cold water on my face. Leyton-Hughes doesn't answer. He starts talking to Craig and Claire.

I open the door and start running cold water in one of the sinks. Even with the taps on I can still hear the roar of the burner in the background. I look at the face confronting me in the mirror. My eyes are bloodshot, my skin pale and sickly looking. There's a scratch down one cheek. My lower lip is swollen and there's a tooth mark where I must have bitten it in the struggle. I turn the taps on full force, but the noise of the burner seems to be getting louder, like a jet engine getting ready for take-off. Unable to make the water run faster or loud enough to drown the noise out, I put my hands over my ears, but the roaring seems to be inside my head. The sweat is pouring off me as my head fills with heat and light and I start to feel myself burning, and then—

Nothing. Falling. I'm being sucked down a black hole.

'Logan!'

I open my eyes and I'm sitting on the floor, my head against the sink. Alex is kneeling beside me. Grabbing her arm, I'm hoping she can tell me what just happened. 'Alex, you OK? What's—? Wait, how long was I out?'

'Can't have been long. You didn't look too good, so I followed you in.'

'Fuck, I need to get up. I can't let anyone else see me like this.'

She puts a hand on my shoulder. 'Just stay where you are for a minute, Logan. The rest of the team have gone to the briefing room.'

I slump back. 'I don't know what happened, Alex.'

She shakes her head as if I'm a total twat. 'I do. Think about it, Logan. Yesterday you were at your wife and son's funeral. Now here you are. Being asked to do . . . that.' Alex is phrasing this sensitively, but I'm not sure what she feels more awkward talking about – my family or killing Khalid.

'Fuck, Alex, I'm sorry. I'm OK.'

'You're not OK. But it's fine, we've got you. Your brain needed to shut down for a bit.'

'Well it fucking did that all right.' I pull myself up gingerly, holding onto the edge of the sink. Trying to regain some sort of composure again after looking so vulnerable seconds earlier, I splash water on my face, stick my mouth under the tap and drink like a dog on a red-hot day. It was cold and good.

'Look, Alex. There's something I need to tell you.'

'It's OK, Logan. It doesn't—'

'No, really. This is important, OK?'

'All right. I'm listening.' I never spoke about what was going on in my head, neither did Alex. It's the type of people we are, always hunting intelligence but never giving it away, but this felt right somehow.

'When I took care of Khalid, that was just . . . an operational necessity.'

'I know that, Logan. It was pretty fucking brutal, but nobody has a problem with it.'

I shake my head. 'No, I don't mean that. There's something else. You need to know that I did it because I had to. Not because I wanted to. If there'd been another way . . . I didn't hate him. I wasn't taking revenge for what happened to Sarah and Joseph. I need you to understand that. I didn't like doing it. *I didn't enjoy it.*'

She can see the pleading look in my eyes. She takes a step forwards and puts her arms around me. 'Logan. I believe you, the team knows too. It's OK.'

She squeezes me tight, and I feel the tension leave me. 'Thanks, mate. I just needed you to know.'

'No problem.' She wipes what looks like a tear out of her eye. 'Fucking dust in this place. Now come on, we don't want Leyton-Hughes going all Oxford-Sandhurst on us.'

I grin. 'Posh twat.'

We walk out of the toilets to see Riaz facing the incinerator door, saying some sort of prayer. I feel instantly ashamed that I don't know what he's saying or what his hand gestures mean. Alex grabs my arm. 'Come on.' We walk up the stairs and, after a few moments, Riaz follows.

As we take our seats, Leyton-Hughes is standing with his arms crossed and a look like thunder on his face.

10

Go on then Jeremy, give us your worst. He waits until the team is assembled, then lets rip. 'What part of keeping the unit deniable don't you understand?' He stares at each of us in turn, but if he's expecting us to cower in fear, he's in for a surprise. There's no way we're about to take any shit today after what he's just ordered us to do. I'm the one who should be reacting to Leyton-Hughes first but it's Alex who jumps up from her chair and takes a step forwards.

'Meaning?' Obviously this operation and the thing with Khalid has gotten under her skin.

If he's intimidated by her reaction, he doesn't show it. 'The burning phone device you left on the ground,' he barks back. 'You don't leave operational kit out. It's just basics. And it's even more crucial for Blindeye. We haven't got anyone to clear up after us, and if we start leaving clues lying around for another team to pick up, we'll be finished before we've even got started.'

So no 'Well done, team' then. Is this the way it's going to be? The device would have destroyed itself anyway . . . Questioning the decisions we have to make in a split second on the ground from the safety of his armchair? All I can think to myself is that this is the type of fucking boss you get in the normal office world, not in MI5 and definitely not in the deepest deniable parts of intelligence. It feels like Leyton-Hughes is out of his depth here. And I wonder if, when he says 'we'll be finished', what he really means is 'I'll be finished'. After all, this is a big step up for someone who is really just a glorified PA for the DG. Yes, he got results as a traditional intelligence officer back in Thames House, but that doesn't make him a good operations officer. With little or no real operational experience despite his military background, he hasn't been able to see it through our eyes on the ground, the dangers we face and risks we take, all the time. And if it all goes tits-up, there's no safety net. It's not a question of losing your job; it's more like destroying the reputation of the security services and spending the rest of your life in jail – or worse. No wonder he's getting arsey and starting to flap.

I'm about to throw some more oil on the flames by explaining exactly why I had to ditch the distraction phone device and asking him what he would have done in the same situation, but before I get a chance, Alan walks into the briefing room.

'Sorry, boss, I should have told you. I told the guys the devices are disposable if need be. They definitely self-destroy, no compromise. If anyone does get curious, it just looks like a broken old phone, a very burned one.'

Leyton-Hughes pauses for a good few seconds, obviously

trying to decide whether Alan has just undermined his authority or saved him from an argument that would end up with him losing it anyway. But Alan's laid-back, shambling presence has already taken the tension out of the room. I reckon, over the coming days and weeks, we're going to rely on Alan for a lot more than just providing our kit. Leyton-Hughes shares a nod with Alan approvingly, as if chucking the diversion device in the bin was his own idea in the first place, and we move on.

'Right, let's take stock of where we are. One-seven-zero Mill Road looks like the real deal. Alan has run a piece of software on the surveillance footage to confirm if the brothers have been at the house and whether they are still there.'

Alan takes the cue and fills us in on what he's found. 'The reason Iron Sword and Stone Fist weren't seen at the Mill Road address is that the camera on that front door isn't being monitored any more. It's on an extraction list and the camera is due to be removed by the techs from Thames House any day. The cousin, Light Rain, was being investigated years ago. But due to the lack of intelligence gained, he dropped down the priority list. There simply isn't the man power to watch video footage of someone who isn't a tier 1 priority target, hence the extraction. Needless to say, the DG doesn't want to alert anyone by reactivating surveillance on it, so it's down to us to make sure the brothers don't slip through the net again. I've got access to the camera, so we'll know if they show their faces, they are confirmed in that address though, and I'll be monitoring it here with the help of my bit of software I'm running.'

Jeremy takes control again, 'I'm sure I don't need to tell you we need to get up there pronto.'

Riaz raises a hand. 'How long will we be—?'

Leyton-Hughes cuts him off before he can finish the sentence. 'Until we have got control of Iron Sword and Stone Fist, this operation is ongoing. If you need to contact your family to let them know you won't be home for a while yet, I suggest you do it now.' He smiles in a way that makes it clear he has no sympathy for Riaz's concerns.

There are murmurs around the room. Maybe it's just sinking in for the first time exactly what they've let themselves in for. And Leyton-Hughes's breezy, no-nonsense manner isn't helping. If you're going to ask people to go above and beyond the call of duty, they need to know exactly what's at stake. As if he's reading my mind, Craig puts a hand up.

'Is there any further intelligence about what the brothers are planning? We're sure they haven't dropped off the grid because they've got cold feet?' He's putting it politely, but I know what he's really asking is whether we've just killed someone to prevent an imminent terrorist attack, or just to find out whether there is a terrorist attack being planned at all.

Leyton-Hughes's response is instant – and not reassuring. 'Negative. What I'd like is to get some surveillance on them and tie them to a specific address, whether it's this one or somewhere else. When we've pinned them down, we'll engineer a police special forces executive action team to go and arrest them.'

Engineer. Code for, he'll get the information in play while concealing its source. Us. But if he's confident he can do that, why is he sending us up to Liverpool and not a regular A4 team with police backup? Is there something else going on? Some deeper game he's not telling us about?

Claire's spotted the inconsistency too, and it's given her a chance to clarify some things that have been bothering her. 'Boss, sorry. Can we address what we are all thinking here? We were recruited to stay on the ground when A4 couldn't, to do things they can't in order to stay ahead of the game. But are we a surveillance team or an escalation of the executive action teams? You've asked us to be a part of something that is completely deniable, I'm OK with that. You've told us that if caught, we are on our own, no one will come for us. I'm OK with that too. But we need to know what we're going to be tasked with, going forward.'

In other words, was killing the preacher an unavoidable one-off, or is that what Blindeye is designed to do?

Leyton-Hughes doesn't look happy. I can tell what he really wants to do is tell her to shut up and obey orders, but he's going to have to realize that this is a two-way street; we aren't soldiers in the army and we aren't MI5 operators anymore. The DG recruited to get ahead of the terrorist curve. We volunteered for this and we have the right to know every scrap of intelligence about our targets and exactly what our operational parameters are.

'You were all recruited to form a fast-moving, small and deniable surveillance team. But as we saw today, this team needs to be capable of carrying out the actions of a strike group. The people we're going after are too dangerous to be allowed to stay on the streets, even under surveillance. Will your actions save lives – possibly hundreds of lives? Trust me, they will.'

Trust me. The trouble is, I don't. But it looks like that's the best we're going to get.

To prevent any further questions, Leyton-Hughes makes a show of looking at his watch. 'We don't have a lot of time. Make those calls and be ready to change vehicles. Let's get to the target address ASAP.' To make it even clearer that's the end of the discussion, he taps a number into his phone and leaves the briefing room to make the call.

All around me, the team are doing the same, pulling out their phones and leaving this signal-blocking secure room, making the calls they need to people expecting them home at some point. I reach into my pocket but stop short of pulling my phone out, realizing I've got no one to call. If I disappear for a week, there's no one to miss me, no one to wonder where I am or whether I'm safe. Unlike Craig, Riaz, Claire and the others, I have nothing connecting me to the normal world, the world beyond Blindeye; the world of loved ones, next of kin and watching a boxset on TV is fantasy to me. Even Alex, who lives alone and as far as I know doesn't have a partner, is texting someone. I wonder if, for her, it's just a way of making contact with that other world to reassure herself it's still there, that the cruel world of Blindeye, the world of terrorists and killers, isn't the only one that exists.

For me, it is the only one, and finding the brothers is the only thing I can think about. Moving past everyone on the stairs, I'm desperately trying to not look like I'm hurt by this situation.

Down in Alan's tech bay, I can still hear the incinerator burning like a jet fighter taking off, as he sorts out new vehicle keys. I have to raise my voice to get his attention. 'Alan, the van. Have we got decent clean-up kit? It won't happen, but Stormy Weather made a mess in the back. If we end up on the wrong side, his DNA is all over it . . .'

He nods absently without looking up from his task, as if I've just asked him about cleaning up some spilled milk. 'Yeah, don't worry. I'll get it cleaned out here, then I'll take it to the compound and change it. I'll make sure it gets a respray and put into the system as another ops van for Thames House. No problemo.'

'Brilliant, mate.' Alan is still obviously very plugged-in to MI5 and Thames House, and the fact he's a tech and constantly working remotely gives him a fairly plausible reason to be here, there and everywhere without anyone asking questions.

He finishes sorting the keys as the rest of the team file

over. He holds a set out to Alex but she shakes her head. 'I'll take my bike out, the rest go up in the cars, given the area?'

Whoever she's been texting upstairs, Alex is now totally focused on the task. There's only six of us on the ground, so we're going to need a biker. Getting a pick-up and a successful surveillance follow, whether the end goal is to guide a police or Special Forces team in, or get close enough for a vital bit of intelligence, is not going to be easy. If we have a foot follow going straight into a vehicle move, then Alex, on her high-powered motorbike, will give us a chance of keeping hold of the targets.

We all grab spare batteries for our radios along with our keys, and I make a mental note of the cars the team gets into. As before, we'll make an operational plan as we drive. I get into a black Mazda 6 and, thankfully, when I turn on the engine it's enough to finally dull the noise of the incinerator. As the roller doors start to rise, I tap the steering wheel as impatience builds up in me. I need to be kept busy, but know I have a couple of hours driving to do yet, so need to keep a lid on it.

Then, suddenly, Alan shouts and rushes towards the roller doors looking agitated. He presses the button and the roller doors start to come down again. Shit. What now? We turn our engines off and get out of the cars. Alex takes off her helmet and swings it in one hand as if she's about to brain someone with it.

'We have a problem,' Alan starts, as if we hadn't figured

that out already. 'The camera feed shows the brothers leaving the house ten minutes ago.'

There are groans from the team, even Alan airs his frustration. 'I'm sorry, there must be a lag in the feed.' He's trying to do the job of an entire technical support team and it's just not possible, despite his incredible skills. He's still just one person. Alex just manages to stop herself from throwing her helmet to the ground in frustration, and I think the only reason she doesn't is out of pure respect for Alan. A chill goes through me. I can tell from Alan's face that there's more.

'They were carrying two large bags.'

Craig shakes his head. 'And I'll bet they hadn't just done a family shop at Aldi.'

'Fuck.' Riaz sums up everyone's feelings perfectly.

We're all getting our heads around the fact that we've just killed a man for nothing. And not only that: we've just had a pretty good indication that our targets – the ones who could be on their way to absolutely anywhere with no way for us to pick them up again – could now be tooled up with a significant amount of arms or explosives – or both. And there's nothing we can do except wait and see what they do with them. Sure, A4 surveillance jobs come to a dead end sometimes, but the backup the MI5 teams have in terms of technical surveillance and wider targets – it all feeds back into creating a new lead or getting hold of the targets again. We don't have that. We *can't* have that, without revealing our existence.

I can feel rage building inside me. Nothing. It was all for nothing. I'm about to slam my fist into the bonnet of the Mazda when Claire's quiet voice makes me turn.

'Hold on a minute. They left on foot, right? Not in a vehicle.'

Alan nods cautiously. 'They may well have had a vehicle waiting nearby, but the camera was only focused on the house.'

'But is there a vehicle parked outside the house?'

'I don't know. What if there is?'

'Don't you see? Whatever it was they were carrying in those bags, someone delivered it to the house. That's the person they've been waiting for. That's why they haven't moved until now. Whoever else is still in the house, they probably won't know anything about the brothers' plan or even who they are. But the person who brought them what they needed – he must know exactly what they're going to do. And if he's still there . . .'

Leyton-Hughes looks sceptical. 'That's a lot of "if"s. We don't know if there is a car or who it belongs to. You're clutching at straws here.'

Claire shrugs. 'What else have we got? I'd rather clutch at something than wait to see if anyone dies. At least let's find out if there's a car.'

Alan finger-punches furiously into his phone and turns away from us. He's not talking though; from his body position he's looking at the screen, maybe the camera feed. After a minute, he puts his phone back in his jacket pocket and turns around.

'OK, there is a vehicle parked outside. Maybe, just maybe, the driver could be connected to our targets. But if he's still in the house, he sure as hell won't be for very long. Let's get to the address as quickly as we can.'

'And the car?' Craig asks.

'It's a green Toyota Avensis, can't see the registration plate. It's parked directly outside the house. I've got the only access to this camera feed and will let you know immediately if the situation changes.'

Within minutes we're on the road, heading west. I'm behind Alex in the black Mazda, the sort of unassuming car that didn't scream 'police' but had enough juice to keep up with a fast vehicle move if necessary. But she soon peels away, knowing that her added manoeuvrability on the bike should get her there ahead of the rest of us. I know the rough route towards Liverpool, but I prefer to let the satnav guide me to an address three streets over, so I don't have any compromising locations on the car's computer if the shit hits the fan. After everything that's gone wrong already, I don't want to leave anything to chance. I need to zone out a bit to recharge my batteries – there won't be any opportunities for that once we get to the address – but it's hard to relax knowing the clock is ticking and our slim last chance of getting back in the game could slip away at any moment. Luckily, driving as fast as possible without drawing attention to myself takes all my concentration, and a couple of hours slip by without any interruptions from Leyton-Hughes.

The next thing I hear is Alex letting us know she's at the address and trying to identify the car. It makes me nervous. I've never liked having someone in the area without the backing of the team around them. Dropping down a gear, I speed past three cars slowing for an amber traffic light. Pushing harder on the gas, I make it through just before it hits red. 'Alex, I'm figures one minute out.'

'Thanks, mate, I've seen the car.' Alex's speech is clear but I can tell she's still got her helmet on by the way her breath is caught on the mic. 'We can box this in and cover the exits to this street if we get a stand-by from Ops. I'm holding north on Mill Street at the roundabout.'

'Roger that, I'll take south.' As the other guys shout-up their intended positions and ETAs, we get the news we're waiting for.

'STANDBY STANDBY from Ops. Unknown male OUT OUT and into the Avensis. He's solo in the driver's seat.'

Here we go, a hot rolling start. Obviously not Light Rain though.

I switch gears and the adrenaline starts pumping. This is what operators live for, getting the stand-by and getting hold of the target. Let's hope Claire's right and this is our man. 'Vehicle moving northbound, northbound on Mill Street out of sight to Ops.'

Alex comes on again. 'Alex has a long view on this. Vehicle

travelling north, I have control. I can give direction at the roundabout but it will be difficult to go with.'

An A4 surveillance team wouldn't have an issue here; it'd be a standard pick-up, even if they weren't quite in position yet. The sheer size of an A4 team means they can afford to burn one or two operators to keep hold of the target till the rest of the team arrives. But there are only six of us, and we can't afford to lose anyone. I've made good ground coming in from the south and I can see the target. 'Alex, I'm now northbound. I've got a loose eye on Vehicle One. Give him away at the roundabout and I'll take it.'

'Roger that. Five-zero metres short of the roundabout now, no indication.'

'Craig is ready for the east option on the roundabout.' Everybody's chipping in now, the net is red hot and we become one entity, just as a team should. It looks like we all got here just in time.

'Awesome, thanks Craig,' I reply.

Alex again: 'Two-five metres short now, no indication.'

'Claire is further north if you struggle, Logan.'

'Roger, thank you.'

'From Alex, Vehicle One is now at the roundabout, no indication, wait one.'

Hiding my car's profile behind a small delivery van, I wait for Alex's update in second gear, ready to calmly but quickly make ground if I need to. I don't have to wait long. 'Vehicle One is exit ONE exit ONE, westbound, westbound towards Liverpool Marina.'

'Roger that, Ryan has control. Vehicle One travelling west, one up, unknown male driver. Full thick black beard, dark top.'

'Roger that, Ryan. Claire is backing from a distance.'

This is good. We've managed to get control of this guy quickly without a fuss, despite having limited numbers. Without thinking, we'd slipped into standard MI5 surveillance operators' mode, and it seems to have worked. For now, the game plan is to keep hold of this guy in the car and see where he takes us. At least we've got him and we don't have to worry about an A4 team looking over our shoulders. The question is, who have we got? I hope to God Claire's theory is right, and all this isn't misdirection.

'Roger the backing. Speed is three-zero,' Ryan responds. 'Three-five miles per hour going past the tourist sign to his offside.'

'Ops, roger all the last, quick message?'

'Go ahead, no change,' Ryan replies.

'Thanks. Now we've got him, let's stay on this guy. Surveillance only. Ops out.'

Surveillance only. Meaning for now we aren't expected to kill anybody. I'm just starting to feel comfortable, in control, when Ryan comes back on. 'That's Vehicle One STOP STOP STOP on the south side of Northumberland Street. It's a vehicle dead end. I've got this at a distance.'

I'm the closest now, and I have a decision to make. Follow and risk exposing myself, or stay put and risk losing him?

'Control car, permission from Alan?'

Ryan is straight on the net, confidently in control of this. 'Go ahead, Alan. No change. Vehicle is static south side, facing west. Ten metres from the end of the cul-de-sac. Hold on, on the map there's a pedestrian cut through, though.'

Dropping down the gears, I accelerate the car to the north-west side, to try and get into a position to follow this guy if he moves on foot, just as Alan pops up with his message on the net.

'I've got a camera feed on this if you need it.'

'All yours, Alan. Thanks, mate!' Ryan responds.

'Roger that, I have control.'

Sly bastard, I think as I slow down again and park up in a row of cars and blend back into the area. Alan was just waiting for us to get stuck before revealing we had this asset. But I don't care. With our options running out, this is the advantage we need.

'From Alan, no sign of the driver yet, vehicle still static. For information, this is all sorts of illegal, I've back-doored my way into this local council camera. If they notice me on their network I'll likely be kicked off so I'll need someone close to hand it over. I can't be relied on as a secure follow.'

'Roger that, Alan, you have Ryan close in.'

'Logan, likewise.'

'Claire, likewise to the south.'

'Thank you. No change.'

This guy has driven down a dead end. Houses either side of him, the marina to his front. What's he up to? It's easy to start second guessing things when you're on the ground. But good operators assess what they can see, rather than guess what could be happening. I'm on the next street, waiting.

I don't have to wait long for Alan to come back on. 'OK. Unidentified male is out of the vehicle, walking west towards the water and marina. Solo.'

'Roger that, Ryan is out on foot if you need it, Alan.'

'Roger, thanks, Ryan. He's now approximately one-zero metres from the water's edge.

'And now leaning against a post at the water's edge, looking out onto the water, alone, I've got this on a long look.'

'From Ryan, no looks back, he's relaxed.'

I'm not sure where Ryan is, but he must be close by. He's experienced enough to know that with the assistance Alan is now giving, we can afford to give the target a little bit of space.

'From Alan, male has taken something from his pocket and thrown it into the water.'

'Yeah, from Ryan, he's throwing bread to the ducks. And stations, for information, I think there is a drone being flown around locally.'

A few minutes go by. Keeping a low profile in my car, I pretend to talk on my phone while keeping an eye out for this drone and anyone walking past. We're used to blending into the environment, but in my experience it's not just the target you have to be aware of, it's third parties and the things you're not concentrating on that will get you killed. Alan breaks the silence again.

'OK, male now walking back to the car, five metres away.'

'Ryan, roger.'

'Into vehicle and vehicle doing a three-point turn to do a reciprocal route.' Is he just going back to the same address? That's not what we want. I stay parked where I am and wait. 'Vehicle is now back towards the roundabout. Close in, can you? The network I've hacked is about to kick me out.'

'Yes, Ryan has control, thanks Alan.'

'Claire is backing.'

I find it difficult to believe this guy has driven the short distance to feed the ducks, ponder life and return home. Something about this doesn't feel right.

Claire comes on. 'Vehicle is towards home address now.' Her voice is flat. I can tell she thinks her theory isn't panning out. Maybe the brothers were just carrying clothes and personal stuff. And this guy is just a low-level facilitator.

'Ops, roger. Alan can no longer provide technical support, his back-door access to the council network has been blocked. Let's sit and wait on the address. We've still got the camera, but we have absolutely no technical assets coming out of there.'

'Roger that, Ops, from Claire, that's the vehicle now pulling up outside the address. Can you take this on the camera please? It's too tight to sit close in here.'

'Ops has control, that's the unidentified male IN IN to the home address now. I can give a standby on exit.'

'Roger that, Ops, all yours.'

As we all swap our compass-point positions close in to the address, we form a thin but tight iron curtain on the surrounding streets. I can hear more buzzing in the sky, but at different pitches. There are at least two drones in the sky, maybe three. I can see one in the distance to my right. Flying low, it looks like it's at the cheaper end of the hobby scale.

We settle in, knowing it could be a long wait before we see any more movement. But my gut is telling me there won't be. Unless we break down the door and pull the guy out, we won't be seeing him again any time soon. I wrack my brains, trying to think of something we can do to get a handle on him, but after a few hours of 'no change' from Leyton-Hughes watching the camera on the front door, I haven't come up with anything and eventually he decides to call it a night. 'Cease and withdraw. All to acknowledge please. Guys, it's late. The house is in darkness and has been for a while. Go and find yourselves hotels. We'll go again before first light. Hopefully he'll be up for morning prayers.'

That's going to be too late, I just know it. If we pull out now, I'm convinced we'll never see this guy again. But apart from sitting here doing nothing, there isn't anything we can do, unless . . .

'Alan, mate. Just had a thought. Any chance we could do a Bluetooth sniff?'

He instantly sees what I'm getting at. 'Yeah, maybe. I could do a network scan and pull some data – see if we can get a phone for this guy, yeah?'

'Exactly.' It was a long shot, but at least we'd be doing something.

'You'll need to be right outside the address, though. Unfortunately, we can't narrow the search for a network or devices, so you're going to pull all the neighbours' data too. Should only take a few minutes, is that OK?'

He knows it's not his call, but Alan's trying to give me a warning. This is the sort of stuff I thought I would be recruited for. Doing things without warrants that weren't legal because they're not targeted enough. As Alan said, we'd also have to hack the neighbours' networks to narrow our scans to try and isolate this unknown male. Doing technical assaults on the ground is fucking dangerous, because if you're caught it's almost impossible to talk your way out of it. I'm basically going to have to get close to our target in plain sight and hope my cover won't be blown. In other words, it's a throw of the dice.

Thankfully, either Leyton-Hughes doesn't appreciate what a gamble it is, or he's thrown caution to the wind. Or maybe he just likes putting me in dangerous situations. 'Ops, did everyone get that?' he asks. The team acknowledges and I can tell, despite their fatigue, that they want to give it one last go. 'Ops, roger, thank you. I'm conscious of a biker being in that area this late at night. Alex, can you withdraw either home or hotel while the rest of the team support Logan please?'

'Alex, yes, no problem. I'm on comms, though, if you need me.'

Even I have to admit Leyton-Hughes made the right call

there. Alex will start to stand out now. It's hard enough for us to blend into the environment, never mind a biker.

'Logan, do you read Alan?'

'Loud and clear, mate.'

'Roger that, great. OK, shouldn't take too long and I'll talk you through it over the net. In the kit bag is a PDA-style device. I need you to switch that on and log in with your pin number. I can then remote in to see the information you're collecting. I'll use that information to pull some phone numbers, hopefully including this unidentified male. OK?'

'Yeah, roger that and good to go.'

The device, the same size as my iPhone but quite a bit thicker, already has the screen brightness turned down to its lowest, but it still feels like I'm lighting up the entire street and can be seen for miles. I'm parked around the corner from the house, so get out and start walking towards the end of the street. I can't talk on the net now, but my covert message will tell Alan that I'm on foot and, as I pass by the camera, I hope that he and Leyton-Hughes can see me.

'Roger that. OK, I can see the information on your screen via my remote log-in here. Open the application called Gingerbread House . . .'

Leaning against the target house, I fall into drunk idiot mode. A new cover, one that suits this area in the middle of the night. The app is initializing, and Alan is straight onto the net while I pretend to look around and fumble with my watch.

'OK, the signal strength for the second Wi-Fi router

down on your list seems the strongest. It's password secured so we're going to bash the password. The router ID needs to be typed into another application called Unlock.'

Quickly typing the router ID into this new app without looking too sober is a balancing act. Hopefully I'll be on my way, staggering around the block to get back to my car, before our target notices the drunk idiot outside his house.

'That's it, once the application has found the password it'll connect automatically. Then, once inside the network, I need you to scan it for devices that are connected. Don't worry, though, your PDA won't show on their network traffic. Hopefully we've got the right one. Are you OK to stay on if this is for a neighbour?'

I signal back for yes and Alan continues.

'Roger that. OK, password has been gained and you're connected to the network now. I need you to switch applications to one called Inside.'

I can tell these applications have been custom built by Thames House or the geeks in GCHQ – massively powerful but with very basic graphics and user interfaces. Opening up this next application, I hope Alan will see something that will confirm this was the right address.

'Great, OK, there are five devices on the network, two of them are phones; an iPhone and a Samsung. I have the details up here and will do some cross-referencing to get the IMEI numbers from the service providers. I need to be as sure as I can be that this is the right house. Switch applications to Sniffer, please, Logan.'

The street is completely dark, but it doesn't mean I can't be seen. Plenty of people look out of their curtains randomly at night. In my peripheral vision, I think I see a curtain twitching on the first floor of the next house down. I need to speed things up. Maintaining my cover of drunken lost bloke while trying not to make much noise, I open up what I hope is the last app. Last thing I need is a neighbour piling out of a house thinking I'm looking to steal a car or the motorbike in front of me.

'Great, thanks Logan. OK, I can see the same UUID numbers. Try and keep the device as still as possible to let the scanner settle. I need to see the strength signals of the phones it's detecting.'

Alan is still on the net but it now feels like he's talking himself through the process rather than actually talking to me.

'OK, iPad 2 signal strength too low, that will be next door. That iPad wasn't on the network of this house, and the two phones we scanned are showing the strongest Bluetooth signal, meaning they are closest to you. I think we have it, Logan. Wait one – I'm just running a piece of software here.'

I pretend to search for something in my pockets. Still no sign of life on the street.

'Logan, I'm happy we've got it. Thanks, mate. Great job.'

As I move off in a stagger, Riaz is first on the net.

'Logan, I've got eyes on you, mate, Claire is at the end of the next street and will watch you to your car.'

I can't tell them about the neighbour watching through

the curtains, who could already have called the target to let him know there's suspicious activity outside his house. Every instinct is telling me to leg it to my car as fast as I can but I force myself to keep moving erratically. I feel like I'm holding a winning lottery ticket in my hand that someone could snatch away at any moment.

After what seems like an eternity, I make it to the car and fumble with my keys in one last little bit of play-acting, before slumping gratefully into the driver's seat. I rock from side to side as if trying to clear my head and do a quick visual sweep of the street. I can't see anyone.

'Logan is complete.'

'Roger, thanks team, cease and withdraw and acknowledge please.' Leyton-Hughes waits for the team to reply before continuing. 'Alan is interrogating the mobile phone service providers now. It might take a few hours, as it's not exactly an official request. Hopefully by the morning we'll have a mobile number we can use to help locate this unidentified male or use the call and text message history to give us a lead on the brothers. Either way, it's going to take till sunrise, at least. I'll send you all a text message with an update and the time to be on air in the morning. Go get some sleep. Ops out.'

As I drive out of the area I know I've done all I can. Now it's up to Alan. What I need now is food and sleep.

Then we'll see what tomorrow brings.

11

It might seem odd, putting make-up on my forehead to hide the bruises from my brothers in the mosque and those I work with at the hospital. The spies would probably find it funny, if they knew about me. They don't. The closer we get to our goal, the more I pray, to cement the strength I need to overcome the hypocrites in this country. I can't risk someone at the hospital seeing my prayer bruises and taking an interest in me. It's nearly time to meet Mohammed at the cut-through to the park, the spot we arranged a few days ago at last prayers.

I leave my flat and go through the motions of a British doctor's everyday routine. I even quickly update my Facebook status with the usual bullshit positive post: A great win for United last night. Had to watch from bed, I'm already off to work!

If I have appeared on any radar of MI6 or MI5, I'm not doing anything electronically that I can be caught for. No internet chat rooms, no support for my brothers out in Syria, no travel to other countries. Everything I do is quietly whispered to Mo in person. As usual, I leave my mobile phone at the hospital so I can't be tracked or listened to while I'm at home or a meeting somewhere.

The ones who get caught are willing to die; they want the police to come after them. But you can't do any real damage or create change if you kill a few kufar. America and Britain don't send their soldiers into our houses to die. They're directed properly, operations are well planned and ongoing. That's what I'm bringing to the streets of Britain. Only then will the government listen.

It's a five-minute walk to the park cut-through. I know Mo will be on time, he's never late. My shift starts in an hour, it's already starting to get light and if this all goes wrong, I have my tools with me just in case.

Pausing at the traffic lights, I wait for the green man before crossing, just as I do every day. It allows me to take in my surroundings, and any change in my daily behaviour could raise interest in me. The street is still rather busy despite it being the early hours, but everyone is moving normally. As I cross the road I take the chance to look up and down at any cars on the street; no one driving suspiciously, no strange vans around. I'll cross the road again soon, but this is still my natural route to the hospital. The hard rain gives me confidence that I can't be seen by satellites either.

Crossing the road to the cut-through, I glance over my right shoulder; no one behind me, no cars slowing down. I'm clear. I walk onto the dark, overgrown path and spot Mo's outline. He's carrying his motorbike helmet and is bang on time.

'Mohammed, my brother, salaam. You rode down on your bike?'

'I had to move fast, we have a problem!'

Mo is panicked, agitated. I've never seen him like this before.

'OK, we need to stick to the edges of the park and walk slowly so we're not seen. Tell me, what's wrong?'

We're completely alone in the still-dark park, it's just us and the soaking wet grass, but I don't like the tension surrounding Mohammed. If he's had to use his motorbike and get here quickly, something must have spooked him.

'The brothers left the safe house as planned. After they had gone I contacted some people from the mosque who have those little drones, you know the ones? I didn't want them to know the real plan, so I asked them to fly them around the area to see if there are any signs of racist, far-right activity. You know the rumours?'

He isn't making much sense, but I already hate this. My shoes have quickly become sodden from the wet grass and my coat is letting in rain, drenching my hospital scrubs underneath.

'What did you find?'

'The people flying the drones talked to me on walkie-talkies when I got home, they followed two cars that were near the house, I drove to the marina and back. Same two cars followed me and stayed a few streets away from the house. I was being watched. I think they are onto the brothers, who led them to me.'

'They . . .?' I know exactly who it would be, my question doesn't need an answer.

'It has to be MI5, or someone like that.' Mohammed is still panicking.

No, damn it! We've been so careful. I know I'm not being watched. But if Mo is, he could have led them to me. MI5 spreads like a virus, everything I've put in place and worked for could be destroyed. Mo is a good man, but he's made a mistake meeting me. I know what I'm about to do is the right thing. I place my right hand into my coat pocket and I hold onto an inhaler I've modified.

'Mo, don't worry. Have you got your phone on you?'

'Yes, of course, here you go.'

Handing it over to me, he realizes he's made yet another mistake. The biggest mistake. His phone will be used to track him here. Mo turns away and tries to change the topic of conversation, but he knows what's coming; I can't leave anything to chance. The inhaler is quick, within minutes it will all be over for him. Facing away from me, he tries to put half a step between us. It's too late.

I pull the inhaler out and remove the cap, then quickly step towards him and swing my left hand round to grip his face from behind. Almost at the same time, my right hand jams the inhaler deep into his mouth. It cracks against his teeth on the way in. One squeeze, followed by another, and another. It's more than enough; the highly concentrated strychnine will be forced into his lungs quickly. I release him and his body drops to the floor. He's choking and trying to grab a breath, his bike helmet rolls away in the wet grass.

I crouch next to him as his muscles go into spasm. I put the cap back on the inhaler and slip it into my pocket. I can't leave too many signs. This park is popular with dog walkers in the mornings; his body will be found soon. It'll take weeks for toxicology to be able to prove cause of death, if at all. By then it won't matter, my war will have started.

I hold Mo's hand, he's convulsing still. I see this at the hospital all the time, but this is the first time I've induced this type of toxin. His breathing slows and his convulsions become less violent, more of a mild twitching. I check his wrist for a pulse and count the beats, but his heart rate is declining so quickly I soon have nothing to count. I'm actually rather pleased it worked so efficiently. Dropping his hand into the grass, I stand up and make my way out of the park.

The hospital lights are overly bright, as usual. I'm met with a 'Horrible weather, Dr Kahn.'

I nod in agreement. 'Indeed. Horrible.'

12

Shit, I'm late! I wake up in the car park next to the drive-through, jerk upright in my seat and immediately grab my phone to make sure I've not missed any calls or text messages. Nothing. I'm covered in fast-food wrappers and the car is fucking freezing. I turn on the ignition and put the heater on full blast. I came straight here to get some food before trying to find a hotel to crash in, but my body had obviously decided enough was enough and shut down right here. It's 0617 hours, no update.

'Anyone, give Logan a radio check.'

'Loud and clear to Alan.'

'Roger, likewise, thanks bud. Just checked I've not missed an update.'

'Negative, getting there though. Shouldn't be long before LH can give you an update. Alan out.'

I need the toilet and a wash. You have to have a bladder the size of a small planet doing this job, and use every opportunity you can to eat, shit and sleep, because when a target is out and you need to keep hold of them, there are no comfort breaks.

I head straight to the toilets in the fast-food place as the staff prepare for the breakfast rush. The toilets haven't been cleaned yet; it stinks of stale piss in here. I rinse my hands in scalding water then turn on the cold tap, reverting back to what I had to do as a kid to wash my teeth: clean finger and plenty of water. I smile to myself, thinking I haven't come very far from those days living on the streets. On my eighth swig of water my phone vibrates in my pocket, as if it's excited it finally has news: Ch2 Now.

I delete the message to avoid having any compromising texts on me and head straight back to the car. Diving into the driver's seat, I get straight on the net. 'Anyone read Logan?'

'Loud and clear to Craig, mate.'

'Roger, likewise.'

Within sixty seconds the whole team is on channel two, ready for an update from Leyton-Hughes.

'Morning team, update on the phone grab from last night. Alan has interrogated the mobile phone network servers and associated cell towers and we now have a location for the phone. It moved to London during the night, shortly after we withdrew.'

I shake my head. I was right. All that bullshit with feeding the ducks at the marina meant he was onto us. And as soon as we left he made his move. If Alan hadn't managed to get his phone we'd be back where we started.

'This is a prepaid phone, unregistered, so no name. The text history and calls, Alan is shifting through now. Under normal circumstances we'd have a team of analysts sorting this, so bear with us. The last known location before the phone dropped off the cell towers is on the east side of Waterlow Park near Highgate, north-west London. It's a couple of hours drive from your location so please all get down to that area as quickly as possible. Ops out.'

It isn't a couple of hours. It's three and a half hours at least, and that's pushing it. Will our guy still be there? Or will he already have dumped the phone and got himself a new one? I can't shake the feeling that we've fucked up big-time. But we don't have any other options.

I don't bother setting the satnav before I head out of the car park. I'll do it on the motorway once I've got some speed up. I need to try and get ahead of the rush-hour traffic. But there's no point lighting this car park up with a J-turn, wheel-spinning out of the area, so I keep it nice and smooth heading away from the drive-through and towards the motorway. The roads are clear and there are no speed cameras, so I start piling on the power. The only thing that might stop me now is a random police patrol, but that's just a chance I'm going to have to take.

'Guys, you read Alex?'

I could tell from the background noise that Alex was going full throttle as well. 'Go ahead, Alex.'

'Riaz, you got your bike kit in your car?'

'Yes, yes, I was going to suggest that too. My leathers and helmet are different colours, too.'

'Great, I'll meet you just before the M25 so we can swap vehicles?'

'Roger that.'

Smart thinking from Alex and Riaz. If this guy is onto us, changing colours on a bike before London will help us blend in a bit more. I just hope our cars don't stand out enough for him to recognize us.

'Message from Ops.'

'Go ahead, Ops.'

'Does everyone know where the Victor compound is?'

'Ops, Claire. Is Victor the one just before you get to the Mike two-five?'

'That's the one. I'll call ahead at the gates and tell them to expect you.'

This is where Alan is switching the cars with others in the pool, without going through the admins at headquarters. Treated very much like an overflow car storage site, Victor is a relatively low-risk place to change our vehicles, as there will be limited police personnel on-site, then just a couple of mechanics and some admin staff, none of whom will have arrived yet if we're being told to change vehicles.

'Alex, roger.'

'Riaz, roger, heading there now.'

As everyone acknowledges the new location before heading to the last known area of our target, Alan sends a text message to my phone: Change of clothes, all different sizes, in the lockers behind the cars. Good man.

* * *

I keep to the middle lane as much as I can, overtaking the endless stream of delivery trucks at 120 miles per hour and still accelerating hard. At this speed it takes a huge amount of concentration to avoid a collision. But pushing things to the limit pays off, as I make it to the police compound after what feels like only about thirty minutes. Soon I'm past the discreetly positioned armed guards and into the dark building used to hold cars there's no space for anywhere else. Alex, Riaz and Craig have obviously driven hard too, and are already waiting by their cars, deep in conversation. I park up next to Craig and join them. Their expressions are grim.

'What's up?'

Craig rubs his stubble thoughtfully. 'There's some concern the boss is missing things. Have you worked with him before?'

I shake my head. 'Never on the ground. Probably same as you guys, just when he's been the Ops officer. But I don't actually know what physical experience he's got.'

Before I can expand on that, Claire and Ryan activate the doors from the outside and drive in to join us. Riaz gets Claire and Ryan up to speed with the conversation and Ryan instantly piles in with his take on Leyton-Hughes. If Craig was being diplomatic, Ryan isn't bothering.

'I reckon if Alan wasn't holding his hand all through this we'd be fucked. Killing Stormy Weather was a tough call, OK, but it's so fucking off that he's missing obvious operational planning and tactics. Just basics. Like the brothers leaving the address: why didn't he check local transport stations – bus, train, fucking coach depots – to see if they turned up on CCTV? We've got the time they left – surely we can set up a radius and cross-reference it all. They had two fucking great big bags for a start, I mean—'

'Yes, exactly,' Claire chimes in before he can even finish. 'Has he asked Alan to check the cell towers nearest to the Liverpool address and watch any phones that left the area at the same time as the brothers? Like Ryan said, it's basics.'

I get a weird feeling, listening to the two of them. On one hand, they're fuelling my own concerns about the man who's making all the tactical decisions; on the other, they're boosting my confidence in the make-up of this team. These guys are good.

But how good is their boss?

'Look, I hear what you're saying. But right now we have to get to the park. Maybe our boy's found some more ducks to feed. Why don't we ask Alan quietly what he can do about this stuff while we're on the road?'

'Yeah, OK.' Riaz leads the way to the key rack. We don't bother signing for the new cars or writing any details down about the cars we're leaving. Even in a secret compound like this, all that will make us more traceable. Riaz swaps for a bike and puts his kit bags in Alex's car, a dark-blue BMW 1 Series. I take the keys to a grey Nissan Qashqai and make my way to the lockers Alan had told me about. As the cars leave, I quickly shift through the huge amount of clothes, all in sealed bags marked 'Washed': socks, briefs, trousers – everything for a full clean change.

I've no idea if anyone else stayed in a hotel last night or managed to get home, but I notice Ryan and Claire are in different clothes to last night. I throw on a clean T-shirt, waiting for Claire and Alex to make it out of the building before stripping down my bottom half. Riaz is getting into his leathers as I change into clean pants and socks and put a clean pair of trousers on. Wearing the same soiled, stinking clothes for days on end when I need to pose as a street person isn't something I had a problem with, but this feels good – nearly as good as getting some sleep.

Closing up the lockers, I follow Riaz – now on his new bike – out. We'll need his speed if we are operating in London today. Flicking the car's covert radio on, I switch it to the team channel and ask for a radio check. Alan is first to reply with a loud and clear, so I grab the opportunity and call him on my phone.

'Hello.'

A typically guarded response, as all our phone numbers are blocked from appearing on-screen. 'Alan, it's Logan, mate. Can you talk?'

'Yep.'

'Can you talk openly?'

'No, I don't know when I'll be home, probably not till tonight. Did you get that boiler booked in for a service?'

'OK, mate, understood. Is the boss with you?'

'Great, yes that's fine with me.' OK, Leyton-Hughes is obviously within earshot.

'OK, mate, give me a ring when you can or we can speak

in person later.' Hanging up, I know Alan will continue to have a fictitious conversation to completely cover his tracks.

Soon I'm weaving through the traffic towards the park and it's Leyton-Hughes who breaks the silence on the net. 'Message from Ops, all to acknowledge.'

I respond along with the others, but from his tone of voice, I don't think he's about to deliver good news.

'Police are at the park after a dog-walker found a body. Initial reports are giving a description that matches our unidentified male from Liverpool. They've also recovered a phone at the scene.'

I just manage to stop myself from pounding the steering wheel with my fist and drawing attention to myself, but I still shout 'Fuck!' at the top of my voice. A cyclist passing me on the inside glances my way with a look of alarm. Well, the good news, I tell myself wryly, is that our target is still in the same location and isn't going to move any time soon. The bad news is he's fucking dead. And we can't even look at his phone.

'We are working through some options here, but continue to head into the area until we have more intelligence. Ops out.'

Options? What fucking options? We've totally screwed up. Not only did the target spot our surveillance, but now he's literally a dead end. Where the hell do we go from here?

No doubt the rest of the team are thinking the same thing. But at least one of them is trying to stay positive. 'Ops, wait one, it's Alex. Can we see if the brothers used any local transport stations in Liverpool? They left with two big bags, so we can use time and distance to see if they pop up on CCTV, or any phones that moved on the cell towers when we know they left the house. Or any other phones in the area of the park when this unidentified male's phone went off?'

For a few seconds, there's just silence. Then, as we hoped he would, Alan responds. 'Alex, I might be able to help with that.' He hesitates, and I can sense Leyton-Hughes hovering in the background. 'There wasn't any movement on the cell towers, apart from this unknown's phone, that matched the time of the brothers leaving. But I'm working on a lead now. It's just taking some time. I should have something for you very soon – by the time you get into the area of the park. What I'm doing takes slightly longer than doing it officially because, well, I'm not doing it officially, if you get my drift.'

'No worries. Appreciated, thanks, Alan.'

The rest of us chip in with our thanks, but the grim feeling that we're wasting our time remains as we continue towards the park. A few minutes later, Riaz shouts up that he's in the area, and soon we're all taking up natural positions on the surrounding streets. No doubt the rest of the team, like me, have made up a cover story for themselves to explain why they're in the area. No doubt they also know that the best thing about working in London is that most people are too focused on where they're going to actually lift their heads and take any notice of anything that's not right in front of them. But underneath the ingrained professionalism that forces us to keep going and not make any mistakes, there's a growing feeling that none of it matters any more. Since Blindeye went into action, two people have died and we've got precisely nothing to show for it. If I was Leyton-Hughes, I wouldn't want to have to explain that to the DG.

I'm jolted out of my gloomy thoughts by Alan, who sounds surprisingly upbeat. Or is that just his personality? 'Team, update from Alan.'

It's a scramble to be first onto the net to respond to him. Craig was fastest on the button this time. 'Go ahead!'

'Apologies for this taking so long – it took time cross-referencing everything. I checked to see if any phones had been switched off using the cell towers around the Liverpool address. Of the phones that were switched off, two of them were later switched on for two minutes on the outskirts of Birmingham. Judging by time, distance and location, these phones would have had to travel by car.' This is obviously important. Otherwise Alan wouldn't be explaining it all to us step by step, but I can't see yet how this helps us. 'During those two minutes, they both sent a similar message to different phones, which could be girlfriends or partners. The phones switched off again and then in the early hours of this morning switched on again for thirty seconds at a street just south of your position. They've remained switched off since.' Yes! This time I do bang my fist on the steering wheel, but in celebration. But there's still more to come. 'I cross-referenced those cell tower movements with the other databases I have access to and I've got a vehicle registration number for you. Ready for details?'

A car! Somehow the clever bastard's got a fucking car! 'Go ahead, Alan,' I tell him, unable to keep the excitement out of my voice.

'Agar Grove – page sixty-two in your map books. Two minutes south of your current location. The vehicle is a silver Ford Mondeo, X-ray two two one, Kilo Golf Golf.'

I'm already moving, having memorized the grid of surrounding streets, and then Riaz blasts past, swerving into the bus lane to undertake the morning traffic. I follow suit. As we get closer I'll back off the speed and settle back into being a regular driver, but now that we've been given a ray of hope, I'm determined to make these extra seconds count. As I turn into Agar Grove a quick check shows the rest of the team briefly filling my rear-view mirror before breaking off to cover the different positions needed to make sure a vehicle or someone on foot can't leave the street without us seeing them.

'Alex is east on a standby.'

'Riaz, taking a look now . . . STANDBY STANDBY on the vehicle. It's parked on the north side of Agar Grove, facing west at the junction of Marquis Road. Needs checking.'

'Ryan is on foot now, checking.'

I keep going past them, and it doesn't take long for Ryan to get back on the net as I pull into a row of parked cars on a parallel street. 'From Ryan, vehicle empty, vehicle empty.'

He pauses, maybe to get his breath back. 'I've got direct on the vehicle and can give it away if anyone comes to it. I can also see most of the east side of the street, but need someone at the western end.'

'Claire is west.'

There's a covert message on the net, which means Ryan obviously now can't talk.

Fuck, have we overlooked something? 'Ryan, permission please from Logan?'

Ryan continues to remain covert and not talk openly.

'Yes, heard, roger, thank you. Ops from Logan, do we have information the unidentified male was murdered in the park? Could Stone Fist and Iron Sword have done him to cover their tracks?'

It could be, thanks to Alan's technical wizardry, that instead of fucking up, we've lucked out and actually found the brothers. And if they've killed one of their co-conspirators then they're either panicking, or they're so near to their endgame that it doesn't matter. Which means we have to act fast. And we can't afford to mess it up this time. But there's no response from Leyton-Hughes. I'm about to lose my rag when he finally answers, his voice deadpan. 'The police are treating it as an unexplained death, according to the information I've seen. Nothing obvious at the scene.'

'Ryan, do we still have permission?'

Ryan sends the covert message for yes.

'Roger, thanks. Ops, if they're killing people already, we need the go-ahead to take them out.'

Another agonizing pause, then: 'Negative. That's a negative. We need to know what the endgame is first. Ops out.'

No! Every fibre in my body is telling me he's wrong. Why is he hesitating? Does he know something we don't? Or has he just lost his nerve? I'm trying to think of what else I can say to make him change his mind, when Ryan shouts up on the net, breaking his silence.

13

'From Ryan, Iron Sword and Stone Fist out of an address on Agar Grove just west of the car, walking west. Wait one.'

Moments ago it'd seemed like we'd hit a brick wall, and Blindeye's first operation had ended in frustration and failure. It was hard to avoid the conclusion that the brothers had outsmarted us. But now we've got the bastards again, and there's no way we're going to fucking let them go a second time.

Ryan's hushed tones tell us he can't talk openly without attracting attention, but we're keen to let him know he's not alone in the hunt and we all instantly respond.

'Claire is backing from a distance.'

'Roger. Iron Sword is black on blue, Stone Fist blue on blue.' He's still whispering but otherwise calm and in control, telling us succinctly what we need to know to keep lock onto them visually – the colours of their clothing. I decide I need to get into a better position, to help Ryan out, so I move my car around to a side street that covers a cut-through the brothers could potentially use and instantly spot Claire, sporting a very convincing pregnancy bump. A brilliant piece of improvisation; not even the best counter-surveillance techniques employed by the Russians, who are the best in the world at spotting surveillance, would be able to identify Claire as a member of a deniable MI5 team. And it sounds as if the extra layer of disguise is well-advised. 'For information, they are extremely aware. Several look backs already, continuing westbound towards the junction of St Augustine's Road.'

'Claire, roger.'

As the brothers continue to walk down this street, with Ryan and Claire's constant communications keeping us aware of their every movement, I begin to feel the net is tightening. As long as no one's cover is blown, they'll need to pull off something very sophisticated to slip out of our grasp. But as we follow them through a bustling part of the city, that still leaves a big question unanswered. How and when are we going to take them out? There's the age-old dilemma of knowing how much rope to give them. Reel them in too soon and you risk not knowing what their endgame is; too late and you risk letting them pull the trigger. We need to identify every player in this plot. The man found dead in the park was connected to these brothers, we know that. But was he giving them orders, helping them with logistics, or trying to help them in some other way? The trouble is, arresting them is not part of the plan.

There's only one way this can end, and that's with us killing them. And an execution on a busy London street in broad daylight isn't exactly an option. For the moment, our job is to keep control of them, like a regular A4 team. But at some point we're going to have to make a difficult decision, or Jeremy Leyton-Hughes is going to have to make the decision and we'll be expected to carry it out.

Ryan interrupts my thoughts. 'That's both targets into an electronics shop on the north side called Everything Electrical. Claire, can you?'

'Yes yes. I'll give them a minute to settle first.'

With Claire's pregnancy disguise, she'll be able to go close in to the brothers to see exactly what they are up to, before dropping back and changing her profile completely. The team closes in tighter, to provide Claire with some security and to make sure we pick the brothers up as they leave. But what we want to know is what they leave with. Any purchases from an electrical shop could give us the vital piece of intelligence we need to figure out their endgame.

'I'm going in now.'

'Roger that, Claire, we have a tight cordon for you.'

Even I'm almost fooled by Claire's act as she walks in, holding her back and grimacing like someone who's utterly fed up with being pregnant. Suddenly I feel a dark shadow closing over me. She's a fake mum just like I'm a fake dad; she doesn't really have a baby and I don't have a son any more. *Damn it, Logan, focus on the job.* I push the thought aside as Claire comes back on the net.

'Message from Claire inside, the brothers have split up inside the shop. Iron Sword looking at video cameras, Stone

Fist is picking up webcams. Message ends. I've got direct on the exit.'

Why split up? Why not stay together to make sure they are both happy with what they get?

'Ops, roger.'

As London goes about its business on the streets outside, I park up and walk into a coffee shop just east of the electrical shop. The brothers are well covered: Ryan has a view of the exit, Claire is inside, and the rest of the team will be blending into the background and staying out of the way, so I'm going to grab some food and drink while I can. I order my coffee and a toastie and use the toilet while my food is being warmed up. Another message comes on the net from Claire, via Ryan.

'Message from Claire, Iron Sword is buying a compact video camera, on the higher end of the price scale at £600. He's at the counter now, paying cash. Stone Fist still looking at webcams at the other end of the shop. Message ends.'

'Ops, roger.'

Back in the car and wolfing down my toastie, I nod to myself. A typical terrorist purchase. Most often, video cameras are posted to fighters overseas, or used in target reconnaissance. The fact he's paying in cash is another sign they're wary of being traced. Hopefully this information will help Leyton-Hughes develop a plan, while also letting Alan know there are potential technical attack options; if it's electronic, it can be manipulated. Ryan relays another of Claire's messages while maintaining his cover outside. I almost miss him as he stands in a bus shelter, facing the right way for the next bus, completely natural.

'Message from Claire. Stone Fist is purchasing a webcam for cash, paid with a twenty-pound note. Iron Sword is waiting by the exit. Message ends.'

The brothers are certainly on top of their operational security. If I was planning a major attack while trying to evade the security services, this is how I'd do it. Local electrical shops, pay cash, move around, good counter- and anti-surveillance, and no electronic communications at all.

'Ryan, it's Ops, permission to pass a message?'

'Negative, standby standby, that's both out out and continuing westbound on the north side.'

Not for the first time, I'm worried that Leyton-Hughes's lack of operational experience is going to screw things up. He should have understood from Claire's message that Iron Sword was waiting by the exit and we were about to have a move.

'Roger that, Craig is backing, mate. I'll text Claire when it's OK for her to leave.'

Even though the brothers are out, we can't assume they are going to walk clean away or that they haven't taken any notice of Claire.

'Thanks Craig. From Ryan, that's both continuing westbound on the north side, each carrying a black plastic bag from the shop. Guys, if we can have a couple ahead of them at key junctions it will mean we don't have to follow directly behind them and risk being seen. They are looking back on their route now, very aware.'

'Logan, roger, I'll be ahead.'

'Alex, likewise.'

'Riaz, roger.'

I know this part of London well. They're heading straight to Camden Town, with Regent's Park on the other side. We need three times the amount of people we have on the ground right now, at least, to make this a secure follow. And what if Leyton-Hughes gives the order to take them out?

'I'm out and changing profile now,' Claire lets us know. 'Thanks, guys.' Alex and Claire have already shown the range of skills they bring to the Blindeye team, but female operators have another advantage over the males: the number of ways they can change their appearance naturally.

Easing the car out into the traffic, I'm aiming to get ahead to the major junctions and tube stations, while Ryan updates us on the brothers' movements. 'From Ryan, continuing westbound—'

Suddenly he's lost comms, his transmission cut off halfway through. I've no idea what's happened, but Craig is backing so should be able to take control quickly. I turn down a side street just short of the major junction, ready to jump out.

'Ryan's in trouble!' Shit. Craig's tone is still calm but there's a hard edge to it. Leaping out of the car, I start running towards where I think Ryan is likely to be. There's no point diving onto the net saying I'm responding – Ryan will need the net clear. Rounding the corner, I slow to walking pace and use my peripheral vision to try and locate Craig without showing out to the brothers. I can see Iron Sword and Stone Fist, dressed in dark jackets over their shalwar kameez, still walking west towards Camden Town and the major junction. Fuck. We have to keep hold of them, but clearly Ryan needs help. Where the fuck is he? The bus stop was his last location – I focus on that and then zoom out, but there's no sign. What I do see is Craig running towards the bus stop from the other direction as Ops comes over the net. 'Who's got control of the brothers?' he asks, his voice controlled but higher-pitched than normal, as if he's close to panicking. But Alex is straight on, with Riaz backing her up.

'Alex has, continuing west. I'm OK for now, I've got Riaz backing on his bike.'

OK, that means I can leave the brothers to them and concentrate on Ryan. I see Craig sprinting past the bus stop. Where's he going? Doesn't matter, go with him. Ryan needs help. I dodge my way through the traffic, trying to catch up with him. I can't disguise the fact that I'm running as if my life depended on it, so if the brothers aren't working on their own on these streets, my cover's blown for sure. And if they have got backup, did they take out Ryan?

I can't lose anyone else. I won't. If we are being targeted by people working with the brothers, then we have to come out fighting.

Claire drives past me to join Alex and Riaz, no glances exchanged like there would be in the movies, as I close the gap on Craig just before a woman in jogging pants and a dark T-shirt staggers out of a wooden doorway squeezed between two shop fronts. Craig darts past her and barges through the door. It's obvious Ryan must be in there, but I force myself to slow down to a walk, hoping no one paid any attention to Craig or the woman, who's now limping awkwardly down the street. Ryan may be in trouble, but the last thing we need right now is the police turning up.

I push through, closing the door behind me. It's dark, but I can make out a narrow mouldy-carpeted corridor leading to a steep set of stairs.

'Lads! You OK?' I want them to hear me, but I'm not quite shouting, as I don't want people on the street to hear me. There's no answer, but I can hear scuffling from somewhere at the end of the corridor, then a thump, like a body being smashed against a wall and a series of strangled grunts. If Ryan and Craig are fighting for their lives, I have to find them. Now.

I quickly feel my way forward through the gloom until I find a narrow door tucked in behind the stairs and pull it open. Craig and Ryan are struggling with two men in a bedsit that looks as if it was a wreck even before the fight started. A huge guy in a grey hoodie with a shaved head and red, sweating face has Craig in a headlock and is about to smash his head against the wall. I can see Ryan and another, shorter guy wrestling in the corner. I step forward and deliver a short jab into the big man's face to get his attention. With blood spurting from his broken nose, he instantly let's go of Craig, but before he can pull himself upright I grab the back of his hoodie and power my knee up into his jaw with a satisfying crunch, before slamming a right cross into his bloodied face, which puts him down for good. I quickly turn to my left.

The other guy has managed to roll on top of Ryan and is trying to force a broken bottle into his face as Ryan holds onto his wrist and tries to keep away from the jagged glass. Ryan is losing the battle, and fast. I kick the guy as hard as I can in the ribs then grab the hand holding the bottle; I twist hard, breaking his wrist. Ryan wriggles out from under the now-screaming guy, scrambles to his feet and kicks him in the side of the head with his heel. The guy curls into a ball, cradling his broken wrist.

Ryan picks up the broken bottle and for a split second I expect him to start jabbing it into this fucker on the floor. Composure takes hold of him, though, and he adjusts his clothing as he takes a moment to get his breath back. 'Thanks, guys.'

'What the fuck just happened?' I ask him.

He nods towards the bigger of the two men, now lying in a heap on the floor. 'That big fucker there had a woman pinned down on the stairs. I was walking past when the second cunt walked through the door to join him and I saw them attacking her. They tried to run off through the back door when I turned up, but it's locked so they came back and had a go. Let's get out of here.'

Craig holds a hand up, struggling to get his breath back.

'Wait a minute, mate. So it was just random? These guys are nothing to do with us?'

'Nah, just wrong place, wrong time.' Ryan doesn't realize yet the thought process we both had before bursting in here as Craig continues to question him.

'I thought maybe these two were working for the brothers, spotted one of us on the street and decided to take you out?'

The penny drops as Ryan notices the confusion on our faces. 'I'm sorry, guys, I couldn't stand by and let them do that. It's fucking disgusting.'

I shake my head. Ryan's right. I look at the woman's attackers, rolling around like a couple of drunks. 'Cunts.' They're nothing to do with the brothers, but somehow it all gets connected in my head: these lowlifes, the brothers, and the fucker who took my family.

I walk over to them both. 'So you like to rape women do you?' I know what's coming, I can't stop the rage within me. It's like someone has turned the heating up to full, my blood is boiling. Lifting my leg high, I quickly drive my foot down hard on the big man's knee, and it breaks with a loud, rewarding snap. Switching onto the other man, I start stamping on his exposed groin as hard as I possibly can. I want to completely destroy them, to keep kicking until I'm sure they'll never be able to do this again. It feels good. Really good.

It seems like only a few seconds go by before they are both completely unconscious and not reacting to my punishment.

I feel frustrated, unsatisfied with the lack of whimpers or screams.

What's the point in stamping and punching them if they can't feel it? *The bottle.*

Adjusting my clothing, I bend down to pick the broken bottle up. I lean over the two on the floor; they belong to me now. 'Let's do something you'll always remember' I say, but as I kneel down, Craig rushes towards me and hauls me up. The horror in his face brings me back to reality.

I'm out of breath. Am I embarrassed or horrified at how easily I lost control here? Fuck. What's happening to me?

Craig can see I'm struggling, 'Brother, we stay on task. Yeah?'

Looking at Craig, then at Ryan, I'm grateful for them both. They have my back no matter what. But in the pit of my stomach I'm starting to feel like I'm lost. My family was ripped away from me, and maybe my humanity went with them. Hurting these would-be rapists felt good. I'm not sure, now I've tasted how good that felt, that I'll be able to contain it.

But there is a bigger picture here. *Bury it, Logan.*

'Yeah, back on task.'

I walk towards the door leading to the corridor and the stairs and Craig quickly follows suit, but Ryan stops us. 'Wait, not the front. She might have gone for help and be on her way back. We need to go out the back, we'll have to kick it in.'

Craig barges into the door. Thankfully the frame is weaker

than the door itself and as Ryan joins him their combined weight splinters it open. Hopping over the broken wood, we exit onto a little cobbled alley at the back of the shops. Ryan gets on the net as we turn back onto the main road.

'Ops, I'm fine. Just a couple of drunks trying to mug me. No issues or injuries and I'm backing from a distance.' He gives me a nod that tells me he understands he put us in a difficult position, and that he recognizes the effect it had on me. He wants to forget what has just happened. I hope I can.

I give him a nod back to say thanks, but the truth is, I'm worried. I was acting out a fantasy, not behaving like a professional. If they hadn't stopped me, I know I would have killed those guys. And Craig and Ryan know it too.

'Ops, roger, Alex, back to you.'

'Alex, roger, they're relaxed and still continuing westbound past the gym on Parkway, generally westbound towards Regent's Park.'

Shit, things have moved on quickly since our little detour. I need to get back to the car and back in the game. The brothers have too many transport options now they're in Camden and we need every available body ready to go with them. I drive like a maniac through crowded streets to catch up.

'That's Iron Sword and Stone Fist now one hundred metres from the north-east corner of Regent's Park.'

'Roger that, Alex. You have Riaz on the north-west corner ready to react.'

'Logan has the south-east corner,' I add, just in time, as I pass the stately white mansions opposite the park.

'Roger, thanks guys, starting to get busier as we get closer.' It's like a concertina – in and out, giving them enough room, then closing in so we don't lose them.

'Ops, message.' Alex gives Leyton-Hughes permission to pass a message as the first drops of rain start to hit my windscreen. 'Just an update on the unidentified male found dead in the park earlier this morning. Through various contacts we have initial police forensics showing nothing on cause of death. It's still being treated as unexplained. Ops out.'

'Roger that. Guys, if they keep going south in the park, they'll exit close to Regent's Park tube station. It would be easy for these two to disappear.' Alex is right, I'm in a position to go with, but knowing these tricky bastards, they'll split up or draw us into the station and then exit again into the park. I'm starting to think we can't handle this. But neither can we afford to let them go. Talk about a rock and a hard place.

'Roger that, Alex, I'll be in a position to react at the tube.'

'Claire likewise.'

Conscious I'm starting to show out, I decide it's time to look for a new parking space. But too much driving about also looks unnatural and draws the eye. As I hesitate, I look over and see the brothers emerging from the park, mingling casually with tourists and office workers who are blissfully unaware that they are sharing a stroll with two dead men.

'I've got the entrance to the tube,' Claire murmurs, but it

takes me a moment to spot her. No longer the tired mum-to-be, she's wearing old jeans and a woolly hat as she smokes and chats with an old geezer handing out the free papers.

'Alex, roger that, thanks, if they go towards the tube I'll let them run to you.'

If they do get on the tube then I may be out of the game. It's a tense few moments as I wait for the next update from Claire.

'Claire, they've gone past the tube. Both targets taking long looks back now. There's a ton of people out here so I'm good to stay with it, but can we keep leapfrogging ahead of them?'

Everyone responds instantly. You can't presume where a target is going, so you cover the choke points and try and be agile enough to react to whatever they do. We've still got them under control.

'That's a right right and west, now out of the park on Marylebone Road towards the junction of Harley Street.' Alex is still in control but she'll be looking to hand over to someone else quickly now. The majority of the people walking south through the park turned towards the tube, so she'll start to stand out if she follows the brothers. But before anyone can offer to change with Alex, she gets back on the net again. 'SPLIT SPLIT, Stone Fist has gone left and south one street before Harley Street. Iron Sword is at Harley Street junction now and followed that left and south. They have split on parallel roads.'

'Ops, roger, stay on Iron Sword, Harley Street is more open, be careful now, team.'

Bollocks. Here we go again. The brothers only ever split up when they are doing something operational. This could just be a counter-surveillance move, but it's starting to feel like a recce to me. We'll have to ride it out and see.

I cross the busy Marylebone Road and ditch the car near the bottom end of Harley Street. Unless they're going to double back to the tube station, I can help out better on foot.

'Alex, let him run to me, I've got the junction of Devonshire Road, which is the first set of crossroads he'll get to. We'll have to box him in while Stone Fist is out of sight.'

'Roger,' she whispers back. Iron Sword is studying the buildings on both sides of the street. What's he looking for? These streets are full of private surgeries, high-end doctors, the type of place celebrities and people with serious money go to for treatment. Not the sort of street you find two terrorists planning a mass-murder event.

'Logan has control of Iron Sword on the east side, walking south on Harley Street. He's studying every building as he goes past; Ops, acknowledge.'

'Ops, roger, and for information we have no linked addresses on Harley Street.'

I'm getting more and more uneasy. What the fuck are they doing here? 'Roger that, and stations that's a STOP STOP STOP at Harley Street on the east side, at what looks like a cut-through. Any vehicle call signs confirm this?'

'Yeah, Logan, the cut-through leads to the road Stone Fist turned down.'

'Roger, thank you, and yep that's Stone Fist now re-joining Iron Sword, exchanging words and now on a reciprocal route back northbound on Harley Street towards Regent's Park again.'

What wouldn't I give to know what they just said to each other. Now I'm convinced it was a recce. But it's hard to believe they are targeting a private clinic on Harley Street.

Two questions we need answers to: did Iron Sword find the address he was looking for? And what the hell was inside? If he'd clearly indicated one address, we might have a chance of finding out, but with the whole of Harley Street to search we've got no chance. Right now, all we can do is follow them to see where else they go, and my gut tells me that's back to the house.

As the brothers walk the exact same route back, we each have to remember which roads we've used, either walking or driving, so we don't repeat. If the brothers have spotters along the route they'll ping our team returning again, and they'll know they're being watched.

Riaz takes most of the control, following them through side streets and allowing us all to get back to our cars. As I manoeuvre through the maze of alternative streets, I see a police van outside the door where we'd left the two animals that attacked the woman. I hope they're not too late to arrest them for sexual assault. And I hope the woman they attacked gets the help she needs. As for the brothers, it's pretty clear they've completed their recce and are now doing a full route back to the address they left on Agar Grove.

'That's both targets now into the same address they left earlier,' Riaz confirms.

'Ops. Do you read Logan?'

'Go ahead.'

'Boss, now we have them securely at this address, this has got to be our opportunity to stop them. We might not get another chance.'

There's a long pause before Leyton-Hughes responds, and I can sense the rest of the team weighing up the implications of my words. Hopefully they'll see I'm right.

'That's a negative, Logan.'

Jeremy's short response has pissed me off big time. I can't hold my tongue.

'We've got to grab the opportunity while it's still there. That what we're here for—'

'I repeat, *negative*, Logan. I'm arranging for another team to take over through back channels. I can't risk exposing Blindeye any further.'

I can't believe this. 'But that *is* risking exposing the team! How can you pass on the brothers' location and what they've been doing without revealing the source of the information? We're supposed to be completely isolated from MI5. I just don't—'

But Leyton-Hughes has had enough. 'Just leave that to me. All A4 teams are out on other operations, but the DG is going to square things so an armed police CTU takes over from you guys. If and when the opportunity presents itself, they will go into this address and arrest them. You guys aren't equipped or trained for house assaults. Team, further to that, the police obviously don't know you're out there. As soon as you see them plotting-up around the address, pull out and get yourselves home.'

Home.

I park at the end of the street, my eyes fixed on the house on Agar Grove where the brothers are plotting their next move while we wait for the undercover police counterterrorism unit to move into the area. My head feels as if it's about to explode. Is the reason I don't want to go home because I haven't got a home to go to? Is it because I want us to go in and finish the job, to take revenge on someone for Sarah and Joseph? Or is the burning feeling in my gut a growing conviction that Leyton-Hughes isn't running this new team properly?

14

The first car of the police CTU rolls into the area. Then the next, and another, until the whole team of more than ten cars has driven past the end of the street to eyeball the address and check where the associated car is parked. I'm presuming this is be the surveillance part of the team, before they bring in the guys who'll eventually knock the door down. The CTUs are good, probably among the best police surveillance teams in the world. But not MI5 good. We would never put all our team close in at the start of a job. It makes the area red hot. The car that was second past the address returns to get a direct position on the house. A dark-blue BMW 530, six months old, just been washed and polished by the look of it. Driven by a white male, mid-thirties, wearing a black waterproof jacket.

None of the police teams react to any of us close in, which either means our positioning is spot on and we've blended into the environment perfectly, or the police just aren't aware of their surroundings yet. Without any fuss, I move out of my position, taking a longer route than normal to leave the area to make sure I don't drive past too many of the covert police teams.

'Ops, from Logan, CTU is in the area. They have someone direct.' Hopefully my neutral tone of voice doesn't betray the feelings churning inside of me.

'Roger, team – cease and withdraw.'

As the team all acknowledge, I can sense relief that we are about to get some down time coupled with an uneasiness about giving up control. On the drive back north towards the camp, my doubts about everything that's happened start to spiral out of control. Was killing Khalid even necessary? Was it the only way of getting us to this point? Now that the momentum of the hunt for the brothers has gone, the thought that I'm now responsible for killing three people starts to bear down on me, crushing me with remorse. My wife and son died because I wasn't there to protect them; Khalid died because I was told to kill him. But was Leyton-Hughes just tapping into my sense of guilt, knowing it was what I wanted to do?

The drive seems like the longest three hours I've experienced in a long time. I try everything I can think of to keep the morbid thoughts out of my head. Loud music, windows all the way down – anything to stem the avalanche of images and what-ifs. The mind is a dangerous place and I don't want to get trapped in mine. But however much I try and focus on the road ahead or the sting of the freezing air on my face, I can't get the images out of my head: choking the last breaths out of Khalid's jerking body; Sarah being attacked by the thugs in the bedsit and me unable to stop them because I can't let go of Khalid. It's like some awful nightmare – except I'm 100 per cent awake and aware that this is madness. I try and blink the images away, but the truth is I don't want to stop seeing her; it makes me feel she's reaching out to me, somehow. I just wish I could see her smiling and happy – not like this, screaming and afraid.

I'm not far away from the camp, but I have to stop. I can't arrive like this. My face would give away what's going on in my head. I can't risk it. I park up in a little village ten miles from camp. It feels a million miles away from the city we've just come from, with all of its threats and dangers. A row of local shops: butcher's; bakery; fishmonger; sweetshop; a bookshop just off to my left. Everything suggests a close-knit community, where neighbours all look out for each other. The sort of place we all dream about living in. It's hard to imagine anyone plotting mass murder here.

Getting out of the car, the evening air is crisp, and already I can feel my heart rate lowering and my head clearing. For some reason, the bookshop draws my eye again; it looks empty, maybe that's why it stands out.

I peer in the window and see that there are no glossy piles of bestsellers; in fact, most of the books on display look second-hand. I try and read the titles, wondering why I am even looking at a bookshop, since I never read books. I must look as if I'm in need of something, as an elderly lady in a light-blue cardigan opens the door and waves me in with a smile.

I walk in and inhale the smell of yellowing paper and old leather. A gentle heat comes from a small log burner in the corner. The shop is tiny, hardly big enough for a dozen people to browse in comfortably, but the floor-to-ceiling shelves, crammed with books, give the impression that you could find anything you were looking for and, thanks to the burner, there's the cosy warmth of a farmhouse kitchen. Still smiling, the woman places a familiar hand on my shoulder and I try not to flinch. I'm instantly drawn to her but uncomfortable with her gentle touch. Someone is being nice to me; it's the last thing I deserve, especially from a complete stranger. I shrug off her hand on the pretext of going over to warm my hands at the log burner. 'At least you're not going to run out of things to chuck on the fire to keep warm,' I say with a grin, trying to compensate for my rudeness.

'Oh, I wouldn't do that,' she replies, walking stiffly behind me to a high-backed chair, where a black and white cat sits, purring contently. She gently scoops up the cat and sits down. 'I'd rather freeze to death than burn any of these books. One of them might be just the one you're looking for.'

I give her a puzzled look. 'What makes you think I'm looking for something?' I say, then instantly think what a stupid fucking question it is. Why else would I be looking into her shop? But she seems to take the question seriously.

'I could tell, from the way you were staring through the window.' She gets up from the chair, wincing a little. The cat quickly seizes the opportunity to reclaim its place. Before I can stop her, she takes my hands in hers and looks into my face, her brow furrowed as if she's trying to read my mind. Instinctively, I try and shut down my thoughts, afraid of what she'll find there, but, stupid as it sounds, I feel as if it won't do any good, that she can see right inside me. A small expression of pain moves across her face – whether it's a twinge of arthritis or because she's just had a glimpse of my nightmares, I don't know. But then she smiles a sad, gentle smile, and says, 'I think you've lost something too, haven't you, dear?'

'I'm sorry, I don't know what . . .'

But she's not listening to my awkwardly mumbled answer. She turns away to the shelf behind her and starts to run her finger along the dusty spines, as if there's something in particular she's looking for.

'Ah, here we are.' She pulls out a fat volume with a faded green cover and looks at it warmly, like an old friend she hasn't seen in a long time, then holds it out to me.

Wisdom from the World's Great Religions.

I try not to laugh. In my job, you tend to be a bit sceptical about the wisdom of the world's great religions. In fact, you might be forgiven for thinking we'd all be a lot better off without any of them. But she seems so sincere, I don't want to upset her.

'I . . . er, I'm not really the religious type, if you know what I mean.'

'Oh, I quite understand. I was brought up by nuns, you see. Very strict! They put me off religion for a long time. But you never know when it can come back into your life. And there's something for everyone in this book, dear, whatever it is you're looking for. If you're having a hard time trying to make sense of things, I'll bet you the answer is in here somewhere.'

I don't know what to say. She seems like a sweet but rather dotty old lady, who probably says the same thing to everyone who comes into her shop, but on the other hand I can't shake the feeling that she's genuinely seen my pain – that she understands it. I certainly don't want to offend her by telling her what she can do with her book.

I take it from her. 'Oh, OK. Thanks. How much is it?'

'Oh, nothing. It's a bit battered, you see. But the words are all still there,' she adds with a twinkle.

'Come on,' I insist, pulling a crumpled fiver from my pocket. 'This is a bookshop, isn't it? How are you going to make any money if you give them away?'

She shakes her head. 'Read it and bring it back. Hopefully it will have done its job and then I can pass it on to someone else who needs it.'

'Err, yeah, OK, sounds good.' I try to clear the lump that's quickly developing in my throat. 'Thank you. And I'll definitely bring it back, I promise.'

'After you've read it,' she scolds, with a mock-stern expression.

'Yeah, absolutely.'

I give her one last awkward smile then dash out of the cosy warmth into the chill of the early evening, not sure which one of us is crazier.

'See you soon,' she says, over the tinkling of the bell above the door.

Opening the passenger door, I place the book on the seat like it's a box of tarantulas I don't want to sit too close to and move round to the driver's side. *As soon as I'm out of the village, I'll chuck it over the nearest hedge*, I tell myself. But I know I won't. Sarah would give me hell. Starting the ignition, I can feel a tear crawling its way down my cheek, followed by another. That mad old bat might have just given me a tattered old book no one else in their right mind would buy, but the generosity behind the gesture was unmistakable, and it's knocked me sideways.

Bloody hell. The idea of stopping here was to get my shit together, not start unravelling like a ball of fucking string. I shake my head like a wet dog. *Drive Logan. Just drive.*

As I make it to the camp gates I grab the spare jacket in the footwell I'd use for changing the colour of my profile and chuck it on top of the book, before flashing my ID to the guard. I'm not sure if I want any of the Blindeye team to be there or not. They're all I have at the moment, but I don't want them to see me cracking up. I'm anxious as the roller doors slide up and I see the place is full of cars, all the vehicles we used on the operation, including Riaz's bike. Reversing into a parking spot, I scan the building. Looks empty, the only sound a dull mechanical grinding, like a giant mixing bowl in a bakery.

I need to get the book into my little room quickly, just in case I'm not alone in here. I must be the last one back, which gives me a chance to get showered and sorted out. Opening the door, I see my bed exactly how I left it, neatly made. Nothing else out of place here. Even in this building I'm paranoid, though I can't explain why. Sliding the book under my bed, I grab my wash kit and spare clothes and kick off my trainers and socks. My trainers are scuffed and dirty – a reminder of what I did to those two animals in that dingy little bedsit. *Get to the showers, Logan, Wash it all off.*

The familiar hardness of the metal walkway pressing into my feet is strangely comforting. It's fast becoming a friend, this walkway. I realize the mechanical noise churning in the background is coming from the incinerator. Jesus, I'd forgotten all about that death oven.

Stripping off inside the tiny shower room, I lean in to twist the tap, hoping it's the right way for hot. It isn't – it's freezing fucking cold. But after the first shock, I don't bother turning it the other way. Standing under the freezing deluge, the air is sucked out of my lungs and the water cuts into me like daggers of ice. My body's shaking, but inside it feels good. Hot showers are for normal people, people who've done an honest day's work, not killers like me. Once I've dried myself off and got dressed in fresh clothes, I decide to ditch the dirty ones in the washing machine next to the showers and grab the batteries for the radio out of my room, so I can swap them for fresh ones in Alan's tech bay. Simple tasks to keep my mind busy. Things to do to keep the demons at bay.

But, deep inside, I know that rattling round in this place, listening to that damned incinerator, is not going to do me any good at all.

15

I am sitting upright in my expensive ergonomic chair, my hands lightly clasped together on the desk in front of me. The desk, like the chair, is an absurd extravagance. An expanse of polished walnut, empty save for a phone, a laptop, a notepad, three fountain pens lined up neatly, and a box of tissues. In front of the desk are two comfortable chairs, one for the patient and one for a family member to sit in during the consultation. The tissues are there in case the news is not good.

There are two framed prints on the walls: one a vaguely Scottish-looking landscape, the other a bunch of purple flowers in a vase, not very well executed in my opinion. I loathe them both. But I have learned to ignore them and, like the furniture, they serve their purpose, telling my patients that I am solid, reliable, respectable – perhaps even a little dull. As soon as they walk through the door, they can be confident that they are in safe hands.

The thought makes me smile. My next patient is about to find out what a sham it all is. He has sought my help to cure his problems. Instead I will send him to hell.

I press the intercom button to my secretary in the reception area. 'Madeleine, are you busy, or could you do something for me?'

'No, of course, Dr Khan,' she replies brightly, but with an undertone of annoyance. I probably interrupted her filing those garish talons of hers or sending unseemly texts to her boyfriend.

'Thank you. Could you please take those notes around the corner to Dr Kinsella? It slipped my mind earlier. There should be an envelope by the filing cabinet.'

'No problem at all, Dr Khan. It won't take me a minute.'

'Good, good. And Madeleine, since Mrs Choudry was my last appointment of the day, you may take the rest of the afternoon off. There really is no need for you stay.'

'Oh, thank you. If you're sure, Dr Khan?' she almost squeals in delight.

'Yes, yes, absolutely. Off you go.'

I hear her putting on her coat, then there's a pause, and the click of her handbag opening as she no doubt rummages for a mirror to check that her make-up is applied thickly enough. Then, finally, the sound of the street door closing behind her.

I spend the next ten minutes calmly checking that everything I need is in place, then settle back in my chair to wait. After a while, I look at my watch. Three minutes past the hour. It's unlike him to be late, but then again, it's not always easy for him to arrange these visits discreetly. It may be he has had some difficulty concocting the necessary lies.

No matter. I will be patient, even though the next twenty minutes will perhaps be the most important of my life. I note that my hands are relaxed and steady, without the faintest sign of a tremor, and my heart rate is normal – somewhat slower than normal, in fact. When I first began my medical studies, I was always fascinated by how people's bodies betrayed them, showing their weakness. Under the smallest amount of stress their hearts would race, their blood pressure would surge. Whereas I was able to control my breathing and heart rate at will, a well-practised discipline.

There were many things I learned in the camps, but that was a skill I had from birth, and it meant that however long I had to wait, I would remain calm and focused – ready to do the will of the almighty at the appointed time.

The intercom buzzes, and I press the button to open the street door. Another half-minute, and my patient raps lightly on the door to my consulting room and walks in.

He is dressed in a sober, dark-blue suit, subtly tailored to obscure the signs of his mostly sedentary occupation, with some sort of regimental tie firmly knotted over a crisp white shirt and Oxford brogues polished to a military standard – every inch the confident, powerful member of this country's ruling elite. But his face, as I stand and gesture warmly for him to seat himself, tells another story. There is a twitch at the corner of one eye, his skin glistens with an unhealthy pallor, and his tongue nervously plays over his thin lips.

Like me, he is a man with a secret.

I have already made my diagnosis before he has settled himself in the chair, but it's important to maintain the formalities. I want him to be at ease. 'Mr Day,' I say, in a voice oozing with feigned concern, 'how are you feeling?'

'Actually –' he pauses to wipe his forehead with a monogrammed handkerchief – 'I'm not doing terribly well.'

I nod sympathetically, as if drug addiction was an unfortunate accident that could befall the most virtuous citizen, rather than the sign of a weak and corrupted personality.

'The truth is, since our last appointment . . . well, I . . . the first couple of weeks went pretty well. Those tablets you gave me really seemed to be working. I wasn't having the cravings. At least not so I couldn't get through them. I hit the port a little hard at times, I'll admit. You know, just to get through a sticky patch. The pressure of the job, I don't need to tell you.'

I purse my lips and nod, leaning forward slightly over my steepled fingers as I maintain eye contact, the very model of a concerned physician. But inside I feel like vomiting. *The pressure of the job.* Bombing innocent women and children, you mean. And now you want my sympathy. You want my *help.* I feel my anger rising, like smoke, then breathe out and let it drift away.

'All right, Mr Day, of course, I understand. Let's start by talking through exactly what has been happening.'

'Please, call me Philip,' he says, as if he is granting me some generous permission. Even when they are desperate for your help, these people can't help acting as if they are the ones doing you a favour. No matter. He is about to discover how fragile his hold on power really is, for all his sense of entitlement.

'Thank you, Philip. I'm very glad you feel you can put your trust in me. Now, I hope you don't mind me asking, but did you come here alone today, or is there a gentleman waiting outside – one of those young men with the short haircuts and the big shoulders?' I smile conspiratorially. 'I only ask because I have cleared my diary for this afternoon, so we can have as much time as we need, and I wouldn't want your, err . . . guardian, to become concerned.'

He chuckles mirthlessly. 'No, I've managed to give them the slip today. They're solid chaps on the whole, pretty reliable. But you know I simply can't let a whiff of this get out, what you've been doing for me, or it would be the end of my career. You know what the media are like. Bloody vultures. Anything to boost their circulation and damn the national interest.'

I shake my head sadly, suppressing a smile. I'm still astonished that he thinks he is safe confessing his problems to me, as if the rules of doctor–patient confidentiality are unbreachable. Perhaps he thinks he is still back at public school, where one boy telling on another to a prefect would be unthinkable. Well, at least he's right that I won't go running to the tabloids.

'Indeed, indeed. Well, let's start by taking a look at you.' I take a blood-pressure sleeve out of a drawer in my desk. 'If you wouldn't mind just slipping your shirt off, we'll get this out of the way and then we can see what's been going on.'

He takes off his shirt, and I put the pressure cuff around his left bicep. As I start to pump it up, I pause to reflect on everything that has led to this moment. It was four months ago that the Foreign Secretary first came to my clinic here in Harley Street, and I'll admit that at first I didn't recognize him. He had made the appointment under an assumed name, of course, and was dressed quite shabbily. But I think what fooled me initially was that this man was quite clearly ill, whereas whenever I had seen the Foreign Secretary on television, he almost glowed with self-importance, as solid and shining as one of the pompous statues along Whitehall. Well, perhaps there was something to say for the ruling class's stiff upper lip after all. He had certainly managed to mask his addiction so far. But he'd realized that if he didn't do something about it soon, the declining state of his health would become apparent. He had heard about my speciality – a speciality, I might add, that I had pursued precisely with this end in mind: to ensnare individuals in positions of influence – and threw himself on my mercy. I've tried all the usual methods, he told me, but nothing has worked. A friend told me about you, about this new treatment you were developing, so I thought what the hell, let's give it a try. It was in that moment, when he assumed once more the casual arrogance of his public persona, that I recognized him. And I realized that a fly – bigger and fatter than I could have hoped for – had blundered into my web. I now had the chance to hold accountable the very person who was responsible for sending planes and soldiers into our countries to kill our people. And in a way that this country and its corrupt rulers would never forget.

As he puts his shirt back on, I walk across my windowless room to the drugs cabinet. 'Are the tremors getting worse, Philip?'

'Yes, I can normally feel them about to come on, and I've just been popping one of those tablets. But they've stopped really having much effect – even when I take a couple.'

I frown, a schoolmaster disappointed with a favourite pupil.

'Look, I know you said don't take more than the one, but I was desperate. I *am* desperate. I need something else to help me get control of this thing.'

I pat him on the shoulder. His shirt is unpleasantly damp to the touch. 'Don't worry, Philip. There is something we can try. Something much stronger. It has to be injected, though. Once every four or five days, maybe less frequently, depending on how your body reacts to it.'

'Could you do it now?' he asks in a pleading voice.

I pretend to hesitate. 'Well, it's somewhat experimental at the moment. We really ought to do one or two more tests.'

He grabs my sleeve. 'Please, Dr Khan. I'm willing to try anything, to do whatever it takes.'

He's babbling pathetically now, and I'm almost tempted to take a scalpel and gut him like a pig, right here in my office.

Instead, I put my hand over his and give him my most reassuring smile, before turning back to the drugs cabinet.

'If you're happy for me to do it, then I think I may have . . . yes! Here we are.' I remove a syringe from its protective wrapping and insert the needle into an ampoule of colourless liquid. I draw the liquid out carefully, filling the syringe until a drop spurts from the end, then flick it with a fingernail to check for air bubbles. I lean over him and rub the inside of his elbow joint with an antiseptic wipe. Not that I care if he gets an infection, but the ritual keeps him calm, safe in the knowledge that this wise doctor is doing everything he can for him.

'OK, here we go, small scratch.' Watching the needle pierce the white skin and sink deep into a vein, I gently push the syringe and watch the solution disappear into his arm. I give a silent thanks to God. Removing the needle, I ask him to place some cotton wool over the injection site, maintaining the charade right to the end. Then I watch as his eyes close. His mouth opens, releasing a thin stream of drool, and his head falls forward.

I feel a rush of joy, knowing that he is finally in my power. But I can't relax yet. We need to get him out of here while the window of opportunity remains open. Switching my computer monitor over to the feed from the security camera outside, I deactivate the locking mechanism for the rear entrance of the clinic. I can see the black private ambulance waiting already. Two men exit it the moment they hear the door unlock.

Leaving the Foreign Secretary slumped in his chair, I go to the corner of the office and unfold a light wheelchair, along with a blanket, hat and scarf. I position the wheelchair next to his limp body and put on the brakes. The office door opens and two young men, dressed smartly in black trousers and long-sleeved shirts, walk in.

'Masood, Hamza, As-Salam-u-Alaikum.'

I embrace Masood first, while his younger brother Hamza stares at the unconscious body in the chair, like a hyena presented with a fresh carcass. He turns to me, grinning, and embraces me. I can feel the power in his grip, the aggression he is barely keeping under control. He might be physically smaller than his brother, but he makes up for it with sheer force of will. God has chosen his servants well, I think.

Masood places his hands directly under Philip Day's armpits and hauls him onto the wheelchair, while Hamza swings his legs into position and places his feet on the pads, before settling the blanket over him. Masood places the large black woollen hat over the sagging head, then wraps a bulky scarf about his neck. No one would recognize him now. Just another unfortunate sufferer from a debilitating disease being taken from a consultant's clinic to some private hospital a few streets away.

Picking the Foreign Secretary's phone up off the floor, I usher the brothers out with their precious cargo. 'Remember what I have told you. Move slowly. Let God guide you.'

As they wheel him towards their ambulance, I look again at the phone. An iPhone with passcode. No matter, I just need to disable it so it can't be tracked to this location. I drop the phone into my sink and fill it with water while glancing at my computer screen. The feed from the security cameras shows the black private ambulance pulling away and disappearing down the alley.

It is done. Our day is finally here.

16

Down at Alan's tech bay, he's left all the fresh batteries out for us in their charging docks. Just as I start to think of what else I can do, my phone rings, blocked user ID as normal.

'Yeah, Logan.'

'Mate, it's Alex, I'm ringing round everyone to see if they fancy a drink tonight. We're stood down until tomorrow night. You up for it?'

I try not to sound too desperate. 'Sure. Who else is coming?'

'Riaz and Claire might not because they've been away from home for a while, but I think everyone else will be there.'

Funny, I assumed everyone else would vanish back into their normal lives as soon as we were stood down, but I guess we're really a team now, and like any team, there's a need to loosen up and download over a few drinks.

'Sounds good. Where do we meet?'

'There's a town five miles west of the camp. Fancy wine bar near the town hall called Chancers. Know the one?'

'I'll find it. See you there. What's our cover?' There's no

reason to think anyone's going to be curious about a group of people letting their hair down in a bar, as long as they don't act too loud or stand out in any way, but we're playing close to home and it's possible there could be guards or other personnel from the camp who recognize us.

'Yeah, thought of that. We've met our monthly target of untaxed vehicles for the DVLA, so we're out celebrating. Sound OK?'

'Perfect. See you soon.'

I make my way to the bar in a little Ford Fiesta – once I'd made sure there was no operational kit left lying around. I don't want to give Leyton-Hughes any extra leverage over me. The green waves of moorland on the horizon are fading into darkness as I follow the parking signs in the town. I see what has to be the wine bar in a row of shops and trendy-looking cafe-bistro-type places. The outside is painted a glossy black and the inside is bright and cheerful. Not exactly my kind of place, but I guess if you work for the DVLA it might look inviting.

Walking in, I scan the space. There's a long bar area and elevated levels, one step higher, with some tables. Bare light bulbs showing large filaments hang from the industrial steel above, illuminating a crowd of well-dressed punters, laughing and joking over expensive-looking drinks. No sign of the team, so I decide to use the toilets and check the fire exit at the back while I have time. Again, we're not on an op, so there's no reason to think we might have to leave this place in a hurry, but I feel better just covering the bases.

By the time I get back to the bar, Alex and Craig are there, Craig holding up a twenty to try and get the attention of one of the smart young bar staff. As soon as he sees me he abandons his quest and pulls me into a powerful hug, while Alex neatly swipes the twenty-pound note with a grin and slides into a space at the bar. I'm taken aback by Craig's show of emotion. He doesn't have a military background, but he seems like a tough, no-nonsense kind of guy, and I wasn't expecting this.

He pulls away, holding me at arm's length. 'You OK, man?'

'Yeah,' I smile, trying not to get choked. 'Yeah, I'm good.'

Alex is holding out two bottles of fancy lager in one hand and a glass of white wine in the other, a tattoo visible on the inside of her forearm; 'Modus Vivendi' – Method of Living. Craig takes one of the bottles without smiling. 'And my change, if you don't mind.'

'In this place? You must be joking,' Alex laughs. 'This isn't some old man's pub with sticky carpets in the backstreets of Glasgow, you know.'

'We have poncy wine bars in Glasgow too, you know,' he says. 'At least so I've been told.'

I grab my lager and Alex clinks her glass with our bottles. As she gives me a quick peck on the cheek, a waft of coconut and lemon comes from her hair. Apart from at the funeral, which is all a blur, I realize I've never seen her outside of an operational role, where you wear slightly too-large clothing to conceal various kinds of equipment. Wearing a black silk top and black trousers with suede ankle boots, she's slimmer and more delicate in build than I see her every day. I also realize I've never seen her wearing make-up before. She looks good, but it's slightly disturbing all the same.

'Sorry, I couldn't get you a pint,' she says.

'Don't worry. The bottle will come in handier if things get a bit tasty in here.'

She laughs and shakes her head. 'Fucking hell, Logan. Always thinking operationally, right? I honestly don't think we're going to get in a brawl in a place like this. Not unless we start chatting with a bunch of people who haven't paid their road tax.'

Craig clinks his bottle against mine again. 'We'll fucking have those bastards, aye? No one messes with the DVLA.'

I just manage to stop myself spitting out a mouthful of lager as Alan and Ryan walk up to the bar.

'What's so funny?' Ryan asks with a grin.

'Ah, just the man,' says Alex, taking Alan's arm. 'Logan was just about to buy a round, but he was waiting for you.'

The big man, looking slightly uncomfortable in a jacket and shirt with a collar, as opposed to his normal baggy T-shirt, smiles sheepishly. 'Thanks, I'll have a lager, mate.'

'No, no, that's not what she means,' Craig says with a wink at Alex. 'Logan here was hoping you might have some sort of fancy device that would screw up the card reader so it didn't take any money off him.'

'Hmm, I don't know.' Alan starts stroking his chin. 'I suppose there could be a way if you just—'

Ryan claps him on the back. 'He's joking, Alan, you muppet. Come on, I'll get them in. You guys OK?'

We all nod. 'Yeah, we're fine for now.' I tilt my bottle, indicating I've still got plenty. 'You get yours and we'll find somewhere to sit.' As Ryan squeezes himself into a space at the bar, we naturally move over to a booth where there's a wraparound sofa and a big oval table. We'll be out of the spotlight and no one will have their back to the bar, so we'll be able to see everything else that's going on around us. And hopefully we'll be out of earshot of anyone trying to listen in to our conversation. Perfect.

Ryan returns with a tray of drinks, including another glass of wine for Alex and two more bottles for me and Craig. I start to protest, but Ryan waves me off. 'Save you getting up in two minutes, mate.' With his long hair and tattoos, I didn't think Ryan would fit into a place like this, but with his dark suit and black collarless shirt, he looks surprisingly at home. Come to think of it, even though we're off duty, we're still surveillance operators. Blending in is what we do. Alan, the only one of us not used to operating on the ground, is the only one who looks a bit uncomfortable.

Ryan raises his glass. 'Here's to meeting our untaxed vehicle targets for another month. Congratulations, team.' We all smile and clink glasses and bottles. 'Shame Riaz and Claire can't be here to share the glory.'

'What's the deal with them?' Craig asks. I know Riaz has

got a wife and kids at home. Claire's situation is a bit different. I remember Alex telling me she's unmarried with a daughter, and her mum looks after the child while Claire is away at work for extended periods.

'I think they've got stuff going on at home they need to get back for.'

Funny how simple words like that can seem like a punch in the gut.

We chat for an hour or so, avoiding the difficult subjects that are at the back of all our minds, and focusing on the inconsequential stuff. I learn that Craig has a wicked sense of humour beneath that flinty Glaswegian exterior, that he grew up on a council estate (which makes me feel we're quite similar) and got a place to study history at Edinburgh University (which doesn't). Ryan's another one who makes me feel like an uneducated oik. It turns out he's a member of Mensa and is probably smarter than the rest of us put together. He explains he got his tattoo of the koi carp after a trip to Japan. This leads me to discover that Alan, who I thought I knew reasonably well, likes to spend his free time night fishing for carp. I tell him it sounds like the most boring way to pass time imaginable, and he counters by saying that's precisely why it's the perfect training for surveillance work, requiring infinite patience and the ability to stay focused over long periods. Which leads to a whole lot of banter about why Alan sits behind his workbench tinkering with electronics when he could be out on the streets, helping us track down the bad guys. As for Alex? I used to think I knew her pretty well. I know she grew up in a sleepy Wiltshire village, where she was something of a nature girl. I remember being plotted-up for hours in the shadow of a run-down block of flats with absolutely nothing happening, but when we got back to Thames House she had a big grin on her face because she'd seen a peregrine falcon stooping at a pigeon. We've been on a lot of ops together. And she was there for me after Sarah and Joseph, big time. She's probably the reason I'm sitting here and not in a casualty ward somewhere – or worse. But watching her now, as she sits back on the sofa sipping her wine with an amused smile on her face, I wonder. What do I really know about her?

And what, for that matter, do any of us know about Jeremy Leyton-Hughes? Posh cunt, obviously. Eton and the Guards before being tapped up for MI5. And he seems to have slithered up the greasy pole all the way to being assistant to the director general without any notable achievements along the way. What are his secrets? I'm about to put the subject out for general discussion when Craig breaks the spell and finally asks the question we've all avoided so far.

'So, Alan, we haven't had any updates from Leyton-Hughes, but have you got an inside track? Is there any news on the brothers? Have they hit them yet?'

Alan looks pained, like he's been hoping no one was going to ask him about this.

'No, not yet.' He takes a swig of his lager, clearly an avoidance mechanism.

'But . . .' I press him.

He sighs. 'I know the Police CTU that took over from you guys had a loss.'

Alan hangs his head; even though he's not responsible, he clearly feels like he should have told us earlier.

Exasperated shakes of the head and muttered 'fucks' all round. We've all stopped drinking as we wait for Alan to continue.

'I'm sure Leyton-Hughes will be briefing us up later but all I heard from the grapevine is the police teams sat outside the house for hours with no sign of the brothers at all. They eventually breached the address to arrest them but it was empty.'

Ryan jumps in straight away. 'We had them to that address though, did they smash the wrong door in?'

Alan continues with a head shake, almost in disbelief. 'No, it was the right address you had the brothers going into. The person who was watching the front door missed them both leaving and they managed to get away.'

The anger at the table is almost tangible. How the fuck could this happen? Our attention drifts back to Alan, who still has his head bowed. I can see there is more he wants to say. 'Alan, what else happened?'

Reluctantly he continues. 'They searched the address, it was empty. Sent sniffer dogs in . . .' He raises his head to look at us, we know he's about to deliver bad news. 'They found the bags they were seen leaving with at Liverpool. Bags were empty.' He takes a large breath and releases it as a sigh. 'The sniffer dogs indicated presence of explosives in the bags.'

'Where the fuck are those explosives now?' Alex voiced what we were all instantly thinking. Alan's raised eyebrows shows no one has a fucking clue. But if Stone Fist and Iron Sword had two bags' worth of explosives that have been transferred somewhere, it's bad news.

'I think it's just been handed over to A4 now. They're searching everywhere for the brothers.'

'It just goes to prove we should have seen this through to the end.' Alex is furious.

'And is that it for us? For Blindeye? At 2100 hours tomorrow do we get a new target? A new op?' Ryan's giving Alan a long stare, as if he's convinced our tech guy knows a lot more than he's letting on.

Alan freezes under Ryan's concentrated gaze, like a rabbit caught in the headlights. He shuffles uncomfortably, then looks at his watch. 'Blimey, I must be going. I said I was going to . . . I've got to sort some stuff out for tomorrow.'

I think Alan maybe does know something, but I hate seeing the guy in this position. I punch him lightly on the shoulder. 'Just when your round was coming up. Fucking typical. See you tomorrow, mate. Take it easy.'

Ryan takes this as a sign to ease off. 'Cheers, Alan. Thanks for everything. You have a good night.'

We watch him scuttle off gratefully through the other drinkers.

'My round, then,' Alex says reluctantly, but it's going to

take more than another drink to get us back in the party mood.

'So,' says Craig, neatly summing up what we all feel, 'now we just sit on our arses and wait for the next fuck-up.'

17

It's nine o'clock in the morning. I'm sitting in a cafe on the other side of town from last night's wine bar with the sun pouring through the windows, but I'm not in a sunny mood. The night out at the wine bar had started as a much-needed release of tension and a way for a few of the team to get to know each other a little better in a relaxed environment, i.e. not in the middle of trying to keep control of a pair of armed and dangerous terrorists. But after Alan's bombshell about the CTU team losing Iron Sword and Stone Fist, the mood had changed, and we spent the rest of the night speculating about what the brothers' endgame might be, based on everything we had seen of their behaviour, and in particular their recce around Harley Street.

We also tried to come up with plausible reasons for Blind-eye being taken off the board, just when it seemed as if we had an opportunity to finish what we'd started. Although Jeremy has a point about us not being equipped for all-out house assaults and arrests, it still would have been better to keep us on it. Leyton-Hughes has dropped the ball here.

We called it a day around eleven, after Ryan muttered

'politics' darkly to himself, suggesting a world of painful experience he didn't elaborate on. That had finally killed the mood. I'd come to realize he was the sort of person who thought long and deeply before expressing an opinion – clearly it was all churning away in that massive brain of his. All that said, it was good to pretend for a few hours that we were just normal colleagues on the piss. In a funny way, it was actually quite like a training exercise; seeing how well you could maintain your cover in a crowded environment. But reality was never far away. There was a clock ticking back in London, and we could all hear it in our heads, even through the shouts and laughter in a noisy bar.

And one thing I was not going to do was get drunk. I was determined not to lose control; not to say or do anything that would make my colleagues doubt my fitness to do the job. And determined that when I woke up today, it would not be sweating and breathless from a screaming nightmare, but in my right mind. Leyton-Hughes might have stood Blind-eye down, but all my instincts told me that this wasn't the time to relax.

When you're not sure what the hell is going to happen next, that's when you need all your wits about you. Maybe this was just paranoia rearing its ugly head, but Leyton-Hughes giving us twenty-four hours downtime almost felt like an attempt to mess with our heads, to break our concentration. On the other hand, I admitted to myself, that could just be the opinion of someone who doesn't want a break from the job because they don't have a life outside it any more.

On that sour note, I dump three packets of sugar into my mug of tea and stir it until I've created a mini whirlpool. I'm sat in the corner, away from the counter, with a good view of the door, so I clock Alex as soon as she walks in and makes her way over to my table. The cafe is almost full at this hour, but most people are intent on their food, their phones or the paper – sometimes all three. Alex is dressed in jeans and white T-shirt, all trace of make-up gone. This is more like the Alex I know; the glamorous mystery woman of last night has vanished, like Cinderella after the chimes of midnight.

'You all right?' she asks.

'Yeah. You?'

She takes the seat opposite and puts her phone on the table. 'Yep. Been for a bit of a run. There's some nice country round here, actually.'

'Seen any interesting wildlife?'

'Apart from a drunk sleeping it off under a hedge, not really.'

'No wolves or bears, shit like that?'

She shakes her head in mock exasperation. 'You're such a fucking city boy, Logan. If there were wolves roaming the streets you probably wouldn't even notice.'

I laugh. 'Where I grew up, the pitbulls would have made short work of any wolves.' I pass the plastic menu over. 'What're you having?'

'Same as you, I expect,' she says. 'Full English with all the extras?'

'You know me too well,' I grin. At that moment the waitress, a pale-faced, stick-thin girl of about sixteen, shuffles over from the counter and puts a huge plate of sausages, fried egg, beans and fried bread in front of me, before turning to Alex.

'Yeah?' she says, completely uninterested.

'I'll have what he's having,' Alex replies, as the waitress is already walking away.

'Talking of dangerous animals, any news on our guys?'

'Nah, nothing. I keep checking my phone every five minutes. I've just got a feeling, you know?'

At that moment Alex's phone pings with a text message. She reads it with a frown, then tosses it back onto the table. 'Twat.'

I look at her quizzically.

'Sorry. Just some bloke I'm seeing. *Was* seeing.'

'Ah. Sorry. What happened?' I didn't even know she'd been seeing someone, but now I feel protective.

'We'd been going out for a couple of months, and I thought it was going all right. But I didn't tell him who I worked for obviously, and he quickly figured out I was hiding something.' She smiled. 'Guess I'm not as good an operator as I thought. Anyway, he put two and two together and thought I must be seeing someone else. The last straw was when I came round to yours. No way was I going to explain anything that was going on, so he snapped.'

'Shit, I'm sorry. It's my fault, I could try and talk to him, to explain?'

'Don't be stupid. Better to find out at this stage. It clearly wasn't meant to be. Reckon I probably dodged a bullet.'

I can tell she's making light of it. I don't want to think of this guy really hurting her. But I don't press her for any more details. I'm surprised she's even told me this much. Up until now her personal life has been a complete blank to me. I'm trying to think of something else to say when I see her staring at the TV on the wall in the opposite corner of the cafe.

'Logan . . .'

The sound is off, but the scrolling ticker at the bottom is flashing *BREAKING NEWS – HOSTAGE SITUATION CENTRAL LONDON.*

I leave my breakfast and we both move to the unoccupied table directly under the TV. Above the headline the screen is showing a terraced street. The camera seems to be behind a group of several police vehicles, so it's hard to figure out which house they're trying to focus on, but you can see police tape cordoning off both ends of the street and people being evacuated from surrounding houses. Armed police are swarming into the area.

We exchange a quick glance. Alex mouths, *Brothers?* I lean close to the TV, trying to make out more detail, while Alex immediately starts scrolling through her phone. Back in the day, when there was a major event like this, people would huddle round their TVs, or even their radios, to find out what was going on. But social media has changed all that.

It doesn't take her long to find what she's looking for, whispering to me, 'Look, Logan, it's the brothers. They're pushing a live feed out on extremist sites. There's multiple feeds on Facebook and Twitter.'

Passing me her phone, I can see a live video feed of Stone Fist and Iron Sword standing either side of a middle-aged man sitting on a chair with his hands behind his back, presumably tied. His white shirt is stained and missing a button, there are abrasions on his face, and one eye is swollen up. He's clearly been roughed up, and has the blank look of someone in shock.

The man on the left is dressed in military-type black fatigues and is wearing a black and white shemagh around his neck. With his shaved head, thin, feral face and untidy beard I instantly recognize Stone Fist. He's waving a large butcher's knife in front of the man in the chair, while his brother, Iron Sword, is similarly dressed but taller and with a slightly darker and fuller beard, reading from a crumpled sheet of paper held in front of him.

Focusing intently on the screen, I hardly notice the waitress putting two mugs of coffee on the table. 'You sitting here now, are you, or what?'

'Yeah,' I bark, without looking at her.

'Then what you want me to do with your breakfast then?' she asks, as if daring me to tell her to bring it over.

'Jesus, I don't know, chuck it away, give it to your bloody dog—'

'Oi, you can't talk to me like that!' she squeaks, her eyes going wide. 'My dad's in the kitchen. He'll come and—'

Alex quickly steps in, putting her hand on the girl's arm and smiling sweetly at her. 'Take no notice of him. He's just a bit wound up.' She grabs my plate from the other table and brings it over.

'I've got to clean it up now before someone else sits there,' the girl complains. 'It's not like I ain't got enough to do.'

'Yeah, sorry,' Alex says, smile still in place. When the waitress finally turns on her heels, Alex leans over my shoulder. 'What's he saying?'

'The guy in the chair, it's Philip Day.'

'The Foreign Secretary?'

'Yeah. They want the Prime Minister to put him on trial for war crimes. Something about bombing innocent civilians in Syria. If the PM doesn't agree, they're going to do the job themselves.' I give her a look. 'And I think we can all guess what the sentence is going to be.'

'How in hell did they get hold of him? He's a member of the fucking Cabinet! Jesus.'

I glance over at the counter, where the waitress is glaring at us, along with a short, fat man wearing a grimy apron and a couple of days' stubble. It's all beginning to feel a little surreal: a top member of the British government has been kidnapped by a couple of terrorists who are threatening to behead him, and we're about to be turfed out of this cafe because of bad language. All around us, the rest of the patrons are showing little interest in what's unfolding on the TV screen, seemingly more interested in their phones or their papers.

'Any more feeds?' Alex asks, but the live feed instantly crashes. I'm sure MI5 and GCHQ are all over this, working frantically to close down as many live-streams and servers as they can find.

I hand her back her phone. 'Well, at least we now know what their endgame is.'

We turn our eyes back to the TV. The Sky News feed is positioned high on top of some houses on the other side of the street. We can make out police snipers scattered around, and armed police covering negotiators with rifles and ballistics shields.

'How did they get him away from his protection detail?' I ask in a lowered tone, to ensure we don't attract any more attention in here. 'I mean, we've seen these guys in action: they're savvy, all right. Definitely had some training. But no way they'd be capable of pulling off a stunt like that. They'd be taken out before they could get within ten feet of him.'

Alex can't hide her frustration, 'Well, they did it somehow.'

'Not on their own, though. They may be a cut above your average suicidal lowlife, but it takes something special to make the Foreign Secretary disappear in a puff of smoke.'

'Well, we know they had one helper. The dead guy in the park.'

'And the question still remains: who killed him?'

'Leyton-Hughes told us the police found no evidence of foul play.'

'Which either means he dropped dead of a heart attack—'

'Or there are more people in this thing that we don't know about. People with some pretty impressive skills.'

We both chew that thought over for a while. I glance at Alex. She has a fierce look in her eyes, and her knuckles are whitening as she clenches both fists in front of her.

'We could have stopped it. We could have taken them down. That was the point. That was what Blindeye was created for.' She jerks her chin towards the TV. 'So it never gets to this.'

'Well, it's happened now. And it doesn't look like there's anything we can do about it. It's all "lights, camera, action". One great big fucking stage. Time for us to scuttle back into the shadows where we belong.'

Alex clenches her fists harder. 'There must be something we can do. There must be!'

I decide to let her stew. There's nothing else I can say.

Alex's breakfast arrives with a surly look from the waitress and we despondently pick at our food in between sips of lukewarm coffee, eyes glued to the TV, even though we know nothing's likely to happen for a while. The house has been secured. The brothers have made their demands. Now the waiting game begins.

Though it's pretty certain how this is going to end: with the brothers coming out in body bags. The question is: how many people will they take with them? If their planning has been sophisticated enough to kidnap the Foreign Secretary, they'll have prepared well for a siege.

They'd know that the location of their IP address would quickly be identified as soon as they started live-streaming their demands. Of course, that's just what they want. They want to suck in as many police and military personnel as they can.

And all on live TV.

After twenty minutes of nothing happening, intercut with so-called security experts and talking heads back in the studio finding various long-winded ways of saying they don't know anything, I turn my attention to the other people in the cafe. It's full now, with a family of five now squeezed into our old table in the corner, and people are beginning to watch the TV, or follow the unfolding drama on their phones. The place hasn't exactly gone silent, but there's some tension in the air and some worried faces.

Not everyone's focused on the TV, however. I watch as two giggling teenage girls use their phones to take videos of each other. Then one of them starts filming the screen of her friend's phone. Odd thing to do, I think: videoing a video. So you wouldn't be able to tell which device took the original one, I suppose. I go back to my coffee and half-eaten breakfast. But the girls' little trick with their phones sticks in my mind. It's connected to something. I just don't know what. It's like knowing you know the answer to a pub quiz question but not being able to actually remember it.

Then suddenly it hits me.

Two devices, filming the exact same content. Fuck me. The brothers – they bought a video camera and a webcam separately. Why would they need two recording devices? It seemed odd at the time, but it didn't seem important.

I grab my phone and punch in Alan's number.

'What are you doing?' Alex asks, picking up on my urgency.

I make a 'just hold on' gesture as Alan picks up. 'Alan, mate, it's Logan. Where are you? Yeah, me and Alex have been watching it too. That's sort of what I want to pick your brains about. We're at the Central Cafe. It's on the High Street. You know it? Course you do. See you soon.'

'What was all that about?' Alex asks.

'Better wait till Alan gets here. I'm not sure I can explain it twice.'

'Explain what?'

'Nothing. Well, maybe it's something. I don't know.'

Alex doesn't bother pursuing it and goes back to her phone, seeing if she can find any sites still streaming the brothers' video. I fold my arms and start chewing my lip. Maybe this is what night carp-fishing is like, I think: feeling a little vibration in the rod and not knowing whether it's some monster forty-pounder on the end of your line or just a little tiddler nibbling at your bait.

Our food has gone cold and the waitress takes it away, along with our coffee. We watch the endless 'Breaking News' statements on the TV in silence, waiting for Alan to arrive. Customers have come and gone but the cafe is still heaving, and just as we're about to outstay our welcome, I see Alan pull up. I nudge Alex. 'Come on, Alan is here. Let's go.'

We walk outside and instinctively towards a grassy area that has a bench, borne from years of not wanting to be overheard.

'So what's up?' Alan asks.

I look at them both, and they huddle in slightly as I begin.

'Alan, hypothetically speaking, could you film something on a video camera then, with a second video camera or webcam, record the display screen of the first camera to make it look like it was recorded from a different location?'

I've confused Alan slightly here. *Fuck*. I need a better way of explaining this. 'OK, look. Pass me your phone.' Without question, Alan passes me his phone.

I bring the camera up and do the same with my phone, which I point at Alex.

'Look, I'm filming Alex yeah? On *my* phone.' Alan nods in agreement at my basic demonstration. I pass his phone back to him. 'Mate, take a video recording of my phone screen now.' I give him a few seconds as he adjusts and tightens in to record the display of my phone, still trained on Alex. 'OK. Play it back.' Alan stops recording and hits play, and all three of us crowd round to watch his short video.

'With a bit of time and a proper set up, it would look like Alan's phone has taken that footage directly of me, not recorded it from your phone, right?' Alex asks.

'Exactly!' I'm hoping Alan is going to see my point and say it's possible.

'Of course, but I'm not sure exactly what you mean by a different location. Unless you mean something like Face-Time or Skype?' he says.

Bingo.

'Alex is the Foreign Secretary, yeah? I'm filming. Which means I'm here in the exact same place?' Nods from Alan as I continue with my theory. '*You* film the screen of *my* video camera, perfectly still. So all you're recording is the video on *my* screen.'

Taking a moment to look at both Alex and Alan, I try and wrap my idea up. 'What if *you* use the video *you* are taking and live-stream it online. Then we would all assume *you* are with the Foreign Secretary, *not me*. Right?'

I can see Alan and Alex working this through in their heads. 'You're still wondering why the brothers bought a video camera *and* a webcam.' Alan delves deeper into this idea. 'So what you're suggesting is that the brothers are filming the Foreign Secretary in one location with the video recorder, but the live feed goes directly to a TV screen in a completely different location, where the webcam is set up to film the screen. So when you look at the IP address, it looks as if the Foreign Secretary is being held at the address where the webcam is, where all the police are now outside?'

Alex takes her phone and waves it animatedly. 'The live-streams I've seen on social media aren't great quality, so maybe that's how they're disguising the fact it's filming off a screen – to obscure the pixilation and line refreshes you get when you try and film video footage off a TV screen.'

The three of us fall silent for a moment, working out the implications.

'OK, so this is just a theory, right,' I begin tentatively, 'but let's say we have no idea where the brothers are actually holding the Foreign Secretary. And the police are surrounding a house which is completely empty . . .'

'Except for a couple of hundred pounds of high explosive rigged with sophisticated booby traps,' Alex completes my thought.

I nod. 'And the brothers can basically control when the security forces go in, by making it look like they're about to execute the Foreign Secretary. They press the button, and the world's media will show the SAS getting blown to smithereens live around the globe.'

'And when they stop shitting themselves with laughter, they cut Philip Day's throat,' Alex adds.

'You know what,' Alan says, touching my sleeve. 'I think maybe we should tell someone about this.'

18

In Alan's tech bay, waiting for Jeremy Leyton-Hughes to arrive, we huddle around a TV showing Sky News reporters. *'You join us live from Middleton Road in north London. In dramatic scenes, police and Special Forces personnel have surrounded a house where the Foreign Secretary is being held hostage.'*

We all discuss the idea that Stone Fist and Iron Sword could actually be deliberately hiding their real location. Alan still has his ear pretty close to the ground with operations at MI5. Missing the brothers leaving the address on Agar Grove was a massive mistake by the police CTUs – it happens to every surveillance team, but losing control of the brothers this time has likely caused this massive fuck-up.

Claire wants to pick Alan's brains.

'Alan, how easy would it be for the brothers to fake their location?'

'It's not easy, but done properly it could fool everyone, because they aren't looking for it. I can't remember ever dealing with a situation like this from a domestic target. The police are surrounding the house in Middleton Road because the phones from Agar Grove were tracked there, the video footage seems to be coming from that area and the next-door neighbours have reported the sound of voices that match the audio. That's it.'

Claire adds to the theory. 'So, all Iron Sword and Stone Fist would have to do is dump their phones at Middleton Road before moving somewhere else without being seen. They knew we'd track their phones . . .'

Alan nods in complete agreement. 'Exactly. So everything indicates the brothers being where they say they are, at Middleton Road.' He points at the little TV. 'I've had a look at the feeds and done some digging on their various sources. All very sophisticated – if I had more time I'd be able to give a concrete answer – but my initial guess is that the brothers are transmitting out of an address we don't know about via Tor, and the webcam is filming that feed at Middleton Road. From there, extremists all over the world are then putting it all up on their social media and news feeds. And it wouldn't surprise me if the brothers are sending the secure feed directly into Middleton Road with the volume turned right up, knowing that Special Forces are going to be listening in. When they hear the audio, they'll be certain the Foreign Secretary is actually there.'

I want this to be true, but it's just a theory. A good one, but nothing we can concretely back up. Leyton-Hughes arrives and beckons us upstairs to the briefing room, just as the news ticker scrolling across the bottom says *Sources say Foreign Secretary taken hostage, local residents forced to evacuate . . .*

We all move quickly upstairs, eager to get more information on the situation. Ryan closes the door as we wait for Jeremy to start this briefing. Our boss looks calm and a little nonchalant, almost arrogant. 'So you've seen the news regarding Stone Fist and Iron Sword. It's confirmed it's definitely them and they have the Foreign Secretary as a hostage. The house on Middleton Road is a rental property which has apparently been empty for a number of months now. The landlord is cooperating fully but isn't believed to be involved in any way. Now, as with everything we discuss in Blindeye, this doesn't go anywhere—'

Claire interrupts Jeremy, 'How the hell did they manage to snatch a government minister?'

Jeremy shrugs his shoulders. 'We have no information on that at this stage. Let's just assume the PM isn't very happy with the DG, or CTU. She's handed over everything to the police negotiators and Special Forces teams, who are looking at ways to breach the building.'

'On that, boss, I have a theory I'd like to share with you.' I hope Jeremy will listen to Alan's reasoning closely enough to allow us to rule our theory out at least. The tech positions himself and us to make his demonstration. 'Something's been troubling me ever since I saw the dodgy quality of the feed the brothers are putting out of this mock trial.'

Leyton-Hughes nods, frustrated, while checking his watch. Alan lays it out in simple terms for him.

'I think the brothers are spoofing their location. The guys had them buying a video camera *and* a webcam. Everyone, including the police and intelligence agencies, think they are holding the Foreign Secretary at Middleton Road. I think they are routing the stream directly into Middleton Road from a completely different address to make it look like they are there. When, in fact, they could be miles away. There's potential for this to go massively wrong.' Alan is determined to hammer this point home. 'If the sniffer dogs are right about those two massive bags having explosive residue in them, the news crews will broadcast the Special Forces teams breaking into the wrong address and being blown up. All on live, twenty-four-hour news. All from British soil.'

Fucking hell, he really does paint a picture, but Leyton-Hughes doesn't seem overly taken by it.

'Firstly, A4 found a van that was rented and paid for by a card registered to the Agar Grove address parked up not far from Middleton Road, outside a police station. Bomb disposal deactivated a viable device with around ten kilos of explosives.' Confused looks fill the team, including Alan. Only ten kilos . . . out of two massive bags?

Jeremy continues, 'The IP address of the brothers' exact transmission location would have been picked up by Thames House, Alan. My source within operations at A Branch had two phones showing up at Agar Grove, which were then tracked to Middleton Road. GCHQ analysed the initial video broadcast and gave confirmation that a video feed is being uploaded to an extremist news site from Middleton Road. Special Forces teams have got audio inside that building after evacuating the neighbours' addresses too. Everything is pointing to the Foreign Secretary being held at Middleton Road.' He's nowhere near convinced, but for the first time I can sense Jeremy being more open to Alan's ideas than he is to any of the rest of us.

'You've got to understand the position I'm in. *We* are in. We're a deniable unit. We are meant to clear up the mess, not create it.' This feels like a plea rather than a rational explanation. 'If you give me something concrete I can maybe do something. *Maybe*. But unless you have any actionable intelligence I can't do anything.'

Alan pushes harder. 'But surely it's something worth ruling out. Two large bags would carry way more than ten kilos of explosives—'

'ENOUGH!' Jeremy explodes, like a man who is trapped on the edge of something he can't get into, or escape from. Frustrated or scared – I'm not sure which.

My immediate reaction is to launch myself between them. Jeremy hasn't made any advance towards Alan but my gut reaction wants to protect the tech. But the boss's aggression dissipates, probably helped along by my ugly mug rushing towards him.

He's backing down, but is still visibly worried about something. Looking around the room, I see panic in his face. As if he's fucked up.

'Team, we have to leave this to the police and Special Forces on site. We, *you*, are stood down until further notice. Keep your phones with you, take a few days off.'

With that, he rushes past me and down the stairs, and he's in his car in a matter of seconds.

This doesn't feel right at all; somehow Leyton-Hughes feels too close to this operation. The inside knowledge he has, I can live with. Both he and Alan still have contacts within Thames House and if Jeremy is taking his orders directly from the DG then obviously he's going to know a lot more than we do. But why won't he entertain the possibility that the brothers aren't at the address currently surrounded by Britain's best armed specialists?

We watch as he drives under the roller shutters without looking back at us. 'Why wouldn't he want to rule this out? If we're wrong, fair enough, but if we're right and nothing is done, the boys in black getting ready to storm that building could be walking into a booby-trapped massacre. All of it on camera. Iron Sword and Stone Fist could easily carry more than just ten kilos of explosives in two large holdalls. If this is part of their plan, the truck is such an obvious plant. These guys are clever, they knew the truck would be found.' The entire team agrees with me. 'Alan, I've got an idea. Everyone will need to be on board though.'

Each of the team gives me a resolute nod. *Of course, we're all in.* 'Alan, do you think there is any way of back-tracing the feeds to identify the true source of the broadcast?'

'Of course, given time. GCHQ would have done that already I'm betting, unless . . .'

'Unless what?'

'Unless, given how fast the PM wants a result and all the

evidence pointing to this one address, they've completely overlooked trying to double-check the route source.'

'Logan, what you thinking of doing?' The look of concern on Riaz's face is genuine and shared across the group, even by Alan.

Running my hands over my stubble, I can't believe I'm going to say this. 'Going to the DG and asking him to buy us some more time. It's moving too fast and there are too many variables not being looked at.'

'No chance, you'll be spotted, mate. I know one of the guys on his protection team. Top people protect him, mate. And you can't walk into Thames House anymore,' Ryan says.

He's right, the DG's team are good. And I'm meant to have completely left MI5 now – I can't get inside headquarters anymore. 'Alan, do you know the DG's home address? You must do . . .'

He nods like a naughty schoolkid who knows he's about to do something incredibly bad. I knew I could count on him. 'I'll meet him at his house,' I continue. 'Ask him to buy us some time. You guys cover for me, in case anything comes in from Jeremy; I'll have my radio with me so I can give the odd acknowledgement, so it sounds like I'm with you guys if Leyton-Hughes is listening in. Alan, is it possible for you to find the source of this video feed while running our ops?'

'Of course.' The confidence of a man who's spent a lifetime on jobs like this, completely off-book.

'Logan, say you manage to get to the DG without being

stopped by his team and he rats you straight out to Leyton-Hughes. Then what?' Riaz has a point.

'Well, I guess I'm stacking shelves at the supermarket for a living.' That gets smiles all round, apart from Alex; she knows this is risky. 'Look, seriously. If they have the right house surrounded then great, hopefully they'll get the guy out of there and leave the brothers for dead. But what if it's a massive trap and those bags they were in Liverpool with were filled with explosives? Where are the rest of those explosives now? Killing a Cabinet minister and multiple police and Special Forces in one op? It would be the greatest achievement of any terrorist on British soil. Stopping that is worth the risk.' They all agree. 'No electronic references to me or this conversation now. Nothing outside this room. I'll be as quick as I can. Alan, you have the DG's address?'

'I do. I've been there once, when he first moved in, to do an eavesdropping sweep and make sure none of our Russian friends had left anything there. I also installed his alarm system.' Another smile, Alan is such a sneaky bastard but an absolute gold mine of resources. 'You know Tony Blair's residence on Connaught Square?' The team all stop breathing at the same time. It's like waiting to get hit in the face; you know it's going to hurt, but your hands are tied and there is nothing you can do about it. 'Four doors up from that. Black front, white door, dome security cameras along the roof line. Let me get something you'll need to get in.' Alan walks down to his workbenches. The enormity of it all starts to become apparent and I lose the ability to make light of what I'm about to do.

The team doesn't really say much as we wait for Alan to reappear. We're all trying to weigh up the pros and cons, but ultimately we all know this theory has to be ruled out. I try and reassure the team as well as myself. 'Blindeye is designed to do things no one else would do. Things that are just too risky, or completely illegal.'

The nods of agreement from the team are comforting, until Alex quickly adds something to my statement. 'And the outright stupid . . .'

Alan rushes back in, slightly out of breath from running up the stairs. 'OK, this acts like a . . . never mind. It'll take too long to explain. Press and hold this and it'll make sure no alarms go off right before you enter.'

I can see the team in my peripheral vision and feel their anxiety as Alan tells me the plan for breaking into the DG's house. *Fuck me.* I'm either going to be shot on sight or arrested. But the level of risk I'm taking is nothing compared to the guys in black kit waiting to storm a house, potentially rushing to their deaths. Not to mention the Foreign Secretary we still have to save.

'Now, he has a terraced extension at the very top of the house. Some of the houses around there are flat-roofed, but he has a pitched roof extension. With tiles.'

That's my way in, through the terrace. 'How do I get up there without being seen?'

This small detail doesn't seem to bother Alan. 'Easy, you

can climb, right?' Looking over to Alex, I keep composed; the team needs to know I have conviction in what I'm about to do, but the sense of unease is really evident on her face.

'There's a posh deli on the corner. Much lower roof line than the houses. Get onto that, use the ledges and arches on the building face to climb up. Some of the houses on the corners might still have the cast-iron drainpipes too. You'll figure it out, you'll need this.' He hands me a small but quite heavy rucksack. 'Should be enough tools in there for you to force a fairly quiet entry from the roof. Good luck.' That was it. Alan walks off with a smile and a pat on my shoulder, and an attitude that says, *Get on with it*.

Bollocks. Not only have I got between six and twelve armed police from the Met's Parliamentary and Diplomatic Protection Unit a few houses down, permanently looking for dodgy fuckers like me, I've also got to circumnavigate the DG's team and any sort of alarm system on his house. After climbing onto the roof and finding a way in.

No time to waste; I can worry about it on the way down to London.

'Right, guys, see you in a bit.'

It's already dark on the roads, and the signs for the South and London light my way down the motorway as I try to maximize my speed in between speed cameras. I've got my radio on, just in case Jeremy suddenly calls us in, so I can make up the necessary excuses then pretend to be on the ground with the rest of the team.

As the miles disappear and I get closer to the end of the motorway into London, I visualize what I can remember of the houses around the DG's. I didn't know he lived near Tony Blair. I fucking wish he didn't. Having a controversial ex-Prime Minister on the street isn't conducive to breaking and entering.

Still nothing on the radio, no text message alerts from Jeremy either. So far so good. After three hours of driving I make it into the area of the DG's house in the posh streets to the north-east of Hyde Park. Midnight. I'll have to park up before I get to Connaught Square so I don't light the whole place up with my headlights.

It's all parking permits round here and congestion cameras everywhere, but given I'm not going to be that long, hopefully I can risk it. Nestling the car in between an S Class Mercedes and a 5 Series BMW, I kill the lights and engine. I put my phone in the glovebox and grab the black bag of tools Alan gave me, before zipping my dark jacket up. As long as my movements are natural, I shouldn't draw too much attention to myself. But I have to be quick.

Surrounded by houses that are worth millions of pounds, with cars outside to match, it's eerily quiet here. I can't quite believe how quiet it is. When I was with A4 surveillance teams, we hardly ever operated in posh areas like this, always in dingy, rough areas. I feel incredibly out of place.

I wish I could have made something else of my life, and had whatever these families are experiencing all around me. I wish I just had my family. *Focus, Logan!* Stopping at the junction of the square, staying out of the street lights in the shadows, I can see the posh deli Alan mentioned. I walk past and turn left onto Connaught Square. There's a fenced private park in the middle, guarded by these opulent townhouses. I can just make out the DG's front door, white against the black facade of the house, further down the street.

I was hoping for some cast-iron drainpipes that I could climb up to get through the higher windows while hopefully evading any security lights. But nothing. Using these precious few seconds to decide if there is an easier way onto the roofs without climbing onto the deli first, I see a wafting sheet of plastic at the bottom of the street, just before the corner, past the DG's house.

Plastic sheeting dancing in the wind halfway up one of these tall houses can mean only one thing: scaffolding. That's going to be much easier to climb than anything else, especially a deli roof.

Ah shit, I'm committed down this street now, right past the DG's house and any cameras his protection team might be monitoring. Keep moving, just a normal guy. As I move past the black-fronted house and the DG's gleaming white door, there isn't any obvious hint of protection details.

I know they are here, ready to respond, but with this being a residential area, they clearly try to keep a low profile. I don't visibly react to the DG's house as I continue to the scaffolding, but I notice there is a small light on downstairs. As far as I can tell, upstairs is in total darkness.

I pause a few metres away from the scaffolding. The

plastic sheeting is meant to hide the renovation work from the street, but tonight it'll provide me with some cover. I've just got to get on with it. No one around, not that I can see, anyway.

Looking up from next to one of the main corner poles, I can see a rough route to the middle. Once I haul myself up onto this initial ledge, about nine feet above the ground, there are connecting ladders to each platform. I jump up to grab a cross piece of scaffolding and I'm suddenly very aware of how heavy this bag is; it's like doing chin-ups with a sack of potatoes on your back. *Got to keep the noise down.* Pulling myself higher onto the cross piece, I manage to hook my arm over and position my hands to pull my upper body onto the platform.

I squat down on the first ledge, quickly assessing any re-action in my environment. No shouting, no people rushing out of their houses to challenge what I'm doing. To be honest, at this time of night, if anyone is walking around they won't notice me once I'm another level or two higher; a combination of being hidden by the plastic sheeting and the fact that people just don't look up anymore.

I can see through the first-floor windows of the house; it's empty, gutted inside. A couple more levels to go and I'll be at the top, then I'll hopefully be able to get onto the roof of this house and right across to the top of the DG's house.

The next few levels are tackled quickly, using the ladders the builders use during the day, with the challenge now to remain quiet. Every clang from a pole and creak from a wooden board forces me to pause and reassess my environment.

At the top of the scaffolding, I can see there's a four-foot gap from this roof to the next. No point thinking about falling; just get on with it.

As I leap across, I catch sight of the very bottom, the bits of rubbish and leaves that have been blown into the gap and haven't managed to escape, waiting to be cleaned out. Landing on the pitched section on the next roof, I no longer have the safety of the scaffolding beneath me. *Come on, Logan, four houses to get across.*

Lifting myself up and quickly getting my legs over the lip of the roof line, I land in the gutters on the flat portion of the roof. Looks a fairly easy route, got to stay quiet, this house below me is empty but the others probably won't be.

London's skyline looks completely different from up here at this time of night. The noise carries totally differently up here too, without as many sound barriers. It feels like I'm on a private tour.

I hop over various obstacles – low joining walls, chimneys and air-conditioning units – until I make it to the terrace extension on top of the DG's roof. No lights on. Two window openings. No curtains or blinds. This extension has been built to lift the ceiling of the hall below and let in some more light. I can just see the carpet in the hallway and stairs leading down. Looks quiet and still.

Fuck. Once I'm in, where am I going to go? I don't know where the DG will be. Probably in bed, but where is his bedroom? *Don't think about future problems, just solve what's in front of you.*

Breaking the window will be noisy and won't give me a chance to see the DG before his protection team are on me. Crouching down next to the tiled extension, I slide my bag of tricks off my shoulder and quietly place it down next to me.

There are various bits of kit inside, from crowbars and a rolled-up fabric ladder to electrical boxes. Some of this I've no idea how to use. Looking at the window again to weigh up my options, I notice the hinges are on the outside.

I check them over quickly; the hinges have been fitted here to oppose their counterpart on the opposite side, which should prevent people like me simply lifting the window up off the hinges and getting in. It's all held in place by a variety of security screws, some of which I don't even recognize. Bollocks. I doubt Alan has anything remotely quiet to get me in here.

Struggling to see much in the darkness, I dig around in the bag and find a box of screwdriver heads. *Please have something in here, Alan.* Opening the small box up, I see all manner of driver heads, including one that looks like it's been custom-made, with serrations around the edges and top. I wonder . . .

Placing this modified contraption over the security screw heads, I can feel it immediately bite. Perfect. This thing will undo anything. I place a screwdriver handle onto this bit and start to quietly undo the screws.

Shit, wait. Alarm. I unzip my jacket pocket and pull out the box Alan gave me, with no idea what it will do or how it does it. All I need right now is for no alarms to go off. I press the button and put the box away and get on with undoing the screws, eight in total. The window is already leaning away from the frame, only held in place by the catch attaching it to the adjacent window.

I slowly pull it away and have my gap into the house. It isn't huge, and I still have to drop down onto the stairs without making too much noise. I can't shake the feeling this is about to go very wrong, very fast. Poking my head inside the window, I wait for that alarm. Sirens. Shouting bodyguards. Nothing.

The drop below me to the stairs is a good eight feet. I'm no cat; wherever I land it'll be noisy, even with the DG's thick-pile carpet. I pull the fabric ladder out of the rucksack and start unrolling it. It's around six feet long. Should do the trick. Securely fastening one end around the window frame, I drop the ladder down into the house.

No time to think about how stupid this is, I'm going in, now. The ladder bends and strains as it takes the weight of my first foot inside the house. Moving as quickly as I can, I'm holding my breath. I'm facing the wall so I can't see the main space behind me; just the plaster, this ladder and the rungs beneath me. Desperate not to get my feet tangled and caught in the fabric, I keep lowering myself down. Almost there. Keep going.

Shit. What's that noise? Sounds like the bottom of the

ladder is banging against the wall. *Stay still, Logan!* The noise is getting louder. Fuck! It's footsteps racing up the stairs behind me, growing louder. Haven't got enough time to get back out. *Shit, Logan, think!*

The footsteps are almost on me, and I hear the unmistakable sound of a top slide being cocked on a pistol. 'Don't fucking move!'

19

'I'm not trying to steal anything, I swear!' My protestation of innocence doesn't quite go to plan as I feel a sharp, hard jab straight into my right kidney, buckling my body.

'Slowly, move down the ladder, SLOWLY!'

One of the DG's protection team. The fact he's giving me commands and punching me instead of putting two 9mm rounds into the back of my head is a good thing, but fucking painful. Rotating away from the wall, I move down the last four rungs of the ladder to yet more barking.

Six feet tall. Stocky. Clean-shaven. Polo shirt. Trousers. Smart comfortable shoes. SIG Sauer 228 aimed directly at my head. There must be cameras round here that I missed. The barrel of his weapon doesn't falter in its aim. If I twitch the wrong way he's pulling that trigger twice. I need to disarm him mentally, not to get out of here, but to stay alive.

Think Logan, THINK!

I've got to get the DG to appear, but I can't tell this guy who I am or anything about Blindeye. Who could I be, sneaking into this house, who doesn't pose a threat?

'My dad. I've come to see my dad.'

Fuck knows how I remembered this. The DG is probably old enough to be my dad, just. He mentioned having a son briefly at the underground garages when he tried to recruit me. Maybe it will be enough to get him up these stairs. I'm hoping it will put enough doubt into this bodyguard's mind that he doesn't shoot me. We all have a past, and if the DG hasn't seen or heard from his son for years, it could just give enough plausibility for me to survive the next few seconds. Please God, make this work.

No doubt another member of the protection detail will be guarding him now. It's gone noisy, I need to do everything I can to get the DG up here to see my face without screaming Blindeye at the top of my voice.

'With your right hand, I need you to unzip your jacket and show me you're not carrying anything you shouldn't. Do it now!'

'Dad! DAD!' I shout as hard as I can without being aggressive. I need the DG to see my face.

It's not working. The pistol lurches towards me. Fuck. Using all my ability to try and live this cover, I plead, 'Please don't shoot.'

Angling my head, I try to project my voice down the stairs. 'DAD! I need you!'

I see it coming but let it happen. The leading foot of this bodyguard ploughs into my groin, forcing me back against the wall as the pistol edges even closer to my head. I can't get into a fight with this guy. I'd be dead in seconds.

'DAD, PLEASE!'

Just as I'm about to be barked at again, the DG pops his head around the corner at the bottom of the stairs. 'DAD, IT'S ME! ME!'

There's another guy trying to force the DG back into cover, but he resists while he takes a second to realize it's me. His face turns to thunder as he disappears. I can hear low mumblings, sounds like he's briefly explaining all this to his wife. Then he reappears. Walking up the stairs in a dressing gown, face like thunder.

'Thank you, Edward. I can deal with this.'

The bodyguard relaxes slightly as the DG is now along-side him. 'You sure, sir? I can escort him out?'

Looking at me then back at the bodyguard, the DG re-assures him. 'It's fine. Let me talk to my son up here for a moment, please.' Edward presses the de-cocking lever on his pistol to bring the hammer forward before he holsters the weapon. It's still made ready as he moves back downstairs.

The DG takes me by my arm, rounding the corner of the hallway so we can't be seen by anyone downstairs, and whispers with venom. 'What the fuck are you doing here, Logan?'

'Sir, I need your help. The hostage situation with the Foreign Secretary, we need to buy some time to work a theory out.' He tries to interrupt but I refuse to relent; we haven't got the time. 'We think there's a possibility the brothers are at a different location and the strike team waiting outside, ready to breach, could be walking into a trap.'

The DG holds his hands up; he's not getting this. 'Slow down, I'm not sure what you're talking about.'

'Sorry, of course. OK, we saw Iron Sword and Stone Fist buying a video camera and a webcam, and the true location of the video feed hasn't been found yet. We also saw the brothers leaving an address in Liverpool with two large bags. Large enough to carry five times the amount of explosives found in that rental van. We think it's a set-up, and if they try and rescue the Foreign Secretary the brothers will blow the building up, and then kill him at a completely different site, before slipping away.'

He's trying to absorb what I'm saying but it's still not sinking in, I can tell. 'We?' His question shows all over his face as the cooler air flows in through the gap I've made in the window.

'Blindeye,' I respond.

Silence. He peeks over the banister to make sure no one is at the bottom of the stairs listening, then faces me again. He's wearing the same steely look he did at the covert garages, when he first recruited me. His voice takes on a different level of seriousness and an even lower volume, guaranteeing only I can hear what's about to be said.

'Logan. I haven't authorized your team to start on *any* operations yet.'

Holy shit. He's not the type of person to joke. I can't think of a response.

'Who the fuck has been giving you operations? What have you been doing?'

'Jeremy Leyton-Hughes. He's running our ops. He's the conduit between you and us, right?'

'Jesus Christ. We haven't told him anything. You're meant to be on standby to react.'

I reply with my own 'We?' this time.

'Yes. *We!*' He doesn't like having to explain himself but knows he has to now. 'Blindeye has been set up to be used by me and my counterparts at Vauxhall and Cheltenham. Tell me now, what have you done?'

I had no idea Blindeye was at the full disposal of MI5, MI6 and GCHQ. This is bad. Fucking hell, Leyton-Hughes had me *kill* someone. 'Boss, if you haven't authorized any of the jobs then he's playing his own angle. But right now we need to buy time on this hostage situation. That strike team can't get blown up and the Foreign Secretary will not get his head cut off on British soil with the whole world watching.'

An angry sigh leaves his lungs. 'How sure are you that the brothers aren't at this house? And how can you be sure they have more explosives than those put in the van we found?'

'We're not yet, we just need a bit of time. We have no intelligence to say they have more explosives than you found, we have no intelligence to say that they purposely left the hire van there to be found, so they could trick Special Forces into thinking this is a straightforward hostage situation. Is there any chance—'

He cuts me off. 'I'll speak to the PM now, keep your phone on.' There is no need to ask if he has my number. He's in charge of MI5, of course he has my fucking number. Looking up at the missing window and ladder, he ushers me downstairs.

'I left my bag on the roof,' I explain.

Another sigh of frustration. 'I'll sort it, you need to leave.'

Walking down the flights of stairs towards the front door, I can't see any of the protection detail, but their presence is felt. Almost like they are purposely staying hidden from me. Maybe the whole son story played out. Well, that's the DG's problem to handle.

As the DG opens the door to let me out, he makes sure he stays behind it so he's not seen from the street. Edward appears again from a side room. 'Edward, my son left a bag on the roof, can you collect it and bring it straight to me. Don't look inside it, please.'

'Of course, sir.' Edward runs upstairs to retrieve the bag, and presumably to fix the window I've removed.

The DG nods at me to leave, and I can tell he's in work mode. 'Go. I'll be in touch.'

I make my way straight back to the car; I need to get a message to the team. I leave the engine off and take my phone out of the glovebox to type a text message. I need to be careful, in case Jeremy is monitoring our phones.

Alan, Alex, fancy meeting up in London for a bit of R&R? Ran into an old friend down here who's doing a big event, tons of people. Fancy it?

Send. Hopefully they will see the references – old friend, big event, tons of people – and read between the lines that I've managed to speak to the DG and we're on.

It takes less than a minute for Alex and Alan to reply to the group message.

Alex: I'm in. Setting off now. Find us a hotel close by?

Alan: Yep, see you in a few hours.

Great, now we're covered. Just. Although I think it's Jeremy who's probably covering his arse right now.

Now we just need to work out if the brothers really are in the Middleton Road address, where everyone thinks they are, and then work out if we are being played by Leyton-Hughes and, if so, just how fucking dangerous this situation is.

But first, I need to find a hotel.

20

I kill the engine in the chain hotel's car park on Dalston Lane, just north of Middleton Road, and send Alex and Alan another quick text message:

Hotel E8 3DF. Parking N1 4BY. Booking under Mr Davies.

Making sure I get my grab bag from the boot with the essentials – toothbrush, clean pants and socks, phone charger, spare top – I pay for parking and move quickly towards the hotel.

This place is used by travelling sales reps and contractors from all over the country, arriving at all hours. This is nothing unusual for the front desk. The receptionist pays me no interest until I start talking. 'Hi there, I booked a couple of rooms online, one twin, one single. Mr Davies . . .' It's the first time I've used my fake identity.

She smiles professionally. 'Have you got your reference number, Mr Davies?'

I give her the number and get two key cards in return; one

for me and Alan to share, one for Alex. Not that we will be here long. I get a reply from Alex:

Thanks mate, we're probably about 3/4 hours away.

Perfect, time for some sleep. I send a quick reply as I head to mine and Alan's room. As I drop my bag inside, I can instantly feel my body shutting down. There's nothing I can do to stop it. Feels like I've been running on empty, fuelled by adrenaline for so long now. It's times like this I fall into soldier mode. Admin. Get your admin sorted before you get some sleep. Door locked and on chain, chair butt up against the door. I grab a glass from the side and balance it just enough on the arm rest so the slightest of movements will make it fall. Phone on charge, volume turned up.

After using the toilet, I fill the other glass with water from the tap and move towards the beds. Two singles. I'd love to strip off and climb in, to sleep for hours, but I know I've got to remain sharp, ready to react. Collapsing on top, I don't feel very sharp at all. Allowing my eyes to close, I whisper to myself, 'No nightmares. No nightmares. No nightmares. No . . .'

The sound of my phone receiving a text message acts like an electric shock to my body. I bolt out of bed; it's Alan. We're here. Replying immediately, I send my room number and move to the door. Taking the glass off the chair and shifting both out of the way, I wait behind the door, listening.

Removing the chain, I hear more than one set of footsteps and wait for the knock on the door. Doesn't take long.

I let Alex and Alan in with a smile; they look as tired as I feel. No one says anything yet. Alan immediately opens his backpack on the bed and takes out a handful of small pouches made of the same material we used to block Stormy Weather's tracking anklet. We each take one and place our phones inside. Alan takes all the pouches and places them in the bathroom. He even closes the door. It's finally time to update them both.

'So I saw him. It's good and bad news. The good news is he's getting us more time, I don't know how much, so we have to act fast. But there's a problem. The DG hasn't given Leyton-Hughes the authorization to use us yet. We're meant to be waiting for our first job.'

'What?' Alex can't believe what I'm saying. 'How, and more importantly *why*, would he have us going on operations that haven't been approved or directed by the DG?'

Alan looks genuinely shocked, a frown appearing on his face that shows how angry he is at being deceived by Jeremy.

'I met the DG inside his house. I asked him for more time to find out whether or not the brothers really are at the address being surrounded or not. I told him about the large bags carried away from the address in Liverpool, the video camera and webcam we saw them buy, and that's when he stopped me to say he hadn't authorized Leyton-Hughes to start operations yet.'

Alex sits back on the desk, shocked, as Alan slumps on the

edge of the bed, wringing his hands and staring down at the floor.

'He also said it's a joint agency team. Him, the DG from Vauxhall and the West Country.'

The anger spewing out of Alan very nearly affects the volume of his voice, but we still need to keep quiet here. 'So everything we've done so far has been off Leyton-Hughes's own fucking back?'

Nodding slowly, I reply. 'Yes. But the DG knows now, he said he'd deal with it, and asked us to find out if the brothers are at this house or not and to keep my phone on.'

He puts his rucksack onto his shoulder and gets ready to get straight back to the search, presumably from the back of his van. But he looks dejected. 'I'm nearly there. I'm almost positive they aren't at that address. From what I can tell, all the neighbours around the house have been evacuated. There is very little internet usage in that defined area now, apart from large data packets being constantly received. There's near constant upload as well, but that always starts slightly after data comes in. I haven't identified if that's the actual feed of the video yet. If there's anything you can do on the ground, it would be really helpful.'

As he moves towards the bathroom to get our phones, he has an idea. 'Of course, fucking hell.' Frantically removing his backpack and sliding his laptop out of it, he places it on the desk next to where Alex is sat. 'Guys,' he whispers to prevent his excitement raising the level of his voice, 'while looking at the GPS movements of the phones MI5 traced to the house in Middleton Road, I had a look at the call and text history.'

Alan opens up a file I don't recognize in a format I've never seen before. He sees the confusion on my face. 'Ignore all this, it's cell tower information, but here is the actual message. We don't know if this is definitely one of the brothers, because no names are used and this side of the conversation is on an unregistered phone. Look here.' Alan points to the screen as we huddle round.

You betta get rid of it. I ain't paying for shit. It's not mine

Alan moves his finger past another load of data to show us the next few replies.

It is yours. I don't want anything to do with you. Stop texting me.

Bitch you better get rid of it

Blocked your number, goodbye.

'I do have an address and name for you for the polite side of the conversation: Emily Gordon, 63 Grosvenor Road, Borehamwood.'

Brilliant, we have two leads now; Alan working on the electronic side of things and a possible ex-girlfriend to see. Although we still don't know if this is definitely a text message sent by one of the brothers, as the phone could've been stolen. They are extremely good at keeping their operational security tight. 'Alex, why don't we go and see this Emily Gordon, see if she knows the brothers? It's a long shot, but worth trying.'

Alex agrees. 'Perfect. If Alan finds the true source of the video feed and it is different to the house they have surrounded right now, it can't be that far away, can it?'

'Good idea,' Alan replies. 'I'll stay here and do my thing and that way I can cover for you with Leyton-Hughes if he tries to call you in early.'

Packing my phone charger up and grabbing my bag, I ask Alan one more thing,

'Alan, I take it the Foreign Secretary wasn't carrying his phone?'

Alan's head shakes in unison with his sinking shoulders as he mutters, 'His phone is dead.'

There's a sense in the room, although no one says as much, that we are doing the right thing. The rest of the team are holding back in case Blindeye gets called in, they can cover for us. But we've been set up by Jeremy Leyton-Hughes, and to what end is unclear. We were designed to operate independently, to be the deniable solution the DGs needed, but so far everything we've done has been built on one big lie.

We're all tired; the driving takes its toll on you. Hollywood and glossy TV shows would have you believe you can just hop on a private jet or helicopter and can cover hundreds of miles in a matter of minutes. But think about your daily commutes. An hour? Two? More? Imagine doing that all the time, travelling three hours to find a target and then following them all day, sometimes ten hours, eighteen hours non-stop, and then travelling back to get a few hours' sleep before getting back out on the ground again. It takes a huge amount of energy and resilience, and right now we need every last bit of our reserves. If we don't keep pushing and find out for sure what's happening, a lot of people could die. Not to mention the huge propaganda victory we'd be handing to terrorists all over the world if the brothers succeed.

Thankfully, Borehamwood wasn't a long drive at all, but we still arrive at the crack of dawn, too early to go banging on doors. Alex and I sit outside her address for as long as we dare wait before knocking on the front door. It's 6 a.m., and the morning sun is already climbing its way up. Emily Gordon is likely going to be pissed off with this, I would be too, if I had two people knocking on my door at this time of day.

It takes a while, but eventually a heavy lock is operated and a woman in her mid-twenties, wrapped in a thick dressing gown, peaks out from behind the open door.

Alex takes the lead. 'Emily Gordon? I'm sorry it's early, but we have some questions for you. Can we come in?' This is a bold move, because we aren't police, nor do we have any police cover IDs.

She could call our bluff at any minute. 'I already told you lot everything I know.'

Bingo. Alex has found the right route in and can push for the answers we need. 'Yes, and we do appreciate it, Emily, but we have a couple of urgent questions to ask you. Then we'll be out of your way, I promise. A lot of people could get hurt if we don't get to talk to you.' Alex is playing on Emily's maternal instinct. Emily must be in the very early stages of her pregnancy, no bump showing underneath the dressing gown. She reluctantly lets us in and invites us to sit on a cold leather sofa.

Emily looks tired as she covers herself up with a large blanket on a chair opposite us. Alex dives right in, not giving Emily the thinking time to ask for our IDs. Special Branch must have been here after MI5 went through the text messages, to rule her out as an accomplice. 'Is he the father?' Nodding towards her stomach, Alex is fishing for her to open up by appearing to be sensitive.

'Hammy? Yeah,' Emily replies with an ashamed look on her face.

Hamza, Stone Fist. 'When's your due date?' Alex says, smiling, trying to keep her onside.

'Not sure exactly, I'm only ten weeks.' Tears start to well up in her eyes. I need to play along with Alex's sensitive side here; I walk the short distance from the living room to the kitchen and get a glass of water for Emily before sitting back down on the sofa.

'Thank you,' she mumbles.

'It's no problem at all. Emily, we need to find Hamza as soon as possible. I know you've gone through this with our colleagues but if there's anything at all that you can remember, an address, a favourite place he would go, friends he stays with sometimes, anything. Specifically in the London area.'

I'm leaning forward to show how keen I am to get an answer and to try and break down the barrier that some Special Branch officers might put up. She's about to be a single mother, living in a rented house. There are a lot of people living in these situations that don't like or want the hassle of talking to the police.

Her mouth opens like she's about to say something, something she hasn't shared with anyone yet, but she instantly retreats. Alex notices it too. 'It's OK, you're safe.'

'You don't know him. Hammy and his brother are connected to a lot of people. Gangs, if I say anything he can get to me, even if he's in prison.'

'It's OK, you'll be protected. I promise you.' A lie Alex knows she can't back up, we can't offer her any protection.

'The only way Hammy is going to cause me trouble is if I ask him for money to help with the baby or if I talk to the police. And I ain't doing either. I don't know anything about what he's doing now. It was a one-night stand and I've been paying for it ever since. I didn't even know at the time that he was just out of prison.'

I feel sorry for her, I do. It was probably a very drunk night, two people having fun. It happens all over the world, every single day. We've all done it, but when your one-night stand turns out to be a terrorist hell bent on a massacre, and the father to your unborn child, that's got to be a complete nightmare. As much as I feel bad for her, we need to push a bit harder. I was following Alex's lead on this but I could get the call from the DG at any minute saying our time's up. Push too hard and Emily could shut down completely, take too long and we could pay the ultimate price.

'Emily, if you help us we can assure you he will be put in a category A maximum security prison. He won't be able to hurt you.' Shaking her head with a dismissive smile, Emily clearly thinks Stone Fist is connected enough to make her life hell even from there. She's thinking about the baby. She needs convincing.

There is no way in hell I'm about to hurt this woman to get her to cooperate. I don't have it in me, and I know the thought isn't crossing Alex's mind either. I can picture in my head without turning the news on what's happening with the hostage situation. Philip Day will still be strapped to a chair and the news crews will be constantly filming the police outside, specialist vehicles turning up and leaving, commenting on every single movement.

She's not going to help us. Alex looks at me, thinking something over, then turns back to Emily. 'What if we could guarantee your safety, one hundred per cent?'

'How? You know how many people he knows, drug dealers, people who own guns. All over the place. Not even you police can touch him.'

'I know that. I know nearly everything about him, apart from one thing; if there's another address in the London area he mentioned at all. Think back to that night you met him, was he bragging about his life at any point? Anyone in his family? Friends? If there's anywhere he mentioned that you haven't mentioned so far, think!'

I can see Emily's eyes searching for something, trying to think of a piece of information she hasn't shared with anyone yet. Finally she gives us a thread to pull on. 'Before we came back to mine, he was saying he'll take me to a boat his friend has in London. One of those canal long-type boats.'

Alex leans in. 'Where?'

'I've got to look after my baby, I've said too much. He'll find out. You can't protect me.'

Alex turns to me, holding her hands up in a 'what now?' gesture.

She's given it her best shot with the 'good cop' routine. I guess now it's the bad cop's turn. I move forward with a determined look on my face and Alex puts a hand out to stop me. She thinks I'm going to use force. 'It's OK,' I say, reassuring Alex. It's true; I'm about to do something desperate, and I have done some horrific things lately, but I'm not going to lay a finger on a pregnant woman.

'Emily, listen. The people you spoke to before were Special Branch. We're not Special Branch. We're not any kind of police.'

She looks scared, like a kitten backed into a corner by a

pitbull, frantically looking for a way out. 'Then who are you? What . . .'

I smile in the hope it calms her. 'We're the ones who stop really bad people. The worst types.'

She looks confused. 'I don't know . . . what are you saying?'

I take a step closer. 'What I'm saying, Emily, is that people like us, our job isn't to arrest the likes of Hamza and his brother. It isn't to send them to prison. Our job is to find them. And *kill* them. And if you tell us where we can find them, that's what we're going to do. I promise you.' There is genuine fear in Emily's eyes. I can't work out if she's frightened of us or the brothers.

Alex steps in to try and ease her anxiety. 'Think of us like pest control.' Emily's gaze flicks over to Alex and the vaguest of smiles creeps out.

I seize the opportunity to push a bit harder. 'Tell us where they are and you'll be safe. You can have your baby in peace. If we can find Hamza and his brother, you won't see them, the police or us ever again. You can be free of all this.'

She looks at me, trembling, and I feel her eyes boring into my soul. She's trying to see if I'm telling the truth. I look back at her, and I know she can see I mean every word.

A subtle nod; she is choosing her unborn baby's life and giving us Hamza's death. Ultimately, it's an easy choice to make for any mother.

'He kept saying it was black, shiny like a piano.'

Now she has opened up, Alex is leading again. 'Where is this boat? We need a location.'

'Millwall Dock, near the O2 Arena. He said we could stay in the boat after going to a concert there.'

It's our only lead, but we have to run with it. I get out my phone and walk into the kitchen to ring Alan as Alex continues to reassure Emily it will all be OK. It's a risk talking to Alan on the phone. I'm fairly sure Leyton-Hughes trusts Alan, but he doesn't trust me, and I have to assume he's listening to all my calls. I use some veiled speech in the hope Alan knows what I'm getting at.

'Hello.'

'Hi, Alan, mate, that boat I was telling you about, the one to rent out. It's available now if you want? Gorgeous, long canal boat, black and right near the O2 Arena at Millwall Dock.'

A brief pause, no more than a second, before Alan continues the act. 'Great, thanks Logan! I'll check some dates and see if I can get two days off. I'll ring you back in a bit and you can pass me onto the owner?'

'Definitely, only thing is it sometimes takes a while to get hold of him because he's always stoned.' I give a little chuckle. 'It's hit and miss whether he's there or not, but I'll see you later, bud, for those drinks.'

Hanging up and walking back to the living room, I know Alan has understood all the references, even the fact I've told him it's Stone Fist that's the link in the text messages. Alex stands up. 'We should go, Emily. Thank you for everything and I'm so sorry to put you through this stress.'

Standing up and wiping the tears from her eyes, Emily follows us to the front door. 'If you're not normal police, then . . .?'

I open the door for Alex and let her out first. 'Thanks again, Emily, good luck with everything.' No need to answer anything we don't want to. It was a dubious call whether to tell Emily we are going to kill Stone Fist. We killed Khalid to make sure we stayed completely invisible, but killing the brothers would be something different. Emily had made one small mistake but has the chance to create something brilliant out of it all, and if we manage to get to Stone Fist and his older brother and kill them, then Emily will be free to raise her child in safety without looking over her shoulder.

Back on the road, we're starting to hit rush hour, but we need to get across London to the docks. As Alex accelerates hard, we talk about this being the most difficult part of it all. Locations. Terrorists are never next door, you always have to go to them. This had been even more taxing in Blindeye, because there's so few of us. There's another reason why we've been darting about all over the place; because Jeremy is running operations on his own, with his own agenda. If the DG or his counterparts in MI6 and GCHQ were directing us, maybe we'd have been on longer-term jobs. Hopefully we'll get the opportunity to find out.

Alex's skilful driving means me make great ground. As we

pass signs for Camden Town and make towards Bethnal Green, my phone starts vibrating with a call. I answer, immediately putting it on loud speaker so Alex can listen in. 'Hello?'

'Logan, it's me. Have you found anything yet?' The director general, Alex recognizes his voice too. 'Potentially. Stone Fist got a woman pregnant after a one-night stand. She's not connected to this but when they first met he told her about a boat his friend has in Millwall Dock, near the O2. Alex and I are lightning towards that now.' *Lightning*, the term used to describe travelling to a location as fast as possible.

'OK, any technical to back that up?'

'Alan, our tech guy, is working on that now. He can't be sure yet, but the Wi-Fi data usage out of the Middleton Road address shows that before any data is being uploaded, it's being downloaded first.'

Truth be told, MI5 and GCHQ would be able to do this much quicker, but on such a fast-moving operation, and with everything indicating the Foreign Secretary is at Middleton Road with the brothers, then it's likely the data patterns wouldn't be checked. When the stakes are so high, the officers in charge are sometimes a bit reluctant to divert assets to triple-check everything.

'Logan, you have two hours. That's all the time I could buy you. If you don't have anything by then, they are going to breach the house regardless.'

Fucking hell, that gives us virtually no time at all to locate the boat once we get there, never mind hatch a plan to rescue the Foreign Secretary Philip Day. 'Understood.'

The line goes dead.

Alex and I exchange glances as she keeps navigating the traffic at high speed. We need to get down there and sort this situation out, then we need to prepare for a fight of our own.

My phone rings again as we take the junction for Millwall Dock. 'Hello?'

'Channel sixty-seven.' Call ended.

'It's Alan, want's us on channel sixty-seven.'

Alex keeps her eyes on the road as she replies. 'Sixty-seven is one of the peer-to-peer channels; only two radios can be on that channel at the same time. That's why he's asked you to use it – no chance of Leyton-Hughes listening in.'

Flicking the channel selector round, to sixty-seven, I transmit to Alan. 'Go, we're on.'

'OK, I haven't found the exact source of the transmission yet; it's being bounced around everywhere and because GCHQ and MI5 are removing the feeds constantly it makes my job harder. *But*, through various extremely illegal techniques I won't bore you with, I've narrowed it down to being highly likely at one of the internet exchange points on the Isle of Dogs, also home to Millwall Dock.'

'Brilliant, mate, thank you. The DG called us, he bought us some more time, but not much. Just under two hours now.'

'They're breaching in daylight? Fucking hell, there's a PR

statement for you. Right, I'll keep digging, Jeremy is going to want to call a briefing at some point so I'll cover for you both. If he rings either of you I'm going to tell him you've had a break-in at your aunt's house in Shoreditch, Alex. Logan is helping clear up the mess because you're very shaken. Speak later. Good luck guys.'

'Fucking hell, Alex, we need to get these two.' Alex's driving ability was second to none. Being a biker definitely helps her assess gaps and other drivers quickly, to avoid getting boxed in by traffic. 'Mate, ordinarily I'd say split up and cover more ground. But if we find them and have to act I'll need you.' There's no telling what the brothers will do if we find them. The plan will be to locate the boat, see if they are on it and try and get some armed police into the area quickly. But we need to identify them first. No one will react without us getting eyes on them, not when so much is at stake, both strategically and politically.

'Check the glovebox,' Alex says mysteriously. 'Should be a couple of lock knives in there.'

'Nice.' Two spring-loaded lock knives, five inches in length. 'These will do.' We arrive at the docks and park the car up in a resident's reserved spot; we get out and take in our surroundings. The place is huge, but there can't be many black canal boats here.

As we walk alongside the water we still can't be sure the brothers are acting alone; they could have counter-surveillance dotted around here. We still need to live our cover. I hold my arm out and Alex links hers around it. We walk along, arm in arm, looking very much the loving couple out for a morning stroll on a slightly cloudy London morning.

The smiles on our faces might look real, and it's true I've had worse covers than linking arms with a beautiful woman, but we're focused. We don't have long; we have to rule this out one way or the other. There's a massed rank of boats, but none of them is ours.

'We'll have to try on the next side.' Picking up the pace without looking in too much of a hurry, we walk round to the other side of the marina. Boats of all shapes and sizes sit on the still water. 'Logan, dark shape over there, before the yacht. See it?'

'Yeah, I see it.' We move closer, still roughly seventy-five metres from it, the dark craft still obscured by higher boats at this range, as my phone rings again.

'Hello.'

'Logan, anything?' It's the DG.

I move the phone around to my other ear and angle it towards Alex's head so she can listen in, our heads locked together as we continue to walk towards this dark boat.

'Alan has said the source of the video feed of Philip Day is almost certainly coming from this area, where the boat is. We have a possible for the boat now and are checking.'

'Logan, I've just finished the COBRA meeting. The PM wants this wrapped up and has authorized a breach by the SF team. They're ready to go. You have thirty minutes. Nothing else I can do. I'll text you my number. If you find them, ring me!'

Thirty minutes. There isn't time to keep living our cover. We break our arm link and start running towards this dark boat. Getting closer, I can see it's definitely much lower than the others and looks heavily strapped to the mooring, ready for some sort of repairs or refurbishment.

'It's the only black canal boat here, mate.' Alex is right, there's nothing else even remotely similar. Slowing to a walk, we study the boat. All the windows are covered up; normal enough for a restoration, especially if tools and equipment are being left unattended at any point. Moorings around here will cost a fortune, so covering up any work inside makes sense too, keeps the area looking smart. Clearly Stone Fist has friends in affluent places, maybe another drug dealer? For now, I don't care who pays to keep this boat here, all I care about is getting Iron Sword and Stone Fist.

'Looks dead, right?' Alex agrees, but we need to know for sure. I put my hand into my coat pocket and grip the knife as I step down onto the mooring, thumb ready to press the button and shoot the blade forward out of its casing. Alex stays slightly back, out of view to anyone opening the small boat doors. Stepping on, I give a friendly 'Hello' and notice how steady the boat is; rock solid, no movement at all.

Nothing, no response. I give the door a knock and try another greeting, 'Hello, anyone home?' I try the handle: locked. *Listen.* I can hear the clanking of the surrounding boats as the rock on their moorings, but nothing from inside. Fuck, this isn't it. Twenty-five minutes, we need to find this black boat. It must be on the far side, the one place we haven't checked yet.

As I turn towards the edge of the boat to step back onto the mooring, we both hear a thud and a mumbled shout, like someone yelling through a gag. I look over at Alex, she knows this is it. We've found the Foreign Secretary.

21

I resist the urge to kick in the door; I have to contact the director general. Trying not to react to the gagged whimpers or screams we've just heard, we start to walk off. If we pile in now, we could die without telling the DG there's a strong possibility we've found Foreign Secretary Philip Day. The brothers win, and those about to breach the house fall into a huge trap.

Alex and I have got to be quick now. I open the blank text message the DG has just sent me and ring the number as I step back onto the walkway alongside the boats. It only takes one ring for the DG to answer.

'Yes, what do you have?'

With my back to the boat, I whisper just loud enough for him to hear me. 'Found the boat, blacked out. Locked. Definite sounds of a struggle inside, though. We need backup.'

'Logan, get in there now. According to the audio, they've just started to beat him, which matches what you've just heard. They are going to kill him any minute now. Leave this call open – put your phone in your pocket or something. I need to listen in as I sort this side out. I can't call off

Special Forces until you know for sure. The PM isn't about to stand by and let Day be murdered on British soil.'

'Understood.'

'Logan, I know you're not armed, but get in that fucking boat now!'

Putting my phone on speaker, I place it into a chest pocket on my jacket so the DG has live audio of everything we are about to do. I pull out my knife and turn back towards the boat. I look at Alex, there's no time for a plan. She knows it too, pulls her knife out and activates the spring. The blade makes a reassuring dull click as it extends. No pedestrians around us for at least thirty metres or so, definitely the quieter end of the marina, and the boat is cocooned among these larger vessels either side.

I nod towards the back of the boat, where Alex is positioned. Instantly, without thought for her own safety, she gets ready to step onto the boat. If today is going to be the day I die, I'm going to do it fucking properly.

Whispering into my jacket pocket, I hope the DG can hear me clearly. 'Going in now. Me and Alex.' I need to make as much noise as humanly possible, to draw the brothers to me and create some chaos. Hopefully Alex will respond to that.

The door is locked, I know that. Likely barricaded. The windows either side are my best option, even though they're blacked out. I'm dead anyway, doesn't matter if I get cut to pieces climbing in. I take a step forward and plant my right foot, heel first, into the lower quarter of the pane. Without offering any resistance, the glass breaks into disjointed triangles. The window is large enough for me to enter, and I crouch to climb through. Knife out, my left foot leads me inside the boat. I'm expecting to be shot straight away as I struggle for a foothold, a firm point on which to transfer my weight and bring the rest of my body into the cabin.

The blade of my knife is tucked into my side, close to my chest, ready to use. The only people that will die today will be Stone Fist and Iron Sword. And, quite possibly, me. I'm ready for that.

I bring my trailing right leg inside the boat. It would be pitch black in here if it wasn't for the hole I've created letting sunlight stream through, but even that doesn't offer much visibility until my eyes adjust. I've entered the kitchen of the boat, the remains of it anyway; it's partway through renovation and the skeleton frames of the cupboards, shelves and sink line either side of the galley, leading towards a sectioned-off area, right in the middle of the boat.

Thick black sheeting follows the shape of the ceiling and walls, right down to the floor, nailed on tight. No light leaks through, but I know the Foreign Secretary must be behind the partition. I can't hear Alex on the other side, or any other movement. Taking a second to look at my surroundings, I see a cable snaking its way out from under the black sheet down towards the kitchen frames, before disappearing where the sink should be. With no sink fitted yet, I can see directly down inside the unit.

The cable leads to a black box; looks like a remote router

or signal booster. Whatever it actually is, if the brothers are behind this curtain about to kill someone, this is likely being used to transmit that footage. No time to think about the pros and cons. I lean in and saw at the cable. It takes three hard slices for my knife to cut through. I've been in here ten, maybe fifteen seconds. Too long, and far too noisy. Walking up to the black fabric, I drive my knife into the right hand side of it at head height, and slice down to provide a way in. It's not fabric after all, more of a rubber material, like pond lining. But the sharpness of this blade cuts through it easily.

The light is instant, as is the barrage of insults. 'WHAT THE FUCK ARE YOU DOING?' 'WE'LL FUCKING KILL HIM, DON'T FUCKING MOVE.'

It's them, the brothers. I can't see the Foreign Secretary, but I need to draw the brothers towards me and away from him. Fuck, I need to be near Philip Day in order to protect him, but I can't see him. I take a step back and both brothers, now dressed in black shalwar kameez and holding large butcher's knives, get on an aggressive footing. *That's it, keep coming you fuckers*. The volume these two are shouting at is definitely loud enough for the DG to hear on the other end of the phone, tucked in my jacket pocket.

They clearly think the game is over for them, but they've come prepared to die. It's a win-win for the two brothers, who are now hacking and ripping at the rubberized black material that was being used, until moments ago, as a make-shift prison and courtroom. As I take another step back, I know I'm going to run out of room soon. Iron Sword is first in line to tear me to pieces, but I can see the Foreign Secretary now, tied to a chair in a bloodstained orange jumpsuit, exhausted and petrified as a video camera connected to a TV screen on the floor stands watch over him with a menacing, blinking red LED. Thankfully I've cut the transmission, I hope.

Buy some time, even if it's just five more seconds until the DG can get a strike team here, or at least to call off the incursion by Special Forces. 'I thought it was empty.'

'WHAT THE FUCK ARE YOU DOING HERE?'

'I just wanted some tools, kitchen stuff. To sell.'

I'm trying to give the impression I'm more frightened than I am, some junkie on the rob. The slightest element of doubt will buy me a few seconds. I couldn't care less that I might be about to die, as long as my death can save others. It's about time I die, I just need to carve these two up before I do.

'YOU FUCKING POLICE? YOU HERE FOR HIM?'

'No, don't call the police, I'll go, I can't go back inside.' Taking my last step backwards, I can see an element of doubt starting to creep into Stone Fist, probably not enough to convince them to let me leave, but that doesn't matter. I just need a window. Stone Fist taps his brother on the shoulder with his non-knife-wielding hand. Iron Sword is still pointing his massive cleaver at me, the tip of his blade now only a metre away. But he half turns his head towards his younger brother, as if to question his judgement, and that's all I need. *Go now, Logan. GO.*

I push forward off my back foot and bring my left hand towards the handle of his knife, almost in slow motion, and I force his hand down towards his groin – there's no way he'll start swinging a butcher's knife around in that area. This twists Iron Sword's body into his younger brother, in turn putting a barrier between Stone Fist and me. With no time to target where I'm putting my knife and make sure Iron Sword is no longer a threat, my first strike is to the middle of his back, towards his right-hand side, straight in and deep. My fist slams against his ribcage, but I need a lot more hits in the next two seconds or so, before the adrenaline surges around Stone Fist and makes him superhuman.

Iron Sword screams like a wounded animal. The noise a human makes when they are being stabbed, not once but multiple times, is unforgettable. I twist the knife out before plunging it in on the same side, further down into the area of his kidneys, again pulling it out with a twist. This time the twist wraps part of his shalwar kameez around the blade, and I have to use a bit more force to pull it out, ready to use again. Still holding his butcher's knife and his right hand by his groin, I plant my left shoulder into his body and continue to work my blade down his torso. He's already starting to go limp. I drive the blade of my knife towards his arse, hoping to hit his rectum. I think I've hit slightly above it, but a six-inch blade, twisting on its way out, has almost the same devastating effect as a direct hit. This scream is the loudest; not the sort of scream you make when you hit your finger with a hammer or drop something heavy on your foot, the sort of scream that lets me know he's begging for mercy, for it to stop. He knows his time is done.

Driving my knife up into the left-hand side of his ribcage at the back, I know at this point he's got seconds to live. I twist the blade out and strike him one last time to the neck, giving his brother an eye-level view of what it's like to see this level of violence exacted on someone you love.

This is the last straw for Stone Fist; the shock that had paralysed him for the past few seconds is now making him unpredictably strong. He lurches forwards, trying to grab me, but the dead weight of Iron Sword makes me completely unbalanced and I fall back into the locked doorway. The weight of me and Iron Sword breaks the door open, easily snapping the wooden two by four braced across it. Fuck, I'm pinned down. Iron Sword is heavy, too heavy on top of me. *Get out, get away and stand on your feet!*

Kicking my feet out, I catch Stone Fist in the knee, buckling him to the floor. I catch sight of the Foreign Secretary's orange jumpsuit, but I can't tell if he's still in the same position or not. Too much happening.

As I keep kicking, I manage to connect with Stone Fist again as he's pawing at me. I wriggle free, shuffle away from Iron Sword's bloody body and manage to get to my feet, knife still ready to go. On the outside of the boat, on the other side of the broken door, I quickly look around me; there's still no one walking past the boat, but more importantly, still no police. Where the fuck are they? I re-focus on the doorway, because Stone Fist will be coming through it and I need to put an end to this.

Ducking down, I look back into the boat through the broken doorframe, over Iron Sword's body, to see Stone Fist running towards me out of the darkness. Like a monster running out of a cave. I can't run. I can't stand still. I've got to charge back at him. *Now, move Logan, MOVE!* Just as I start to run towards him, I notice something in his hand. It's a Beretta 9mm pistol—

The thump of burning metal into my chest is followed by messages to my brain carried by countless pain receptors. It's excruciating. I instantly lose my balance and stumble backwards. I can't see any signs of the orange jumpsuit. I can only see Stone Fist, arm stiff, straight aiming to take another shot as he holds me with his free hand.

I need to pull him towards me. If I get him outside, hopefully the police will be here any minute and can take him out. I manage to grab him by the scruff of his garment with one hand and drag him outside, holding his pistol hand away from me with the other, the loud crack of him firing another shot off ringing past my head. That one doesn't connect, but my arm is starting to go numb near where the first bullet ripped through my upper chest. I've lost my knife.

Logan, just fight a bit longer. I trip and fall backwards over the broken wood and plaster. Shuffling back, using the heels of my feet, my hands slide on the broken glass. *Keep moving back, Logan.* The pain from the glass cutting into my palms is nothing compared to the pain in my chest and shoulder.

I'm still facing Stone Fist as he gets ready to fire again. Come on – get out into the open. He tries to pull the trigger yet again, but the smile of vengeance he has across his face is replaced by a look of anger. The pistol hasn't been looked after properly – what looks like surface rust obviously goes deeper, causing a stoppage. It buys me a few more seconds.

Every bit of strength I have left forces me to shuffle back against the side of the boat, leaning against the small lip that would normally be used to stop people falling in as they take in the view on a calm canal. I'm using it to prop my body upright, ready for my final fight.

My body is starting to go into shock. *Hold on a bit longer, Logan.* Stone Fist looks back towards the broken doorway, seeing his brother. This is not how he imagined passing to the afterlife. I can't wait to get off this world. Won't be long now.

The first of his punches lands on top of my head, and as more rain down they hurt, but are nothing compared to the hole in my chest. I don't see them coming, my body is shutting down. Somehow he's picking me up and throwing me across the boat towards the mooring. Adrenaline will do that for you. *Come on police.* Trying to hold him close to me in a desperate attempt to frustrate his punches, I'm spun round, my chest slams onto the side of the boat and my head hits the concrete mooring. I think he's trying to smash my head open like a walnut. I crawl out of the boat onto the mooring to get some space, trying to find a second to regain some sort of fighting position. My phone falls out of my jacket pocket onto the concrete. The screen is black. I don't think it's connected to the DG anymore, the call must have ended during the struggle. I've lost all fight, no more energy to continue.

Hurry up and get on with it, you fucker.

Wrapping some rope around my neck, Stone Fist drives a knee into my back and yanks my head backwards, the force of the rope cutting into me, closing off my wind pipe. My left hand has instinctively come up to try and free myself, my right arm still unresponsive, but I'm hoping the pain will soon stop.

What the fuck is he shouting? It's incoherent but the volume nearly deafens me, pulling me out of the increasingly black tunnel I was slipping into. Out of the corner of my eye I spot Alex holding the Foreign Secretary, still in his orange jumpsuit, as they run as fast as they can towards some buildings in the distance. Alex is propping him up – being held captive for the last few days has sapped his energy.

Fuck, if he goes after Alex, it's game over. I can't have her die. My vision goes, starting to blur out.

Logan, get up. Move.

Sarah? I'm cold, the darkness is swarming around me.

'I'm done. Sarah, I'm done.'

No you're not. You won't die today. You can't die. People need you. Alex needs you. MOVE!

'I'LL FUCKING KILL YOU!'

Stone Fist screaming threats brings light back to my vision. I need to get him before he gets to Alex.

My life is worth nothing now, but she has something to live for, surely. Stone Fist's grip on this rope is too strong to break – the lack of oxygen to my brain is shutting me down. My left hand flails around for anything to help me, got to be something. Please, Sarah, help me. Please.

I feel the sharpness of the ridges first. A screw, hard to tell what length, maybe four inches. I don't care. Grabbing it, I jab it into Stone Fist's shin, and the rope slackens, but I still can't breathe. I have maybe two more strikes left in me; pulling the screw out I know I've hit bone because of the effort needed to extract it. Again, into his shin, straight into muscle, and one more go. Just as I strike down, Stone Fist moves and the screw plunges into his calf muscle. His knee releases the pressure holding me down and he gets up, limping but still fuelled by adrenaline as he starts running after Alex.

No fucking way, I can't let her die. Pulling the rope from my neck, my lungs get some much-needed oxygen, but my vision is badly affected. Stars start to form a cloudy haze over everything. I can't stop coughing, my windpipe feels like it's been crushed irreparably.

I can hear Stone Fist shouting, he's on the marina, running with a heavy limp towards Alex and the Foreign Secretary. *Logan, just thirty more seconds then you can die.* Don't let him touch Alex.

Staggering to my feet, I try and breathe through my nose, hoping it will stop me coughing. It doesn't, but I get one last surge of adrenaline as I see Stone Fist battling to get past a delivery truck that's blocking his path. He's only ten metres away now, his black shalwar kameez flowing in the breeze; this truck has given me one last opportunity to stall him and let Alex get out of here with Philip Day.

Using every last bit of strength and will I have, I bear down on Stone Fist as the truck moves out of his way. I can't see Alex or the orange jumpsuit of the Foreign Secretary. But I can see the terrorist. I need to pin him down as long as I can – five metres away. *Sprint, Logan, sprint!*

Dipping my left shoulder into his ribcage, I drag him down with my left arm. Our bodies hit the floor, and I try and wrap myself around him to make it impossible for him to get up, but the way we fall, he ends up with the upper hand and is almost sat on my waist. Before I know it, the punches rain down into my face. I wrap my legs around him, locking my feet together in the hope this slows him down when I'm gone. The pain of the first punch isn't in my eye socket, where he connects, but in the back of my head as it slams against the hard concrete, the force transmitting through my skull.

He tries to stand up but I keep my legs around his waist. I told you, I'm going to die properly today and Stone Fist is about to find out I'm a relentless little fucker. The damage he's doing to my face now is out of frustration; he knows he's lost. But soon the punches stop and his hands and fingers dig into my throat, once again crushing my windpipe; this time he has his thumbs into my Adam's apple.

My legs are still locked around him but my arms are flat

out beside me. I'm no longer able to fight, I can't see anymore, the only things I can hear are the grunts of Stone Fist as he strains to take my life.

I hear two cracks almost at the same time and Stone Fist's body flinches explosively, collapsing to my side. Then silence. A second later, I see the barrel of a black rifle, or maybe this is the tunnel. No light at the end of this one.

22

It's dark. Pitch black. I'm sure my eyes are open. Aren't they? Unable to see anything, I'm in agony. In my right arm. The ribs on my right side. And my chest. I've never felt pain like it. Taking a breath, it feels like molten lava is being poured into my heart while someone is crushing my chest. Which doesn't make sense. Because I'm dead.

If so, why am I still feeling pain? Isn't that supposed to stop when you die?

I've never been dead before. Maybe this is how it works, you take the pain from when you're alive into death with you, as your baggage? In which case, dying is really not what it's cracked up to be. And there's something else that was supposed to happen. Something else that's not right. But I can't remember what it was. *Damn it, Logan, remember!*

It's like my brain isn't getting enough power.

Slowly the darkness starts to change. As if someone's turning a dimmer switch. Shadows suddenly appear out of the gloom. Rows of . . . books? Then one of the dark shapes gradually turns into a person. An old woman. She looks familiar, somehow.

The books, of course! I'm in the bookshop. Her wrinkled face brightens and she smiles at me. I begin to feel the rest of my body, the parts that aren't in agony. I'm sitting in the chair by the fire, feeling the heat coming from the burning logs as they crackle, it's hypnotizing. Peaceful.

I open my mouth to speak but I can't remember how. I don't know how to make words any more. Like my tongue is pinned to the top of my mouth. All that comes out is a feeble groan. The old woman puts a hand on my arm. 'She's over there, silly. Where did you think she'd be?'

I follow her gaze, to a bookshelf. Everything's suddenly very bright now. A woman is standing with her back to me. She's got long blonde hair and she's holding a little boy by the hand. Together they're scanning the bookshelf, looking for something together.

The little boy has a mop of dark, curly hair. Like mine when I was his age. He lifts his hand and touches a book with his finger. 'D is for . . .'

'Daddy!' says the woman, and they both turn towards me, grinning. I still can't speak. Ice-cold tears run down my cheeks, the only thing stopping them freezing is the heat from this fire.

'It's all right, darling,' she says, moving closer. 'There's nothing to say. I know you wanted to join us, so we could be together. I wanted it too. But it wasn't time. It's not *your* time. Sometimes it's like that.' Sarah always has a way of putting a positive spin on things. I love her for that.

I blink my eyes to try and clear the tears. She's still there.

She's so beautiful. I just want to reach out and touch her, but I can't seem to move. The heat from the fire is becoming hotter, it's distracting. Desperate to block it out, I focus on her as the smile turns a little sad.

'I'm sorry, darling. This is just a visit. While you're in between. We'll have to go back soon. But I want you to know we're OK.' She ruffles the little boy's hair. 'And Joseph's happy. You'd be proud of him.'

'Big boy!' he says, catching my eye and chuckling.

I stare at him. This is my son. God, I love him. The tears in my eyes are doing their best to ruin this for me. Absorbing every detail like a drug addict savouring his last fix, trying not to blink, so I don't miss a moment, but he's already starting to fade. Sarah scoops him up in her arms. Joseph's elephant teddy bear dangling down. 'Come on, you. It's time to go. But we'll visit Daddy again soon, won't we?' Joseph smiles like he's just been told it's Christmas Day. She turns to me and smiles. 'Goodbye, Logan.'

Wait, please. I mouth the words but don't make a sound, and before I can plead with Sarah to stay just a second longer, they're gone.

Fuck.

The pain is excruciating.

It's feels like my heart, stomach and everything in between is being pulled out of my body with meat hooks. The log fire is burning brighter, more furious and no longer peaceful. The fire is frightening. The flames grow larger, more violent as they try to lash out at me like demented whips.

Turning to the old woman, I'm finally able to speak. The frustration has somehow released me. 'I don't understand. That was my little boy. But he was only a baby when . . . when they died. It doesn't make any sense.'

She smiles, and touches my arm. 'Did you read that book?'

Shying away from her gaze, I feel guilty. 'I didn't really have any time. I'm sorry. I meant to, really. I just never . . .'

'That's all right. You've been busy. But one day it might help. It's just stories about people who've lost loved ones. About what happened to them, how they coped. How they came to understand how things . . . work. Between this world and the next.'

I nod, as if I understand what she's talking about. But I'm more confused than ever and starting to be consumed by anger; my family keeps being ripped away from me. The combination of rage and delusion is frustrating. 'Then where am I? What's happened to me? I thought I was dead. Look.' I point to my chest. There's a gaping hole, crusted with bone fragments and dried blood.

'Oh, that,' she says, gently touching the edge of the wound with a finger. 'Yes, that was nasty. But I think they managed to fix it. You just needed some time to gather your strength before going back.' She looks at a small gold watch on her thin wrist. 'Oh my, just in time. I'm afraid I have to be going. It's been lovely talking to you. And at least you know where Sarah and Joseph are now. And you know that they're safe.'

'*Safe?*' I try to get out of the chair but it feels as if I'm tied down. Looking down at my arms, the flames lash around my wrists, pinning me down. Creeping around my chest, circling me, constricting every rise and fall of my ribcage.

I want to ask the old woman to help me, but she's gone, and the rest of the bookshop is fading away, too. I say the word to myself, over and over. 'Safe . . . safe.' As if repeating it will let me remember this wherever I'm going to next. I struggle against the flames, as everything gets brighter. This whole place has been taken over by the fire, too bright to handle. Too hot, it's unbearable. Please let this be the end. Please.

I close my eyes against the brightness. It's like a spotlight is being shone in my eyes, burning into my pupils, my eyelids doing nothing to shield against it, it's like hurtling towards the sun. Then I open them again and—

'Yes, you're *safe*. It's all right, Logan. Everything's fine. You're *safe* now.'

It's Alex. She's smiling, but crying at the same time. I'm lying in a bed in a white-walled room. I can feel a tube coming out of my nose. My right arm is in a cast and my chest is cocooned in tight bandages. More explosions of pain suddenly scream out of my body and I feel my head spin uncontrollably. I think I'm going to be sick. There are more tubes attached to me. I start pulling at them with my free hand, and feel a shocking jolt of pain in my groin.

'Jesus, Logan! Don't do that!' Alex pushes me down onto the bed again. The sudden sharp pain has cleared my head.

My brain is starting to work properly, like it's been rebooted. The dream or whatever it was has gone.

I'm still alive. I've never wanted to be dead more than I do right now. My family being ripped away from me on continuous loop. It's like I'm being punished. I deserve it.

Everything comes screaming back to me, the boat, the brothers, the marina.

Alex is wearing a red climbing jacket. It's the first time I've seen it. A pair of Oakley sunglasses are perched on the top of her head, pulling her brown hair away from her face. She looks composed, even as she wipes the tears from her face with a tissue. Not as if she's just been in a life-or-death struggle with a pair of armed terrorists.

'You're OK?'

She grins. 'Laddered my tights. Might have chipped a nail. Otherwise fine. And all the better for seeing you conscious again. Although I may live to regret that.'

'You probably will. And the Foreign Secretary? How's he?'

'Yeah, he's safe. Properly shaken up, lost a couple of toes during the torture, but he'll recover.' Alex pauses. I know she's keeping the flow of information slow on purpose, so she doesn't overwhelm me. But I need to know everything.

'Did they breach the house? Did the DG get our call? Did he—' A massive wave of pain down the right-hand side of my back stops me mid-question.

'Easy, Logan, what do you remember? Take your time.'

'I remember finding the boat, going in, and the Foreign Secretary in the orange jumpsuit. I cut some sort of cable I thought might be the internet feed they were using. Was that right?'

'Yeah, cutting that cable stopped all the live feeds instantly.'

Thank fuck for that. 'I got into a fight with Iron Sword and Stone Fist.' The horrific details of how I dealt with Iron Sword are vivid and playing in my mind. There's no need for Alex to hear that. She's seen me do enough bad things. I run my hand over the bandages on my chest. 'I remember Stone Fist shooting me. He had a stoppage. I tried to draw the fight towards me. Away from you and the Foreign Secretary.'

Alex adjusts the glasses on the top of her head, scraping her hair back as she fills in her side of the story, 'Yeah, and it worked. I got him out the other end of the boat and ran for it. He was fucked, which is why we were slow, but what you did saved him. Us. And the phone call worked. The DG heard everything.'

I suddenly feel very tired. Whether it's the mental effort of recalling the details of the fight on the boat, or just the relief at knowing we pulled it off, my brain just wants to shut down. But I still need to know what happened while all this was going on. 'What happened at the house? Did the Special Forces guys go in?'

Alex shakes her head. 'Bloody hell, Logan. I tell you, that was very nearly carnage. The DG heard the brothers shouting when you got into the boat. He called the PM and told her they have the wrong address and diverted a strike team over to the marina. They sent bomb disposal into the house.

The footage being fed into the house was in a central room. No window access or outside walls, so they couldn't get a camera in there.'

We were right – that's how they managed to fool everyone. The webcam was recording the video link from the boat and transmitting it into this central room. The armed teams outside would have drilled tiny holes from the neighbours' houses, which would have given them the audio coming from the room, but without getting into the address, they wouldn't have been able to actually see inside.

Alex continues leaning in. 'The door to that room had a pressure plate underneath it. All the explosives were underneath the floorboards. Nearly ten kilos' worth. It would have been a massacre. They called off the breach just in time, the media is reporting a "huge success", and obviously the Prime Minister is using this as an excellent bit of PR.'

Alex and I share a mutual head shake and eye roll as the door opens. A tall, silver-haired figure enters the room, closing the door carefully behind him. Long coat, black thick-framed glasses, royal-blue scarf and a dark-grey flat cap. I don't recognize him at all. Too much hiding his appearance.

Instantly I feel a wave of panic, trying to edge myself further up the bed. I don't like this, I feel vulnerable and wide open to another attack. Alex places her hand on my arm to calm me. She's noticed the distress. As he pulls on the door handle to make sure it's firmly shut, he turns to us, removing his glasses and hat. Then the scarf and coat come off. Fuck. Of course. It's the DG.

Releasing the breath I must have taken in, my chest instantly reminds me I'm still broken.

Alex stands and the DG shakes her hand. 'Afternoon, Ms Winters.' He turns to me. The DG never misses a trick; seeing I was like a cornered animal when he walked in, his tone changes slightly. 'And how are you feeling, Mr Davies?'

At first, I just stare at him blankly. What is he on about? Is it me who's being stupid? Then the penny drops: he's using our cover identities. He sits in the chair Alex has just vacated. 'If anyone asks, I'm your Uncle Jeffrey, although this is going to be a brief visit which hopefully won't draw too much attention. Ms Winters told me earlier you had started to drift in and out so I wanted to check up on you myself. And, of course, to thank you for what you did.'

Before I can splutter an embarrassed reply, he continues, 'Of course, the person who really ought to be thanking you is Philip Day. He's making the most of his new status as a national hero whilst claiming he can remember nothing of the abduction. If the PM goes, I think we can expect he'll be trying to step into her shoes. Well, that's politicians for you. Anyway, how's the shoulder?'

Placing my hand on another set of bandages, I offer up an obvious but polite reply. 'Bit bloody sore, but to be honest I don't really know the extent of the damage.'

Alex jumps in again. 'Luckily the bullet went straight through his upper right chest, just under the clavicle, missing his lung and scapula by a whisker. But it's done a fair bit of muscle damage to his back, so even after the wound heals, he'll be doing physio for a while. There's damage to his neck and windpipe, too. The surgeon who operated on him said he's lucky to have survived.'

'Well, you look like shit.' The brutal honesty is what I needed to hear. I imagine it's one of the reasons why the DG has risen through the ranks to be in charge of MI5. I hadn't looked in a mirror yet but I could see the DG looking at my neck and around my eyes, where I'd taken a pasting. I feel uncomfortable with all the attention, so try to divert the conversation onto another topic.

'Boss, how is this being handled? Did I compromise our team?'

'All taken care of. The Foreign Secretary has signed a gagging order and been given a few lines that he can say about you two and what happened. There's a media ban on talking about the actual rescue itself, although we have used the usual channels to fake a leak that you are both military personnel attached to Special Forces. But so far so good. The police turned up with a medical team and managed to get the pair of you, along with the Foreign Secretary, out of harm's way before the people's press turned up with their mobile phones. Nothing on social media, thankfully.'

'And what about here, the hospital? What's the cover story?'

'Victim of a carjacking, Mr Davies.' I can nearly detect a hint of a smile from the DG. He loves all this cloak and dagger stuff. Nodding his head at my injuries, he continues: 'Hence the bruising and gunshot wound.'

'I hope the bastards didn't get away with my car, then.' Alex and the DG both smile at my attempt to make light of the situation, and I can feel my body wanting to laugh, but the combination of the bandages restricting my chest and the fact my body is barely functioning cause me to start coughing.

Every forced, uncontrollable cough is pain, pure pain. Desperate to stop it, I close my mouth. Alex can see me struggling but the DG beats her to it with a plastic beaker of water and a straw.

'Sip it. SIP!' Like a father to his son, I listen and try to follow his order, not wanting to disappoint him. The violent cough turns into a mild splutter as I get it under control.

No one speaks for a moment, giving me time to settle again. There's a growing tension as Alex and I simultaneously figure out the real reason the DG is here.

Finally, Alex asks, 'And Jeremy? Leyton-Hughes?'

The DG makes a sour face, as if he's been wrestling with this problem for a while. 'I suppose one could say all's well that ends well.'

Rubbing his hands in a revolving motion, like they're mimicking the swirling thought process in his brain, it's the first time we've seen the DG hiding his real thoughts and having a clear tell. If Alex and I were playing poker against the DG right now, we'd be all in.

Choosing his words carefully, he continues: 'Initially he

said that he was simply providing a level of deniability by not informing me what Blindeye was doing. And that pulling you off Iron Sword and Stone Fist was purely an operational decision, a judgement call.'

'One he got wrong,' Alex mutters.

'Well, I think there was more to it than that.' The DG is opening up, probably realizing there is nothing to be gained by lying to us. 'After further . . . conversations, he admitted the truth. He had a direct line to the PM's office. A young chap he was at Eton with.' He shook his head. 'Something I should have been aware of. Basic bloody intelligence. Fucking Etonians.

'Anyway, once you chaps had run the brothers to ground, Jeremy decided that instead of taking care of them quietly, which was the whole point of Blindeye, there might be an opportunity for something more public – in short, a propaganda coup for the PM. So he and his pal cooked it up between them. The irony is, of course, that in the end that's exactly what they got. Thanks to you two.'

Alex is seething. We knew the risks becoming part of this team, but to be treated like pawns in some power game was eating at her.

'Instead of the almighty bloody screw-up they almost created.'

'Indeed.'

'So what happens to him now? And his friend? Did Jeremy tell him about Blindeye?' Alex wants blood.

'His friend got what he was after – a big promotion. As

for Jeremy, we'll see. Blindeye remains operationally secure. It's got to be handled very carefully, as you can imagine. Despite him trying to run this himself, he is perfectly placed for this role. So for now, he stays in position.'

Alex and I share another look, we both know there is something between the lines, but we can't read it.

He continues: 'Craig, Ryan, Claire and Riaz are all in the area. No one knows about them or you, but they are providing a ring of steel around the hospital just to be sure. And, of course, now you're awake you'll have someone to talk to.'

As the DG leans in to my bed, he addresses us both with a smile that catches us off guard. 'I'd quite like to have Jeremy shot, to be perfectly honest, but we'd probably best not go there.'

Matching his smile, Alex replies, 'I know a guy . . .'

He stands, buttoning his camel-hair coat. That's obviously as much as we're going to get as far as Leyton-Hughes is concerned.

'One more thing . . . In case the death of Stormy Weather is preying on your mind . . .' The subtle shift in Alex's posture is minute, but I see it. She's still uncomfortable with what I did in the back of the van.

The DG pauses by the door to continue. 'Now that you understand Jeremy was working off his own bat without my say-so, you still did the right thing. Had I been aware of the situation, I would have given my authorization. It's not easy, and we don't do these things lightly, but it was for this kind of operational –' pausing to find the right word his eyes flicker until he picks one – 'flexibility that Blindeye was set up. You have nothing to punish yourself for.'

He places his hand on my arm in a way that says he knows the hurricane of pain I'm in, not just physically but emotionally. I realize I'm a different person than I was a month ago. Tapping my arm, he signals that's the last he's going to say on the matter.

'Now, recover quickly. As soon as you're well enough to be moved, we'll get you to a more discreet facility. In the meantime, you won't see anybody in uniform about the place, but Ms Winters and the rest of your friends are here making regular visits around the clock, just to be on the safe side.'

He leans down to shake my good hand before he goes. No more needs to be said. From the intense look in his eyes, he knows the burden he's asking us to bear. In this split second, I get the sense responsibility weighs heavily on him.

With his coat buttoned up, his flat cap and glasses back on, he approaches Alex, wrapping his scarf around his neck to cover the lower part of his face. Shaking her hand, he lowers his voice and leans towards the side of her head, just enough to make it difficult to hear, but my hearing is the only thing that's sharp right now and I can just see his mouth over the top of his scarf.

'I'll square everything away. Get him fit. Quickly. There is a war coming.'

Alex is ready to get back out on the ground, but her focus on the DG's eyes is broken by a light knock on the door.

'Ah, I expect that'll be your doctor.'

EPILOGUE

'How's the pain, Mr Davies?'

'Yeah, my shoulder's a bit sore. And my arm.'

'Well, now that you're fully awake, you'll be needing more pain relief. I'll have a nurse give you something when I'm through.'

I gently probe the wound. *A carjacking*. That was what the police said when they brought him in. But I wonder. It could be coincidence, I suppose, but he was brought to A&E soon after the live feed from the houseboat was cut. With a gunshot wound to the chest, a deep cut to the forearm from a knife, bruising and laceration around the throat and various other cuts and bruises. I have seen these kinds of injuries before. To me, this man has been in a fight to the death. I don't know what happened on the boat. You cannot trust the government lies on the television. But somehow they discovered where Masood and Hamza were really holding the Foreign Secretary. And somebody slaughtered them.

And now this man is here. And the woman who watches over him. And when she is not here, I believe there are others who take her place. They are subtle, but years of

323

watching out for the spies, studying their tactics, has taught me to remember faces.

'Can you move your fingers in this arm? Can you make a fist for me?'

As he grimaces with the effort of obeying my instructions, I could take his life now as easily as crushing a bug. Because that's what I believe he is. An insect. Masood and Hamza would instantly be avenged. Has he been delivered to me in this miraculous way for that very purpose?

As my fingers move to his throat, I hesitate, even though righteous anger is coursing through my veins like fire. What if they catch me? His friends who guard him so carefully. What if they are watching me somehow now?

No, I must put my anger aside and be patient. They think that killing the Foreign Secretary and ambushing the soldiers was everything. But that was only ever the first part of the plan. The second part is beyond their worst imaginings. And I need to remain free to make it happen. When it does, I will make sure they are the first to be slaughtered.

I pull my hands back. 'I think that will do for now, Mr Davies.' I smile reassuringly. 'But I'll be seeing you again soon.'

ACKNOWLEDGEMENTS

I want to thank Luigi, Wayne, Alex, Bill and everyone at Pan Macmillan for being so positive, patient and understanding during the clearance process which is, and always will be, incredibly important to me. You and the entire team have allowed me to write how I want right from the start and I look forward to many more books with you all. I hope *Capture or Kill* does you all justice.

I'd especially like to thank the Security Service and DSF. I'll never break my life-long oath to you and I mean every word when I say: We are the best in the fucking world! *Regnum Defende.*

Coming soon . . .

I SPY: MY LIFE IN MI5

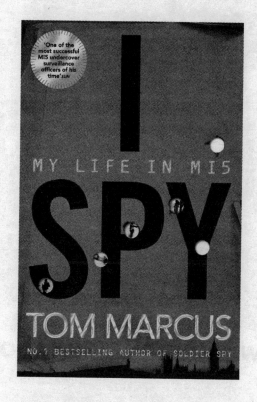

The explosive new memoir from
the author of the phenomenal number
one bestselling *Soldier Spy*.